Mother Not Wanted

Timothy Fish

Mother Not Wanted

Cover design by Timothy Fish.

ISBN-13: 978-1-61295-000-6

Contact the Author:
bookcomments@timothyfish.net

Author's Website:
http://www.timothyfish.com

Fort Worth, Texas 76134

Mother
Not Wanted

After seventeen hours of listening to the wheels of the train and feeling the gentle rocking of the car, it no longer had power over her. It no longer threatened to pull her into sleep. Though she knew that it meant they were that much closer to the end of their journey, Amber was glad to see the suburbs of Dallas sliding past their window. Just one more stop and then on to Fort Worth, a city she'd avoided far too long. She knew she wouldn't be welcome, but it was time to put things right.

She reached over and rubbed Lizi's back. The young girl was either sleeping or staring out the window. Amber couldn't tell which. Perhaps she was dreaming of a magical city where cows roamed the streets. Amber hoped Lizi wouldn't be too disappointed that Cowtown was a city like any other and people didn't have cattle grazing in their front yards. There were already so many things that could disappoint Lizi during the next few days—many more than any twelve year old should face. Amber hated to add even one more.

Lizi straightened in her seat, pushed back the worn blanket and stretched her arms above her head. "How much longer?"

"Another hour or so." Amber could only assume that what another passenger had said was right.

"To Cowtown or to the house?" Lizi put the emphasis on the word *cow*.

"To Fort Worth." Amber ran her fingers through Lizi's hair to break the tangles. For the last time? She tried not to think about it. She knew what she was giving up by bringing her here. No one would know the difference if they got off the train and bought tickets back to St. Louis. Amber wished she could convince herself it wasn't the wrong thing to do. Lizi would have a better life in Fort Worth than she'd ever had in St. Louis. "I don't know how long it will take to get to their house. We have to find it first."

Lizi turned to stare out the window again. Amber pulled out the last of the cash and counted it one more time. It came out the same as before, but knowing there wasn't enough for tickets on the next northbound train helped steel her resolve. They had enough to get to Fort Worth, and ride a bus to where they were going. If things went well, they would have a place to spend the night. It was just wishful thinking on Amber's part that she would find an extra few bills so they could spend the night in a cheap hotel—one more night with just her and Lizi. But the end would come sometime.

"Amber?" Lizi turned back and looked at her. "What if they don't like me?"

"They'll love you." Amber tried to reassure the girl, but she knew that Lizi couldn't hear confidence in her voice. You couldn't walk in off the street, say "here's your granddaughter" and expect someone to believe you without question. Being less than honest about the situation wasn't going to help either. But if they found out, what could they do?

"Can we go over what I need to say?"

"You just have to be yourself. I don't want them knowing I taught you to cheat people." Amber picked up Lizi's discarded blanket and folded it.

"But you said that we have to do what we have to do," Lizi said.

"Yeah, but not this time. You just be yourself and I'll worry about the rest."

Lizi took the folded blanket from Amber and put it in her lap. She ran her hand across it and traced the holes with her finger. "Tell me about Holly."

The rainy night so many years earlier flashed into Amber's mind. She could still see the image of the smaller woman standing in front of her with rain drenched hair, begging for her help.

"Your mother loved you very much. She had lots of friends. One was…"

"No, I want to hear about Holly, not her friends."

"Just to be on the safe side, when we get there, try not to call your mother by her first name." Amber stared out the window on the other side of the car. She looked past the man reading a book and out at the industrial building bathed in sunlight. She wondered if she'd already told Lizi more than she should. "Maybe we shouldn't talk about her here. Some people may not understand her like we do. We don't want people knowing more about us than they just have to."

"So it is a scam. You just aren't letting me in on it." Lizi turned sideways in her seat and leaned her head against the window.

"No, it isn't a scam. Not completely anyway." Amber took the blanket from Lizi and tied the length of rope around it. She wished they had a larger blanket. It would come in handy if they turned them away and they had to sleep outside. "Even if it were, now isn't the time to be planning. Now we just follow this thing through and see where it goes. I'm not even sure things are anything like Holly described. You remember I told you she believed stuff that wasn't true. We'll have to wait and see how the Jacobs remember her."

"Then tell me about one of Holly's friends." Lizi sat forward, eager to hear a story. "Tell me about Bennie."

"Alright," Amber said. She tried to remember some of the stories Holly had told. "Holly saw Bennie a lot. You weren't much over two—one night I woke up and heard this terrible racket coming from the other bedroom where you two were. I could hear you crying, but it sounded like she was throwing things at the wall. I got out of bed to see what was going on. I opened the door to the bedroom and switched on the light. You were on the floor and Holly was standing near the window. 'What'd you do that for?' she asked. 'You can't catch an elf with the light on. Bennie almost got away with Elizabeth this time.'"

"Was Bennie really trying to steal me?" Lizi's eyes twinkled with the thought.

"Holly sure thought he was." Amber twisted sideways to face Lizi more easily. "I came home from work the next day and Holly was setting up cardboard boxes all over the house. There was hardly any room to walk through."

"What were the boxes for?"

"Traps," Amber said. "At least, that's what Holly said. She checked them every morning for two weeks, hoping she would catch Bennie. I made her get rid of them after that."

When they disembarked at the Fort Worth station, Amber looked around for something that would give her information about the bus routes. She didn't have to look far to find a map, but when she saw the jumbled mess of colored spaghetti showing nearly forty routes, she wasn't sure it would help. She must have looked confused because a stranger asked her if she needed help. Maybe he was a worker. Maybe he was just a friendly person. She didn't know, but she was glad to have his help. She showed him the address she had written on a slip of paper.

"We're trying to get to this address."

The man looked at the address and then at the map. He looked at the paper again and then he looked back at the map. "I don't think where y'all are goin' is on this map."

"It says it's in Fort Worth." Amber pointed to the city at the bottom of the address.

"This map don't show all the streets. Then it could be the bus routes ain't made it out that far. Fort Worth's like a giant monster that swallows up everything in its path, but city services take a while to make it into some places. I used to live in the country, until they decided they wanted to incorporate my land." The man handed the slip of paper back to Amber. "Let me get my Mapsco. It'll show more."

After a few minutes, the man came back with the Mapsco. "This'll have it in it."

The man looked up the street and flipped to the right page. He pointed to the street. "Here it is."

"Where is that?" Amber asked. "We're not from around here."

"It's outside 820." The man pointed to the route map. "This map doesn't show it, but it should be right here. The buses don't go there."

The road he mentioned looked like a wide freeway. "Which route should we take to get as close as possible?"

After looking at the map for a couple moments, the man pointed to two routes. "You'll have to switch buses, but this will get you close. If you get off at this bus stop, that should put you within a mile or two of where y'all want. But are you sure you want to take the bus? They've got some money over there. I'd think they could afford to send someone to pick you up."

"It's kind of a surprise." Even though the man was being nice, Amber didn't want him knowing what they were doing. She thanked the man and then went with Lizi in search of the right bus.

On the second bus, Amber and Lizi were the only passengers for most of the trip. When the bus driver discovered they knew little about Fort Worth, he began to unload the extent of his knowledge—or his ignorance. Amber didn't know enough about the city to know which.

"We've got it good over here in Fort Worth." The man looked at his left mirror before he changed lanes. "We don't have as bad of traffic as Dallas has, but we get the benefit of all the stuff they've got over there. But then Fort Worth has some nice stuff too. Our zoo is better. At least, I think it is. And the Cowboys are over here now—or closer than they used to be. Do y'all watch much football?"

Amber indicated that she didn't.

"My wife does. She's a big fan. It's nice having the 'boys over here now—Arlington really—but I figure anything in Tarrant county practically belongs to Fort Worth. I buy 'er season tickets every year." The driver slowed the bus to come to a stop.

"Isn't that expensive?" Amber thought about the small amount of cash she carried with her—the last of everything she owned. The last time she'd heard someone talking about attending a Rams game, he'd spent more than she carried with her.

A Hispanic woman with two young children got on the bus. The driver spoke to her in Spanish. She smiled and spoke to him in a friendly tone. They found a seat closer to the rear of the bus.

"Not so much." The driver put the bus in gear to pull away. "It's my Christmas present to her every year and we don't spend money doing other things. I know some folks that spend a lot more on golf than we spend on football. Me—I just don't see spending money to chase a white ball around, when it always comes back to the same place."

Amber nodded, even though the driver couldn't see her.

"Now if I had money like the Bass family..." The driver said the name like he expected Amber to know who they were. She didn't. "My wife's related to them. I keep telling her she ought to go ask them to share a little of that wealth. She say it ain't proper."

"Maybe so," Amber said, "but I couldn't fault you if you did. We're on our way to do something like that, now."

He looked back at them in the mirror and raised his eyebrows ever so slightly.

"This next stop is the one you want." The driver brought the bus to a stop once more. "I hope y'all don't have far to walk. They were saying it's supposed to get up to 104 again today. I'll be glad when we get past this hot weather, but it's just started."

The driver let them out in front of an apartment complex and drove away. Amber could see a car dealership a short distance down the street, but they wouldn't walk past it. Instead, they turned the other direction and followed the street past an older middleclass neighborhood. They found another dealership a short distance down the street. Amber could feel the afternoon sun bearing down on them, even before they made it to the drive of the dealership. She could see the freeway over their heads a short distance away. She could hear the noise of the traffic zooming past. With her bag in hand, she walked in that direction. They would have to cross under it to get to the other side.

They followed the frontage road south. They could see a field with cedar and mesquite growing wild to the west, but no cows. Lizi thought it odd. "How can it be Cowtown without any cows?"

"I'm sure it's because they used to drive cattle through here." Amber gave her best guess. "Maybe they have cows somewhere else."

Lizi seemed appeased, but the heat had already begun to slow her walking pace. The sun hung high overhead and the trees were too short and too far from the road to offer shade. Amber took Lizi's small bag from her and added it to her own load. She hadn't considered that neither of them had had anything to drink since lunch. That had been before they reached Dallas. In the heat, carrying a heavy bag, she felt ill and wondered if she might faint.

Just before they reached a stone fence enclosing a large wooded area, they crossed a creek, or a river. It was almost too large to be a creek and too small to be a river. Amber looked ahead and saw water shooting high from a fountain next to a small stone building. She thought they could make it to there, but it also looked so far away and it was uphill the whole way. Her lungs couldn't take in enough air. She wondered if Lizi had the same problem. Amber tried to tell herself that the water from the creek might be dirty, but she knew she wasn't going to talk herself out of stopping there. They left the road and sat near the water's edge.

They had shade there. The water ran clear. Amber tried not to think about what they couldn't see. They dipped their hands into it and drank from it. The water wasn't cold, but it felt cool as Amber let it run down her throat. She hadn't realized how thirsty she had become. They sat in the shade of the mesquite for several minutes.

"Let's get moving." Amber stood up.

"Do we have to?" Lizi put her hand in the water and let it run across her fingers.

"We need to get out of this heat." Amber could tell that Lizi was taking it better than she was. Amber hadn't been prepared to carry what little remained of their possessions through triple digit temperatures. The worst of Lizi's problems was that she was tired after so many hours of traveling.

By the time they reached the little stone building, Amber felt ill again and wondered if the heat was causing the problem or if the water had something in it. The gate blocked the road, but there was enough room for a person to walk between it and the fence. They walked through the opening and up the short rise where the road came to a T. To the right, the road went down to go around the hill. To the left, the road had a steep incline as it went up. From the map, Amber knew they had to go to the left, but the map hadn't shown her how steep the hill was. She feared she would never make it to the top, but she was sure that was where she would find Fox Jacobs.

"Hey! Where do you think you're going?"

Amber turned around to see a white haired man coming toward them. She had seen him inside the stone guard house, but she didn't think he looked up from the small television he was watching. She had thought that if they hurried they could be out of sight before he noticed them. It would be hard to explain their presence and Amber wanted to reach the Jacobs house as quickly as possible.

"We're going to see Fox Jacobs," Amber said as the man neared them.

"You and everyone else," the man said under his breath. "I'll have to see if you're on the list."

"We have to be on a list? We thought we'd drop in and surprise him." To her knowledge, Amber had never been on anyone's list and she certainly wasn't going to be on anything this man had on his clipboard.

"The people who live back here don't like surprises." The man took up a position between them and where they wanted to go. "I'm going to have to ask you to leave. Unless you can call him and tell him you're here."

"I don't have his phone number. Couldn't you overlook it this once? We've been traveling all day to get here." Normally, Amber would have seen it as a minor setback. They would be able to introduce themselves to Fox Jacobs eventually, but the long day traveling, mixed with the heat and the fact they were nearly out of money made her desperate.

"Come on now. Out you go." The man gave them a gentle push toward the entrance. "Don't make me call the cops."

Chapter Two

"Mr. Jacobs..." the reporter began, as he pulled a pen from his pocket and wrote something in a small notebook.

"Call me, Fox," Fox Jacobs said. "Everyone else does."

The reporter nodded. "I can appreciate that you don't want to say anything about what you're announcing today until you can tell everyone, but if you don't mind, I'd like to talk to you about something else."

"Okay," Fox said, "what is it you want to know."

"I went back and looked at the last time you were in the news. I couldn't help but notice that it's been a year, this week, since the accident. I covered it when it happened. How have you and the family been holding up since then?"

Fox looked up at the picture hanging on the wall. The faces of his grandchildren stared out at him, frozen in time. They would never grow older than they'd been the day the picture was taken. They'd always look so happy, with their lives in front of them. "I don't want to talk about it."

"You must have known it would come up."

"I'm done talking for now," Fox said. "You can wait for the announcement like everyone else."

The reporter looked like he was going to remain in his seat for a while longer, but he slipped the pen back in his shirt pocket and closed his notebook. He stood up and extended his hand to Fox. "Thanks for your time. I would like to talk to you some more when you're…"

Fox shook the man's hand. *When you're what? When you're feeling like talking? When you man up and can talk about it without crying?* Maybe the reporter would have the good sense to stay away from the subject the next time they spoke. Maybe people thought a year was long enough to get over something like that. It wasn't.

The reporter left and before Fox let himself think too much about the faces in that portrait Steve came in, along with Jack Abrams.

"It's almost that time, isn't it?" Fox looked at his watch. In less than a minute it would be the appointed time. "Are we ready?"

"Grayson isn't back yet," Steve said.

"He left?" Fox tried to keep his anger to himself, but there was no reason for Grayson to leave when they were making a big announcement. The press had even shown up. Okay, so it was just a guy from the Star-Telegram and a cameraman from one of the television stations, but that was worth something. And to have the company department heads there too. "He was just here a few minutes ago. We can't make this announcement without him."

"I'm afraid that's my fault," Jack said. "Celia needed a ride and he was kind enough to go pick her up."

"He should've sent someone else," Fox said. "We need to make sure we're all on the same page before we go out there."

"Oh, I wouldn't worry about it," Jack said. "We'll make it through it. Besides, this might lead to something better anyway."

"How's that?" Fox asked.

"You know," Jack said. "Two family businesses coming together and merging like this—it might not be a bad thing if the two families merged too. Then we could all keep it in the family. I don't think those two are opposed to the idea. You didn't think all that time they've been spending together has been all business, did you?"

Fox walked over to the window and looked down the sun drenched street. He didn't see Grayson's car parked below and it wasn't coming down the street. "I won't say that hasn't crossed my mind, but I really don't think Grayson will let it go very far—not after what happened with his first wife."

"I didn't realize he was married before," Jack said. "Do you mind if I ask what happened? I suppose he's divorced now."

"Widowed," Steve chimed in. "His wife ran off and then she killed herself. She had a few screws loose."

"Yeah, I suppose so," Jack said. "I can see why you think he might be afraid to marry again, but how long's it been? Everyone gets lonely. He might get tired of living alone."

"If he had time," Fox said, "maybe he would, but he works an awful lot, and with this merger, I don't think things will get much better for a while."

"Then maybe it's up to you and me to take some of that workload off of him."

"No," Fox said, "Not me. I turned most of that over to him last year. And he does an excellent job. I think you already know that or you wouldn't have agreed to this merger. I keep my hand in so I know what's going on, but I've found it's best to just let Grayson do his thing."

Even as he discouraged Jack's thought, he imagined family gatherings with Grayson and Celia there with young children. Trying to encourage Grayson would only make him back away, but if the family business was going to stay in the family, they had to have an heir. One generation and out wasn't Fox's idea of a legacy. It only made sense that the business should go through Grayson. Of the three kids, he was the oldest and the one who hadn't sold most of his share of the business already. But none of them had children—not any more.

Fox looked at his watch again. They were already late. If someone didn't do something, the two members of the press would be leaving to find a better story. The employees would stick around longer, since they were getting paid to be there, but even some of them would head back to the office because they had work that needed to be done. Fox was just about to go out to stall when Grayson walked through the door. Celia was with him.

"Sorry I'm late," Grayson said. "Are we ready?"

They all left the quiet of the office to stand in front of the small crowd gathered in the great room.

It wasn't the first time the leadership team had been invited to Fox's house. He used to invite them at least once a year, but that was before the accident. What a difference a year could make. Last year, they'd all turned to Fox to tell them where the company was headed. This year, Fox felt like he was sitting on the sideline in his own company. Of course he and Grayson discussed things, but no one seemed to know it. As they made their way through the crowd, people stopped Grayson to ask questions. No one asked Fox anything.

"Can I have your attention please?" Grayson took his place in front of the group. He stood on a short platform that was in the small cove in the corner of the room. It normally held a lounge chair, where Fiona would soak in the sun streaming through the windows, but on occasions like this it worked well as a small stage.

The people turned to face him.

"I'm sure you're all ready to eat," Grayson said, "but we've got a few things we need to get out of the way first. I'm sure you've all heard rumors that we've got a big announcement to make. We wanted to tell y'all first, so that when it comes out you'll be able to answer any questions your teams have. But first, my father and I wanted to take this time to recognize some people who have done an outstanding job during the past year." Grayson turned to Fox. "Dad."

Someone shoved a stack of service awards in front of Fox. As he took them, he recognized his secretary. He didn't know her very well; Grayson had hired her. Fox took his place on the raised platform and looked down at the awards. The first few had names written at the top with the number of years of service next to it. Fox read these off and handed them out, but he came to one that just said, "John Sayers." He read the name and looked at his secretary. She looked back at him as if she didn't realize he was struggling for words.

Grayson stepped forward and addressed the gathering. "John has been working on some of our research projects. He had an idea that has as much as doubled the battery life on some of our products. We've recently secured a patent."

Everyone clapped as Fox handed John his award, but Fox felt uncomfortable. He looked down at the few remaining awards. Each, like the one he'd give John Sayers, had only a name penciled in the top right corner. Fox didn't bother telling the others to wait for them, but he grabbed his oldest son by the arm and pulled. "We need to talk."

Grayson followed Fox out of the great room and down the short hall to where they were out of view of the guests. More importantly, they couldn't be heard.

"How am I supposed to hand these out?" Fox waved the remaining awards in front of his son. "I don't know what these guys have been working on. I hardly know them."

"I sent you an e-mail," Grayson said. "It had all of that stuff in it. Didn't you read it?"

"If you sent it, I'm sure I did," Fox said. He wasn't at all sure that he had. "I just wasn't expecting to be the one doing this."

"I can do it if you'd like," Grayson said. As he did, he fumbled through a folder he had in his hands. He looked at one page and then another before he pulled out a loose sheet of paper. "Here's that e-mail I sent you. You can read it off of here, if you want."

Fox took the paper and looked at it. In very clear terms it laid out the reason that each of the recipients was receiving an award that year. Fox was torn between letting his son do it or reading from the sheet of paper. There was no way for him to memorize it all in a few moments. He had to do one or the other and either way seemed like he was admitting he wasn't competent enough to run the company.

"Here we are trying to pull off this merger and we look like bungling fools," Fox said.

"No, I don't think so," Grayson said. "Besides, it's not like…"

Fox knew why Grayson stopped. Once the merger took place, Fox would be less involved in the company than ever, so what did it matter if he looked like a fool. But for Fox this was a matter of pride and an opportunity for an easy out. The merger would put the company in a lot better shape. People would look at the strength of the company when Fox turned over the reins of leadership and they wouldn't talk about how he had ruined the company. And they wouldn't talk about him stepping down because he couldn't handle the loss of his grandchildren or because he needed more time to care for his wife. No, this was going to be his final act that would make the company something to be proud of. It would work, if they could just get through the announcement. They had a long way to go, but it would be much harder for Jack Abrams to back out of it once they'd made a public announcement. Of course, if Grayson and Celia were dating, that was even better.

It was as if Grayson read Fox's mind when he said, "I don't think you have anything to worry about. Jack Abrams may not need this merger as much as we do, but it's not without its benefits. They're still struggling with improving their reputation after what happened with that recall last year. They need us because people respect us.

"Let's keep them thinking that," Fox said, "at least until the paperwork is signed."

The guests were growing restless by the time Fox and Grayson returned to the great room, but they quieted down as soon as Fox stepped back on the platform. This time, he had the paper in hand. He didn't read what Grayson had written word for word, but he added his own flavor to it, hoping that people wouldn't notice that he didn't know why they were giving these people awards. But it looked like these people had served the company well.

When the last of the awards were given out Fox began to say, "Now for what you've all been waiting for," but out of the corner of his eye he saw Grayson waving him off. "Aren't we ready for that?" Fox asked.

"No, we decided it would be better to eat first," Grayson whispered. "It didn't seem right giving them awards and then saying, 'Oh, by the way, we're going through a merger, so you might get demoted or get laid off.'"

"We'll do the announcement later," Fox said. "Let's eat." He wasn't sure who "we" was, but he couldn't fault the logic. He just hoped the news guys didn't get tired of waiting around and decide to go look for something more news worthy. Another hour wouldn't hurt. It didn't seem like anything could happen in an hour that would make Jack Abrams change his mind. But he had no way of knowing about the storm coming.

Chapter Three

The white haired guard stood outside and watched for quite a while as Amber and Lizi walked away from the entrance to the gated community. Amber kept looking back at him. She hoped he would go back inside, but he just stood there watching them.

"What're we going to do now?" Lizi asked.

"Don't worry, we'll find a way." Amber already had an idea, but she couldn't do anything while the guard was looking. "Haven't I always told you it isn't good to plan in too much detail? We couldn't have anticipated this."

They didn't walk the direction from which they had come. Instead, they turned to the right and continued to follow the frontage road up the hill. Amber hoped they wouldn't need it, but she began looking for some kind of shelter for the night. On the other side of the freeway, she saw a building with a cross above it. The building was a jumbled mess of angles. It was probably the ugliest church building she'd ever seen, but it had an awning covering one of the entrances. It would protect them if it rained. Amber looked at the sky. It didn't look like they would see rain anytime soon. The grass had as much yellow and brown in it as it did green. There were several bridges that crisscrossed each other up ahead. Amber didn't like the idea of sleeping under a bridge. The traffic would keep them awake. There were several acres of grass between the roads. If it wasn't so hot, Amber thought it might be nice to sleep under the stars. Then it would seem more like a camping trip than being homeless. All the same, she willed the guard to go back inside.

Amber looked back at the guard one more time. He still stood there with arms crossed, watching as they climbed the hill. A Hummer drove along the frontage road and crossed the little bridge where Amber and Lizi stopped earlier. It made a right and stopped in front of the gate. The guard went to talk to the driver.

This was the chance Amber had hoped for. They just needed the guard to look the other direction for a short time. She grabbed Lizi by the arm and pulled her off the road toward the fence. It was mostly stone with vertical wrought iron bars every few yards. The bars were too tight for them to squeeze through, but Amber thought they could climb over the eight foot fence.

With Amber's help, Lizi climbed to the top of the fence. Amber handed the bags to her and she dropped them on the other side before jumping down. It was a little harder for Amber to cross the fence by herself, but she found a foothold in the stone and pushed herself up. She looked down the hill toward the guard house. The guard raised the gate to let the Hummer through. He walked back to where he had been standing before, looked up the hill along the road, turned and went back inside. Amber dropped down to join Lizi.

Lizi pulled at her jeans and tried to pull them around to the front. "I think I ripped my pants."

"Turn around and let me look." Amber could see a small hole that looked new. It might have come from Lizi climbing over the fence, but the jeans had little holding them together anyway. She didn't want Lizi fidgeting with the hole, making it bigger, before she could make a repair. "I don't see anything wrong with them."

"Are you sure?" Lizi tried again to look for herself.

"We'll look again later, but we need to get moving before someone sees us." Amber picked up the bags and began walking up the hill. The trees on this side of the fence gave them shade they hadn't had before, but they needed more than the partial relief from the heat the trees gave them. Amber's mouth felt dry and she still felt ill. Even if Fox Jacobs threw them out, Amber hoped he would be kind enough to give them something to drink.

Lizi looked around at the trees. "Do you think this could be the fairy wood Holly told you about?"

"No, this neighborhood is too new for that. I don't think they would know anything about these trees." Amber didn't tell her that she knew because she had been the one that made up the stories about little people with butterfly wings hiding in the trees when she had run out of Holly stories that interested Lizi. Holly's fairies had rested on her shoulders, not in the trees.

"Tell me about the fairies." Lizi kept looking for the miniature people.

"I'll tell you a story at bedtime." Amber told Lizi that for her own peace of mind as much as Lizi's. She could only hope that she would be there to share a story with Lizi at bedtime.

They stayed in the trees for as long as they could. It forced them to take a steeper route up the hill. While they still had the cover of trees, Amber noticed a police cruiser creeping along the street. "Get down!"

Amber pulled Lizi behind one of the trees and they stayed there until the car disappeared up the hill. They climbed some more and came to the clearing. As they neared the top of the hill, the houses forced them to walk along the street in the bright sunlight. The policeman had moved on, but nothing would keep him from returning.

"Is that a castle?" Lizi pointed to the first house they saw.

"Hardly." Amber knew the house must have looked large to a child. For that matter, it looked large to her. The house must have sold for more than a million dollars. It shouldn't have surprised her, even with what little she knew about Fox Jacobs. They hadn't traveled this far to visit a poor man.

They walked past the first large house and then another. Trees grew behind the homes on the north side of the street, but few shaded the drives that circled fountains or well-tended flowerbeds and even fewer grew near the street. The south side of the street had even less to hide the big Texas sky and the sun still hanging in the southwest corner. Amber kept looking for the police car to return and knew the officer would ask them more than a few questions. He would want to know what they carried in their bags. It would be very obvious, if he looked inside, that they hadn't stolen any of it from these people. These people probably threw better things in the trash. But if someone looked through their bags and found Lizi's birth certificate it could cause trouble. If she hadn't wanted it available to show Fox Jacobs, Amber would've found a hiding place for it.

Each time they came to a different house, Amber hoped it would be the right one, but then felt let down when it turned out to be the wrong address. The police officer couldn't stay hidden in the side streets forever.

They came to a house covered with stone that looked more like a castle than any of the others. Round tower like structures with cone shaped roofs adorned several corners of the multifaceted house. Lizi, with energy that Amber didn't have, ran ahead to look for the number on the mailbox.

"Is this it? It looks like a princess lives here!" She stopped at the mailbox and looked at the number. Her shoulders drooped and she walked more slowly forward. "It isn't the right one."

Amber noticed the police cruiser making its way along the street toward them. She began to think about how she would answer his questions and only glanced at the number on the box. She took a few steps past it and had to look back. "Lizi, this is it."

"It is?" Lizi looked back for just long enough to see Amber nod her head before she cut across the grass toward the front door.

Amber walked along the drive. This was the first time she paid attention to the cars parked on the drive. It had the appearance of a party. She didn't know whether that would help or hurt their cause. At no point had she planned to crash a party.

Lizi stopped at the front door and waited for Amber. The police officer parked his car on the street and came up the walk toward them.

"Ma'am!" Amber heard the man say, but she pretended not to hear.

"Ring the doorbell Lizi." Amber knew she wouldn't get by with ignoring this man a second time.

"Ma'am, can I have a word with you?" The cop didn't give up. He didn't have anything on them. No court would convict them for walking down the street carrying a bag.

"Of course." Amber turned around to face the cop. "I've got nothing to hide."

"Do you want to tell me what someone like you is doing in a neighborhood like this, carrying large bags?" The cop had made it up the walk and across the drive. He stood just under the largest of three arches at the front door.

"Is that a crime?" Amber removed the bags from her shoulders and set them on the ground. She held onto the straps with her left hand and with her right rubbed her shoulders where they had begun to dig into her flesh.

"It could be," the officer said. "I saw someone hop the fence while I was driving past on the freeway. That wouldn't be you would it? The guard said he saw someone matching your description."

Amber didn't say anything. She knew the cop was fishing for information. He couldn't be sure that they were the ones he saw, but she refused to lie and tell him he must have seen someone else.

"Do you have some form of identification on you?" The cop would ask that if for no other reason than to have a suspect if someone did rob one of these houses.

"It's in my bag." Amber knelt down and unzipped her bag. She double checked to make sure the birth certificate remained hidden and then she spread it open wide. Out of the corner of her eye, she could see the officer place his hand on his weapon. She pulled out her purse and stood, leaving the bag wide open so he could see that it had nothing that any of these people would value. That wouldn't keep him from thinking they just hadn't stolen anything yet, but he couldn't arrest her for something she hadn't done—not that she could do much if he did.

She looked at her driver's license carefully before she handed it to him. Amber thought she'd gotten rid of all of her fake ids, but it didn't hurt to check, just to make sure. The cop looked even more carefully, wrote something in a notebook and handed it back to her.

"So why are you at this house?" The officer made a sweeping motion with his hand.

Amber heard the door behind her open as she said, "My daughter's grandfather lives here."

"Does he have a name, so I can ask him to confirm that?"

"Fox Jacobs." Amber could tell that the cop didn't expect her to answer so quickly.

He might have said something else, but the woman who answered the door asked, "Can I help you?"

Amber turned to face her and saw that she had directed her question at the police officer.

"Does Fox Jacobs live here?" the officer asked. "She claims her daughter is his granddaughter."

The woman's eyes scanned both of them, paying special attention to their faces. "I've never seen them before and Dad doesn't have any grandchildren. This has to be a sick joke."

Chapter Four

Most people had finished eating when Fox stood before them again. They seemed like they were in a good mood. He had to ask for their attention several times before they stopped talking and turned to face him.

"One of the reasons we invited you here today is because we have an exciting announcement about where our company will be headed in the next few months. Several of you have met Jack Abrams and his daughter Celia today and I know some of you have worked with him and his company in the past. Today we're excited to announce…" Fox's voice trailed off because he quickly noticed that his audience was turning its attention to something else, beginning at the back and moving toward the front. He could see Abby coming toward him. The uniform of a police officer also caught his eye and between them were a woman and a girl that he didn't recognize. People made a path for them as they crossed the room, but every head turned to follow them. As if the policeman behind them wasn't enough, the mother and daughter wore clothes that even the engineers in the room would recognize as out of style. The seams were worn much more than anything they might have found at Goodwill or a yard sale or wherever they shopped. Fox wasn't one to judge, but he recognized the type. These two were look-ing for money, but how they'd gotten into the gated communi-ty he didn't know. And he didn't know why there was a police-man following after them.

The thing that bothered Fox the most was that the camera-man from the television station and the reporter from the news-paper both had cameras pointed right at the woman and her daughter as they approached. Even if it turned out to be noth-ing, it might show up on the front page of the business section or in a piece talking about the problem of people begging for money. It would make a much more interesting picture than just another drunk standing at a traffic light with a cardboard sign. "Need a meal."

Fox wasn't about to be forced into giving these people money just because he had a room full of people. He hated see-ing people handing money through their windows just because they felt guilty about seeing the guy standing next to their car. If the guy needs a meal, give him a meal; he'll just waste the money. But Fox himself had never taken the time to feed one of those guys a meal. He just assumed they would refuse. But he wasn't going to have anyone begging in front of his guests.

"In my office!" Fox snapped. He left the platform and with a quick pace made his way to his office.

When he reached the sanctuary of his office, Fox looked around to see who had followed. Abby, the two strangers and the police officer were there. Grayson hadn't followed. He was probably trying to explain the strange events to the guests. Someone needed to.

"Daddy, this woman says this girl is your granddaughter." Abby didn't have the look of someone who was trying to hide a laugh, so maybe she believed it. *How odd*. Or perhaps not. Abby took after her mother and had more of the gift of mercy than Fox.

Fox looked at the girl more closely. He saw a resemblance there, but someone could fake a resemblance or highlight the features that looked similar. These two just wanted money.

"Why are you here?" Fox looked at the police officer as he spoke.

"I'm here because I saw these two climbing over the fence." The police officer stepped forward. "If they aren't who they say they are, I'll make sure they move on. I suspect they came in to see what they could steal and when they saw me, they made up a story."

It was as good of an explanation as any. He could see them standing outside talking to the police officer and saying they were visiting his house without expecting the police officer to check it out.

"Are you my Grandpa?" The young girl looked at him with pitiful eyes. It reminded him of Abby when she was a child. She always knew how to make him feel terrible for not giving her what she wanted, but this girl wasn't Abby.

"Of course I'm not your Grandpa!" Fox looked at the woman with the girl. "You picked the wrong house. My sons aren't the type to mess around with someone like you."

"Come along Miss." The police officer grabbed her by the arm.

The woman pulled her arm free. "She isn't mine. She's Holly's"

"A likely story." It took Fox a moment to let the woman's words sink in. It would've been easy enough for a stranger to pick his house at random and say he was the girl's grandfather, but to know to use a name like Holly, that was a different story. They couldn't just send them away with the police officer until they knew how she knew that name. This woman had done her research. Whatever con she hoped to pull, it was well thought out. But why Holly? That was a name that hadn't been spoken in many years and it was never welcome.

"Don't be difficult." The policeman grabbed her arm again. "These people don't want you here. I don't make me arrest you in front of your daughter."

"Wait officer." Fox had to know more and he didn't want the officer walking back through the guests and then people finding out the girl was his granddaughter, if that was even possible. "I'm not sure who these two are, but I don't think they came to steal jewelry. You can leave them with us and we'll figure out what's going on."

"Are you sure?" The officer looked surprised.

Fox nodded. The sooner he got the officer's car, which was surely parked out front, away from his house the better. What were his neighbors thinking? What were his guests thinking?

"If they cause any trouble, call us and we'll have someone out to pick 'em up. I'll stay in the neighborhood for a while, just in case you need help."

"We'll do that." Fox waited for the policeman to leave before he asked the woman any more questions. "Sit down and tell me how you knew Holly."

"I'd rather not talk in front of Lizi." The woman gave a nodding motion toward the girl.

Fox couldn't imagine why she had reservations. "Abby, how about finding some place to keep the girl out of trouble without disturbing the guests? This woman and I—what was your name?"

"Amber"

"Amber and I will talk about this." Fox wondered if the plan had been that Amber would keep the family distracted while Lizi had the run of the place. She could steal plenty if someone didn't watch her. But that didn't explain how she knew Holly.

"Could I have a glass of water or something?" Amber asked. "I haven't had much to drink this afternoon and my throat's dry."

"Have Maggie bring her a glass of water." Fox didn't want Lizi to have any chance to get away from Abby.

Abby understood. "I'll tell Maggie. Then Lizi and I'll find a movie to watch."

After Abby closed the door behind them, Fox gave Amber the sternest look he could muster—the one that used to make his grandchildren cry. Now he regretted using it with them. "What's your connection to Holly?"

"I would rather not talk until I get something to drink. My throat's too dry to talk." Amber spoke with a hoarse voice.

They waited in silence until Maggie showed up with the water. Amber took the glass from Maggie and began to drink it down.

"Will there be anything else, sir?" Maggie asked before she left.

"No, that's all." Fox dismissed Maggie and waited for Amber to finish.

"I can prove Lizi is your granddaughter." Amber fished one of the ice cubes out of the glass and began to suck on it.

"At what price?"

"It doesn't come with a price."

"Of course it does," Fox said. "How much money do you want?"

"I don't want money." Amber spit the ice cube back into the tall glass. "I just decided it was the right thing to do to return your granddaughter."

"So that's what it is, isn't it?" Fox asked. "You don't have the money to raise your own kid, so you thought you'd find a wealthy family who does and dump her off on them."

"It's not like that at all."

"Oh, I think it is," Fox said. "I have a hard time believing someone who'd just abandon her daughter when it gets to be too much for her."

"I don't want to abandon her," Amber said. "Actually, I'm hoping you guys will let me visit her. I'll find a job down here, if I can."

The thought flashed through Fox's head that this was all just an elaborate plan for this woman to get a job. He wasn't sure how she expected that to work. Maybe she thought he'd give her a job because he felt sorry for her not being able to take care of her child.

"I don't know you," Fox said, "and I'm not sure I'd be comfortable with you being around my family."

"That's understandable." Amber took another drink from her glass. "I'll have to live with whatever decision you guys make, but Lizi won't be very happy about it."

"So you would be willing to just leave her with us? I don't understand that. Why would you do that?"

"What choice do I have? She isn't mine," Amber said. "I wish she were, but I'm trying to do the right thing here."

"You realize that if what you're saying is true, we could have you charged with kidnapping."

"You could," Amber said, "and maybe that's what it is, but you won't do it. Just because I'm trying to do the right thing doesn't mean I'm not prepared to protect myself."

"You may have under estimated us," Fox said. "I've already got a team of lawyers ready to go to work at anything I need them to."

"I don't doubt it," Amber said, "But you'll want to avoid the embarrassment. And I don't think a jury would convict me if I show up with proof that Holly asked me to take care of her daughter."

He stared at the woman, not knowing why he had such a hard time just throwing her out. "I know you're lying about something. I can see it in your eyes."

"I never said I wasn't." Amber laughed. It may have been a nervous laugh. Or maybe she wanted to appear more confident than she was.

Fox looked up and saw the family portrait. The eyes of his grandchildren bore into him. If he threw Lizi out and she really was his granddaughter, he would never be able to live with himself, but he couldn't trust this woman.

Amber had followed his gaze and looked up at the picture too. "Are these your grandchildren?"

"They were," Fox said. "Now they're all dead. But you already knew that."

"No," Amber said, sounding sincere, "I'm sorry to hear that."

The door opened and Maggie stuck her head in the room. "Sir, the guests are asking for you."

Fox had forgotten about the party going on in another part of the house. He stood up. "I'm coming."

"What about me?" Amber asked. "Should I take Lizi and go?"

"No!" He spoke more forcefully than he intended. "No, I mean, try to stay out of the way of the guests and we'll talk about this later."

Secretly, Fox almost hoped Amber would use her apparent freedom to steal something. That would put to rest the questions about her intentions. Even if she didn't, Fox wanted Grayson's opinion. It should have been Grayson's problem anyway. The fact that she hadn't approached Grayson directly probably meant she had chosen what she thought was the easier mark.

"Fox," Maggie stopped him before he rejoined the guests. "Should I get a room ready for those two? Lizi said they don't have anywhere to stay."

Maybe that was the game they were playing. Maybe they were nothing more than a homeless mother and daughter looking for someone to put a roof over their heads for a while. They were succeeding, Fox realized. He couldn't turn them out until he knew more about them. "Yeah, go ahead and do that. While you're at it, see if you can convince them to bathe. They stink."

Chapter Five

As soon as Fox went back to his guests, Amber went look-ing for Lizi. The young girl was alone, watching an animated movie on a large screen in a room that had no other purpose. Three rows, with four cushy chairs each, on a terraced floor. Amber sat down next to Lizi on the front row.

Lizi turned away from the movie. "Are we staying? I like it here."

"Whatever happens, I don't think you'll be staying here." Amber grabbed the girl's hand and held it in her own. "You'll be with your father, whoever he is and wherever he lives."

"I don't care. We'd still get to visit, wouldn't we?" Lizi leaned her head against Amber's arm. "Did he believe you?"

"They haven't thrown us out yet, have they?" Amber thought that was saying something. She knew better than to think that Fox and his family would believe a stranger coming in off the street without checking out her story, but he'd had the opportunity to send them away and had not. She only part-ly believed her story herself. It was built on what Holly had told her and what she'd been able to discover on her own. She'd filled in the gaps with a few good guesses, leading her to this house. And just in case they didn't believe her, she'd brought what looked like very convincing proof, but it had been fabricated by a friend. She told herself that she wouldn't use that. She wouldn't have brought it at all if she'd been sure she'd be believed.

"Where do you think he lives?" Lizi still hadn't turned her attention back to the movie.

"Who, honey?"

"My Daddy. Do you think he has a house like this?"

"I doubt it." Amber stroked Lizi's hair. "A house like this costs a lot of money. He probably doesn't make as much money as his father does."

"Did you find out if it's Steve or Grayson," Lizi asked.

"No, I'm still not sure about that." Amber was far more uncertain than she dared let Lizi know. But what good would it do if they were both uncertain. She needed Lizi to convince these people that she really thought they were her family. If Amber was wrong, it would hurt Lizi, but she'd get over it. It couldn't be helped.

"What should I call him?" Lizi asked. "Should I call him Daddy or Dad?"

"Maybe you should wait until you meet him before you decide that," Amber said, "But I don't think it'll matter."

"Father?" Lizi grinned. "Don't rich kids say father all the time?

"Maybe that isn't such a good idea."

Lizi moved her hand and Amber felt something sticky. "What did you get on your hand?"

"Chocolate." Lizi spoke as if it were ordinary for her to have chocolate stuck to her hands.

"Where did you get chocolate?" With their financial situation, chocolate had become a treat that they rarely bought. If they didn't need it, they went without.

"It's on the strawberries. Maggie brought me some. Want some?" Lizi picked up a bowl from the seat next to her and held it out for Amber to take.

Amber picked out one and bit into the berry. It tasted sweet in her mouth. She picked out another.

"Miss?" Maggie came into the room. "I've got a room ready for the two of you, if you would like for me to show you where it is. I put you both in the same room, with it being a strange house and all."

"That'll be perfect." Amber couldn't remember the last time she had fallen asleep at night without hearing Lizi's breathing a short distance away. "I'm sure you wouldn't want to clean another room just because we showed up."

Maggie looked hurt. "There's five other rooms that aren't being used, and they're all clean—all of them."

"So we get to sleep here tonight?" Lizi sat up in her chair.

"Yes, that's what it looks like," Amber said.

They could still hear the noise from the party as Maggie led them up the stairs to the second floor. Amber didn't think the other guests noticed them. Maggie led them to a room that had a king-sized bed. A couple of chairs sat at a table near the window.

"Is this where we're staying?" Lizi stood in the center of the room and turned all the way around, taking it all in. "It looks like a motel room—only bigger!"

"Don't let Fox hear you say that." Maggie carried their bags into the bathroom and disappeared into a closet. "I'm sure y'all would like to take baths. Do you need me to wash your clothes? You do have a change of clothes?"

Without waiting for an answer, Maggie unzipped the bags and began rummaging through their things. She pulled out the few clothes they had and started putting them on hangers or folding them neatly to place on a shelf. Amber snatched her bag away, hoping Maggie hadn't seen something she oughtn't.

"I can do that." Amber hoped she said it in a way that Maggie didn't think she was hiding something. Amber looked in the bag. Nothing important looked disturbed.

"I'm just trying to do my job, Miss." Maggie went on putting clothes away. She held up the better of Amber's two dresses. "I'll iron this for after you get cleaned up. The rest I should take outside and burn."

"You wouldn't dare!" Amber readied herself to snatch her weather beaten apparel from Maggie's fire hungry hands.

"Of course not—not at this time of year. It's so dry out there I'd probably burn down every house in the neighborhood." Maggie finished putting Amber's clothes away and turned to Lizi's. "At least you dress your daughter better than you dress yourself."

"It's easier to find clothes for her." Amber wasn't about to tell this woman that all of Lizi's clothes were gifts from people at church.

Maggie looked more carefully at Lizi's clothes before she picked out a dress. "This will have to do. You can put this on after you clean up."

"But that one's only for church," Lizi said.

Maggie smiled slightly. "Are you afraid someone's going to see you wear it twice in one week? I'm sure you won't be seeing anyone you go to church with around here. But we can't have you wearing rags. Not today."

"What if we went and got clothes? Is there a Goodwill close by?" Lizi turned and looked at Amber. "Do we have enough money for that?"

Amber shook her head and hoped Maggie didn't see her. She wasn't ashamed that she didn't have any money, but she didn't want them thinking that they'd come because she didn't have money. "It'll be okay if you wear your Sunday dress."

Maggie frowned. "I don't think people who shop at Goodwill go to church where the Jacobs got to church."

"But we've got to go to church. Don't we Amber?"

"Yes, Honey, we'll go to church—somewhere. I'm sure Fort Worth has more than one church." For that matter, Amber had seen more than one as they made their way through town, but what she wondered was whether Maggie was correct or if Fox didn't want to be seen in public with them. What if his son was the same way? Maybe Holly's concerns had some truth to them.

"I'll bring your supper up here so you can eat after you bathe." Maggie began running water in the tub.

The sound of gushing water brought back memories of days Amber had time to just sit and soak in a tub. This wouldn't be one of those times, but the tub looked perfect for that. It looked more like a giant bowl than a bathtub.

"The towels are here." Maggie pulled towels out of a cabinet and huge them from a rack near the tub. "If you need anything else, let me know."

While Lizi took her bath, Amber stared out the window. At first, she saw little movement on the street below, but then she saw people walk out to their cars. One by one the cars disappeared down the street until she could see only one car on the drive. The rear wheels of this car rested on the street. A man with hair a little darker brown than her own walked out to the car. Amber heard the chirp as he turned off the alarm and then the delayed sound of the car door after he got inside. The engine came to life and he pulled forward. Amber expected to see him drive to the other end of the drive and pull out onto the street, but the car turned and disappeared as if it had gone through the house. Amber supposed there must have been a drive that she hadn't noticed and she couldn't see from her vantage point.

Lizi came out of the bathroom. "Your turn." Her wet hair clumped together and hung straight down her back.

"Let's see if I can find a comb so your hair won't get all tangled." Amber went to the closet and dug through her bag until she found the faded red comb. It had teeth marks from a dog chewing on it, but it was adequate.

Lizi sat on the bed and Amber sat behind her. As she pulled the comb through Lizi's blond hair, she could smell the scent of lilacs. So different from the medicine like smell of the shampoo they had at home.

Amber was running the comb through her own wet hair when Maggie returned. She sat the tray on the table next to the window. "If there's anything you'll need—I'll be downstairs helping clean up the mess before I leave. Tomorrow's my day off, you know."

No, Amber didn't know. She watched the housekeeper walk out the door.

Maggie turned around. "The family wants to see you after you bathe and y'all finish eating."

Chapter Six

The guests were on their way home and Fox sat at the head of the table, looking at the rest of his family. From another part of the house, he heard Maggie barking orders. Mostly, things that even he could understand, but all that mattered was that the house would be spotless before the maid service left. It was too much to expect Maggie to clean the whole house by herself after a party. He heard the sound of a stainless steel spoon against a pan in the kitchen as the catering service cleared away their mess. Next to him, Fiona's fork tapped against her plate as she picked at her food. She hadn't come downstairs at all during the party. She no longer enjoyed parties the way she once had.

Grayson sat on the other side of him. Celia played with the hair behind Grayson's ears, running her manicured nails through it. Maybe there really was more going on there than Grayson had let on. Next to her, Abby sat quietly — nearly as quiet as her mother. At the other end, Steve sat with a big grin on his face that wouldn't go away. Beside him, Donna looked thoughtful. Something was always going on behind those black eyes of hers, but this time — more than normal.

"She wants money, don't you think?" Abby broke her silence.

"I'm sure she wants money." Fox could tell that by the way Amber dressed. "Just from the clothes they wear, you can tell they either need money or they want us to think they do. But the real question is whether that's all it is."

"She just picked an easy mark and we're it," Steve said with a laugh. "Or at least Grayson is. I'm going to enjoy this."

"But she didn't." Donna touched her husband's arm as she spoke.

"She didn't what?" Fox asked from the other end of the table, fearing that Donna would explain what she was thinking to her husband and not to the rest of them. Fox wanted to hear what she had to say.

"She didn't pick an easy mark." Donna took a sip of coffee. "Just look at all the trouble they went to just to get here. They climbed over the fence. They could've just called or gone by the office. And the girl told Abby that they rode the train from St. Louis. I don't know how long that takes, but why go to the trouble? If they're just wanting money, why not try got get someone in St. Louis to give them money?"

"Maybe they conned so many people there they had to move." Celia moved her chair a few inches closer to Grayson and interlaced her fingers in his.

"Let's say that is what happened," Donna said, "but why come here? They could've picked Dallas or Little Rock or Kansas City. Any large city is bound to have someone they could target. No, they had to know they were coming here before they left St. Louis."

"If they really came from St. Louis..." Grayson pulled his hand free from Celia's grip and began to run his finger around the top of his tea glass. "For all we know, they could be living in one of the houses on the other side of the freeway and decided to come asking for money."

Steve grinned even bigger. "What's the matter Grayson? Are you trying to weasel out of taking care of your kid?"

"Don't be childish!" Donna shot her husband a look. "He's right. We don't know, but I think we could find out easily enough."

"She showed that police officer a driver's license." Abby spoke again. "It looked like a Missouri license to me."

"A driver's license can be faked," Donna said, "and I doubt the Fort Worth police have a lot of experience recognizing fake ids from different states. But that might be a good starting point to see if she's lying."

"I've got to admit that I'm surprised about all of this and I'm sure my father is real happy about it." Celia grabbed Grayson's hand and caressed it, as if to apologize for what she was about to say. "Y'all are treating this like you think she might be telling the truth. Shouldn't y'all know who your own family is? If she's supposed to be Grayson's daughter, wouldn't he be the first to know if it's even possible? I think I know him well enough to know that he's not the type of guy to be fooling around."

"I think I see what you're saying," Donna said. "We ought to assume that she's telling the truth because if she were lying about it she wouldn't have..."

"No, that's not what I'm saying," Celia said. "I'm saying this whole thing is raising some doubts in my mind about what I thought I knew about this family and I know my father is having questions."

Celia confirmed what Fox feared. He could see the whole merger falling through because of this. That was nothing if Lizi really was a lost grandchild, but if it all turned out to be a scam and the merger fell through because of it, things would not be good.

"Not to speak for Grayson," Donna said, "But I'm sure every family has secrets they keep from each other. If this is a scam, I'm sure she's relying on that. If she'd gone directly to

Grayson, it would've been easy for him to deny it and that would've been it, but with her coming here, we all might question if we know Grayson as well as we think we do. We know what he's like when he's around us. We don't think he would do anything inappropriate, but we can all make mistakes. It does make you wonder why she made the claim she did instead of just saying she and Grayson had a one night stand and Lizi was the result."

"Thanks Donna," Grayson said dryly. "I really appreciate your high opinion of my moral fiber."

Donna blushed. "I'm not saying I really think you would do something like that. I know better, but she doesn't. For all she knows, you might have a different girl every night."

"To answer what I think is Celia's concern," Grayson said, "the one thing that keeps me from just saying it isn't true is that she mentioned the name Holly."

"That's part of what bothers me about this," Celia said. "Maybe I should say that what you did before is your business and be done with it, but who is Holly? I know your wife's name was Victoria."

"Yeah, Grayson, how are you going to answer that one?" Steve asked. "Sure, seems like you've got a few extra women in your life to me."

"Holly was Victoria's best friend," Fox said before Grayson had a chance to speak. Grayson looked at his father and must have gotten the idea from the look Fox gave him that his father didn't want him to give a better explanation than that. He spoke only to affirm what his father had said. The rest of the family understood the situation, but Fox wasn't ready to bring all of the skeletons out of the closet for Celia and more importantly, her father to see.

"I can't tell you how much it disturbs me to think about you sleeping with your wife's best friend," Celia said.

"That's not the way it was," Grayson said. "Holly was—let's just say that Holly was a little special. If the girl is Holly's, I'm sure that Victoria would want me to take care of her."

"But the woman is claiming that the girl is yours," Celia said.

"One of ours, anyway," Grayson said. "If she just knew Holly, there's really no reason why she would think it had to be mine. She just said the girl is Dad's granddaughter, right?"

"Hey, leave me out of this!" Steve said.

"It's really sort of convenient. It's possible she knew Holly," Grayson said. "But if we do some kind of test that comes back negative, she could just claim that the child's mother told her one of us was the girl's father and we couldn't prove otherwise."

"Unless we can prove Amber is the girl's mother," Donna said. "No jury would believe she didn't know her own daughter."

"Let's not worry about taking her to court yet. It'll take several days to get any results back, even if we can find a lab that can start right away." Fox wondered if that was what Amber was counting on. "I'm not sure I like the idea of them staying here so long. The minute my back is turned they could grab a bunch of stuff and disappear. But I don't really see any other choice. Until see have some kind of evidence, everything will be her word against ours."

"We could put them up in a hotel." Grayson rested his free hand on Celia's arm. "But then, with a few careless words, we could have some news types asking a bunch of questions."

"Grayson, why don't you just stay here too?" Steve asked. "Maggie will be around most of the time and you can make sure they're staying out of trouble when she's not. That way, Mom and Dad won't have to watch them so close."

"It does seem like the thing to do," Celia said but looked very unhappy about his suggestion. "If the girl was your daughter, you would want to spend time getting to know her."

"Yeah, you're right," Grayson said. "It would give me a chance to get to know her. She might be interested in learning about her mother. But, I can't be here when I'm working."

"This is your ballgame. You decide on the game plan." Fox looked up and saw Amber and Lizi standing a few feet away from the table. How much they heard he couldn't be sure.

Steve turned around to look at them. "Hi, I'm Fox's son Steve. I understand you're looking for the father of your child."

Amber hesitated for a moment before she said, "I suppose that's right, in a way. Are you saying you're the one looking to claim that position?"

Steve laughed. "Sorry, no can do. I'm already taken." He patted Donna on the arm.

"This one's taken too," Celia said, indicating Grayson.

"I'm glad to hear that," Amber said. "I'd like for Lizi to be in a home with both a father and a mother."

Fox had to admit that the woman handled herself well. Either she had nothing to hide or she was good at what she did.

Fiona pushed back from the table, leaving a plate full of food that she hadn't eaten. Fox held his hand out give support if she needed it. She made her way around the table and stood in front of the newcomers. She held Lizi's chin in her hand and looked at her face from one angle and then another.

"Give your grandmother a hug," she finally said. The girl obliged her, but Fox wasn't so quick to trust his wife's assessment. It had only been a month before that she had seen a child in a store and insisted that it was one of the dead grandchildren. Whatever the tests proved Lizi to be, Fox hated to think how it would affect Fiona.

"I'm going back upstairs." Fiona turned to look back at Fox. "I'm feeling a little tired."

"Mom, do you need some help." Grayson rose from the table.

"I'm not as feeble as you think. I can make it." Fiona waved him off.

Grayson picked up his glass from the table and walked over to grab one of the taller chairs from the breakfast bar. "One of you can have my chair."

Lizi walked around the table and sat in the chair Fiona had vacated, leaving Amber to take the chair next to Celia. Celia followed Grayson, grabbed another chair from the bar, and placed it as near Grayson as she could. It put her slightly behind him because there wasn't enough room where he'd placed it between Fox and Amber.

Grayson looked down at Amber. "We've been talking about what you claim. I suppose you have some kind of proof that she's my daughter?"

"I've got a birth certificate." Amber reached into a pocket of her dress and pulled out some worn looking papers. She held them under the table as she looked through them. She handed one up to Grayson. "Here it is."

He looked at it carefully and started to hand it back.

"Let me see that." Fox pulled it from his hand. He looked at it just as carefully. He read parts of it aloud.

"Elizabeth Victoria Jacobs," the paper said. "Mother, Holly Jacobs. Father, Grayson Jacobs." The date placed the birth at about the right time. It also gave the name of a St. Louis hospital and a doctor Fox didn't know.

Fox handed the paper back to Amber. She folded it and put it back in her dress pocket. He wasn't sure how he wanted to handle this. It looked real enough, but it had the wrong name on it. *So much for the merger.*

"You realize, of course, that we know that thing isn't real," Grayson said, as if it was the most natural thing in the world to accuse a woman of lying.

"Oh?" Amber asked. "It looks real enough to me. I didn't fill it out, if that's what you're thinking."

"Perhaps," Grayson said, "but Holly's last name wasn't Jacobs. If you're saying it was, then I'm sure we're talking about a different Holly than the one we knew."

Fox watched Amber to see how she would react, looking for anything in her body language that would give them a hint of what she was thinking. It wasn't much, but he thought he saw her shoulders relax just a little. It gave him the impression that she was relieved, but about what he couldn't be sure. Was she relieved that she'd been found out and it was over? Maybe she was relieved for another reason.

"Well, if that's the way it is, that's the way it is," Amber said. "I was just going on the information I had. I just wish I'd known that before we came down here. It took most of my savings to buy the train tickets. I was trying to do the right thing."

At last, the last shoe was about to drop, Fox thought. Amber would be asking for money for a train ticket. Of course, Grayson being the kind of guy he was would offer to give them money to fly back to St. Louis. They could easily walk away with a thousand dollars in their pocket with no thought of how they'd disturbed the family they'd scammed.

"Don't let that bother you." Grayson said. "I'm no expert on birth certificates. I'd like to get some tests run, just to be sure."

"Amber?" Lizi looked scared.

"It'll be fine," Amber reassured the girl, but then she looked Grayson squarely in the face and said, "If you're positive she isn't yours, I don't see any reason to run the tests. Her mother is dead and I wouldn't have any idea where to look for her father if you aren't him."

"I'd like to run the tests anyway," Grayson said, "Just on the off chance that your Holly is the same Holly we knew."

"But it might be a lot of money." Amber's statement gave Fox something to think about. He wasn't sure if she was saying it because she was really concerned that they might spend money needlessly or if it was calculated to steer them away from anything other than sending them on their way with a pocket full of cash.

"Yeah, I don't know what it'll cost," Grayson said, "but I'm not too concerned about that. I'd rather be sure. If she really is Holly's kid, I want to make sure she's taken care of."

Grayson looked thoughtful for a moment. He started to say something, but closed his mouth and turned to look at Amber again. "How did you know Holly? And how did you end up with her daughter?"

"I met her at work," Amber said. "She came in the diner where I was working to get out of the rain. I she looked like she could use some help, so I offered her a place to stay. I figured I'd let her stay until the baby was born. But it was kind of nice having someone else help pay the mortgage. That was only when she had the money. She had trouble keeping jobs."

"So how was it you ended up with Lizi?" Grayson asked.

"It just happened," Amber said. "I wasn't trying to keep her from her family, but Holly died when Lizi was two. No one ever told me what I should do with her. I'd been taking care of her when Holly wasn't there anyway, so I just kept taking care of her."

"So what made you all the sudden decide to look for her family?" Celia asked. "Did you just recently start looking?"

"I'd rather not answer that," Amber said. "Nothing I can say will keep me from sounding like an awful person who kept Lizi away from her family."

Amber covered her mouth and yawned. Fox couldn't shake the feeling that she was lying about something. Maybe her yawning was just an attempt to encourage someone to change the subject.

"You must be tired," Grayson said. "What time did you leave St. Louis this morning?"

"Eight o'clock last night," Lizi bragged.

Grayson looked at his watch. "Did you get much sleep? That was more than twenty-four hours ago."

"I dozed on the train. Lizi slept pretty good."

"Maybe we should let you go on up to bed. We can talk more tomorrow."

Amber didn't wait to be told a second time. She pushed her chair back from the table. "Come on Lizi."

Lizi took a little longer to leave. "Good night, Daddy. Good night, Grandpa."

As she went around the table calling names, Fox felt sure Amber must have drilled her on this. When she got to Celia, she paused for a moment and then said, "Good night, whoever you are," and then she hurried out of the room to catch up with Amber.

"You can see what kind of impression I made on her," Celia said.

Grayson laughed. "I thought it was funny—whoever you are."

"Well I think I'll gather my things and let you take me home." Celia put her chair back at the bar and left the room.

"Kind of makes you wonder if Amber coached her on how to leave the room," Fox said.

"That thought crossed my mind," Grayson said, "But it doesn't change anything."

Chapter Seven

Amber pulled back the blankets on the bed. They smelled clean and fresh. She knew she shouldn't have shown them the birth certificate. It wouldn't have helped if she'd shown them the real one, either, but at least with that one was on file with the county—if they went looking for it. She shouldn't have come. She'd been so sure that this was the right family. She'd spent hours in the library trying to find them. Her high school history teachers would've been proud, but she'd done something wrong and she wasn't sure what.

She wondered if she should've asked someone to help her, but she wasn't sure whom she could've asked. A lawyer might've done this sort of thing, but she didn't have the money for an attorney. And what could a lawyer do that she hadn't? She had started with the little Holly had told her about her family. Holly wasn't keen on giving out names, favoring instead to use more creative ways of referring to them. The one name Amber did remember Holly using was that of Fox Jacobs, a man she despised because he always chased all the fairies away. There couldn't be very many men named Fox Jacobs in the world and even fewer in Texas. When she'd found this one in Fort Worth, she'd been sure that he had to be Holly's father-in-law. But after having met him and the rest of the family, she began to wonder if Fox had just been a nickname. A fox would scare fairies away, wouldn't they? It didn't matter now anyway. It was too late to try thinking through Holly's logic.

Lizi slipped under the sheets on her side of the bed. "It's big enough for three or four people."

"It's just the two of us." Amber planted a kiss on the top of Lizi's forehead and turned off the lamp on her side of the bed. She walked around to her side, slipped under the sheets and turned off the light. "What'd you think of everyone? Did you like them?"

"I'm trying not to."

"Why?"

"Because after I start to like them we'll just have to leave."

"That shouldn't keep you from liking people," Amber said. "And who knows, your mother may still have been a friend of the family."

"So what?"

"So they might be willing to take you in," Amber said. "They can give you things that I can't."

"I don't need anything," Lizi said.

"I wish that were true, but you know it isn't." Amber stared at the ceiling through the darkness. There was just enough light for her to see the texture. "What do you think of Grayson? If anyone takes you in, it'll probably be him."

Lizi didn't answer immediately, making Amber wonder if she'd fallen asleep, but then she said, "I don't know."

"What about Celia? She seemed nice, didn't she?"

"If you say so," Lizi said. "Do I have to like her?"

"No," Amber said, "but it looks to me like she and Grayson might be thinking about marriage. If Grayson takes you in, she'll be your new mother."

"Why can't you be my mother?"

"We've talked about this," Amber said. "You need to be with your real family."

"But what if they're not my real family? Do I have to stay with them anyway?"

Amber thought of the very small amount of cash she had left. It wouldn't last long. As much as it hurt to let her go, the best thing for Lizi would be if someone who could afford to take care of her would take her in and yet Amber hoped whatever tests they wanted to run would prove there was no connection between Lizi and their family. "I'll tell you what. If those tests they want show you aren't part of their family, you and I'll leave and pretend none of this ever happened. I'll find a job somewhere and we'll find a way to survive."

"We always do," Lizi said.

"Yes, that's right." Amber tried not to let Lizi know that this might be the exception. She refused to do what they'd done before to survive.

"But what if they find out that Grayson's my Dad?"

"I don't think that's likely."

"But what if?" Lizi asked. "Are you going to stay with me then too?"

"I don't see how that would be possible," Amber said. "But don't worry about it. I'll get a job down here and find a place to live. I'll come to visit you as much as they'll let me."

"You could marry Grayson," Lizi said.

"I suppose," Amber said. "If he wanted to marry me."

"You should make him marry you," Lizi said.

"Just how do you propose I do that?"

"Blackmail."

"That's probably not a good idea," Amber said, all the while thinking of ways she could pull it off. It could be done, but it was too big of a risk to take, no matter how much Amber hated the thought of losing Lizi.

Amber let her head sink into the soft pillow. She wanted to sleep, but even after twenty-four hours without much sleep, she was too keyed up. She listened to Lizi's breathing.

They lay in silence for several minutes. Amber heard a car. It could have been someone leaving the house or someone driving past on the street. She heard water running through the pipes. And then sleep—

"Amber?"

"What Honey?" She stirred from her sleep and responded before she was fully aware.

"I don't think they like us very much."

"Who doesn't?"

"The Jacobses."

"They just don't know whether to trust us. Give 'em a chance. They'll come around."

"How long will that take."

"I don't know. Try to go to sleep." Amber listened to Lizi's breathing. The girl had already fallen asleep. Amber closed her eyes and did the same.

Chapter Eight

When Fox crawled out of bed and left the bedroom, Fiona was still asleep. She slept too much these days, but he knew why. She'd never been the same since the day they lost the grandchildren. They'd gone through a year of this and she still wasn't better. Neither was Fox, but he tried not to show it. He tried to be strong for Fiona and the kids. Abby had taken it the hardest. She'd lost her children and her husband in one day. But now she was coping a little better. For a woman who'd lost her children, Donna seemed unscathed, but Donna had always been strong. Steve coped the way Steve always coped. He cracked jokes and made everything out to be a game. He'd sold most of his share of the family business to Grayson and would've used the money to tour the world, if Donna hadn't talked some sense into him. And Grayson, who'd lost the least, was forced to run the business with very little help from the rest of the family.

Fox looked down the sunlit hall toward the bedroom where Amber and Lizi spent the night. He had mixed feelings about that. It's not often that life drops a grandchild in your lap. She could never replace the children they'd lost, but she could infuse life into a family that was in a walking death. But she could also kill any hopes of a merger. Jack would not be happy about the situation.

He descended the stairs. On the landing, halfway down, Grayson stood with a forgotten cup of coffee in his hand, staring at an old portrait, an image from happier times. A younger version of Grayson stood behind a seated Victoria as they smiled into the camera lens. Her long auburn hair flowed in streams of curls and rested on her shoulders before disappearing behind her back.

"They don't look much alike, do they?" Fox touched his son on the shoulder.

Grayson made eye-contact for a moment and then looked back at the photo. "No, not really. Not enough to be certain anyway. I wouldn't have expected Victoria to have a blond headed kid, but I was never sure what Victoria's natural color was anyway—she messed with it so much."

"Wondering if she might have had a baby?"

"No—well, sort of." Grayson turned and walked down the stairs. "I just can't help wondering what happened to Victoria after she left. Who knows, maybe it was beyond what Victoria could do to have children. But Holly might have handled it just fine. I'm hoping Amber can tell me something about that."

Fox followed his son as he walked toward the kitchen. "She might. That's assuming she knew the same Holly."

"I know, but I think it's worth listening to see what she has to say." Grayson dumped his cold coffee down the sink and poured another cup. He sat down at the breakfast bar and briefly looked at the front page of the Star-Telegram before pushing it aside.

"We really need to be careful. We don't know anything about the woman. She may have just made up a story or she heard the story from someone and decided to cash in on it." Fox opened the dishwasher and pulled out a clean cup to fill with coffee. He opened the refrigerator door as he took his first sip of the hot liquid.

"If that's what she did, I know how to handle her," Grayson said. "You taught me well."

The eggs and bacon looked appetizing, but Fox didn't feel like cooking. He grabbed the milk and went to the pantry to get the cereal.

"What I don't like about all this is that we don't know her motives," Fox said. "If we accept everything she said as true—and I don't think we can do that—but if we do then we might assume that she really wants to do the right thing. Or it could be that she wants money. Then we have this merger going on. I have a hard time believing this is a coincidence."

"Yeah, but what's the point," Grayson asked. "Do you think Jack Abrams is looking for a way out? If he doesn't want to go through with it, he can back out at any time anyway."

"Maybe it's not that he's trying to get out of it, but maybe he wants to weaken our position a little. If our company is worth less then he gets a bigger ownership stake."

"That would be a risky move. If he got caught at it, he could be in big trouble. I think it's more likely that someone just wanted to get it on the news. Or maybe one of the employees heard about the merger and wanted to try to stop it."

"How did we do in the news?" Fox asked.

"Not bad," Grayson said. "The newspaper said something about the party being interrupted by uninvited guests. It didn't go into detail, but we didn't tell them much about what was going on. But I did see one blog that wasn't so kind. One of our employees blogged about it. He implied I'd been sleeping around."

"What are you going to do about it?" Fox asked.

"Nothing, I don't think," Grayson said. "He didn't really call me by name and he thought it was with Amber. It's probably better to pretend it never happened than to stir things up even more."

"I don't like our employees talking bad about us on their blogs."

"Neither do I," Grayson said. "But I don't think it'll do any good to fire them for doing that. It'll just give them more to fuss about."

"What do you think we should do about it?"

"Nothing for now, but as soon as we figure out what's going on, we need to make some kind of public statement with all the facts in it."

"Even if it makes us look bad?"

"It won't," Grayson said, "but even if it did, it would be better coming from us than a disgruntled employee."

"The first thing we need to do is double check her story," Fox said. "We need to know how much of what she's saying is true and how much isn't. Maybe we should bring the lawyers in on this. They'll have a better idea of what we can do and what we should do." Fox took the first bite of his cereal.

"I've already scheduled a meeting at one o'clock this afternoon," Grayson said.

"Here or at the office?"

"Here—I'm still not sure I like the idea of leaving those two alone with just Mom in the house." Grayson voiced one of Fox's concerns. It wasn't wise to invite a perfect stranger into the house and leave them to take whatever they wanted.

The two strangers walked into the kitchen together. They both looked well rested and bright eyed. They wore clothes that Fox had never thought a guest in his house would wear. Maybe he should give them some money to go shopping, but he was hesitant to do that because that may have been their plan. Show up; get a few hundred dollars and leave. Their story seemed too elaborate for that, but he didn't want to be made the fool.

"Maggie isn't here, so if you want breakfast you'll have to fix it yourself." Fox felt guilty for not offering to fix breakfast for guests in his house, but he'd already given them a place to sleep. Besides, if they were family, they could fend for themselves like everyone else.

"I'm sure we can manage." Amber smiled at him and then walked over to the refrigerator. "Maggie told me that today's her day off."

"She deserves it," Grayson said. "I don't care how many people the caterers bring, Maggie always ends up doing more work at a party than anyone."

"I've worked a few big parties," Amber said. "I know what it's like. But I was always on the catering end of it."

"She doesn't always show up in time to fix breakfast anyway."

"I don't guess there's any reason she should," Amber said as she began pulling things out of the refrigerator. "Anyone can fix breakfast."

"Try telling Celia that," Grayson said. "I don't think I've seen her within five feet of a stove. If I ever see her fixing breakfast for me, I'll know she wants something pretty bad."

"She doesn't need to." Fox defended Celia. "She has enough money she can pay someone to do the cooking. But I didn't realize the two of you were so close."

"We've been working together on this merger," Grayson said, as if it were nothing. "Seems to me that you've got enough money to pay someone to fix breakfast for you too, but I don't see anyone cooking for you this morning."

"Yeah, but look what I'm eating." Fox pointed to his half eaten bowl of cereal.

"Do you want me to fix you something?" Amber asked. "It's no trouble."

She was either being nice or she was trying to make a good impression. Fox would've liked to have known which. "This is probably all I need, but it's been quite a while since I've had real good homemade biscuits. Usually we have those greasy things that come out of a can or they're so dry they aren't worth eating."

"It'll take a few minutes, but I think I can handle that, if that's what you want."

"No, you don't have to do that," Fox said, but was curious how well she would do.

"Maggie has a cookbook around here somewhere," Grayson said. "But I'm not sure where she keeps it."

"I think I can manage without." Amber opened one cabinet door and then another, pulling out a large bowl.

"Amber never uses a cookbook," Lizi said.

"That's not entirely true," Amber said. "I use one once in a while."

The last time Fox had seen anyone make biscuits without following a recipe, they'd come out as hard as hockey pucks and was anxious to see if Amber would fare any better. He pushed his cereal aside as he watched her work. She put one ingredient after another into the bowl. He could've had the recipe in front of him and wouldn't have known if she did it right, but she not only didn't use a recipe, she didn't measure anything. He knew enough to know that would lead to disaster. He wondered if she was going through with it just to keep up the act, whatever it was. She put the pan of raw biscuits in the upper oven and set the timer. She didn't appear worried at all as she went about frying sausage and eggs on the stove.

After several minutes, the timer beeped. Amber pulled out a pan of golden brown biscuits and set them on the granite counter top. "There you go."

Fox picked up a biscuit from the pan. The heat hurt the tips of his fingers and he dropped it back on the pan.

"Careful," Amber said, "Let me get you a plate."

He ignored the pain, picked up the biscuit and pulled it apart. The steam rose from the two halves and stung his nose, bringing tears to his eyes. He dropped the halves on the granite counter. He could tell from looking at it that the biscuit was soft and flaky.

Grayson waited until Amber had found the plates, the butter and the jelly before he reached for a biscuit. "You must make biscuits a lot."

"I did." Amber put a plate with sausage and eggs in front of Lizi. "I worked at this little diner in St. Louis until the place burned down. They laid all of us off while they rebuild."

"You were a cook?" Grayson asked.

"Part of the time, but most of the time I worked out front. I helped prep when we weren't busy with customers. Nothing difficult—we served stuff like Mom might fix at home."

"My mother never has been big on cooking. Now she won't cook at all." Grayson smeared jelly on his biscuit.

"You know what I mean." Amber sat down with her own plate.

"How long ago did it burn?" Fox asked. He tried not to sound like he was interrogating her, but it was something they could check to see if she was telling the truth. Someone might know her there.

"Six months or so—I thought they'd rebuild right away, or move to a different location, but they still haven't gotten funding. You run out of money quick when you aren't working."

"So you brought Lizi down here because you ran out of money?" Grayson asked. He took the last bite of one biscuit and reached for another.

"Not exactly," Amber said. "Both things happened about the same time, but running out of money convinced me I had to do it sooner than later."

"Why now?" Fox asked. "Didn't it bother you that you were keeping her from her family?"

"Lizi's mother never said a whole lot about her family," Amber said. "I had to dig to find out anything. And I wasn't sure that I could trust her family if I found them. Even now, I can't help but wonder if her family had something to do with her death."

"Are you saying you think we might have killed her?" Grayson's agitation was understandable, but not helpful. "How could one of us have done that?"

"I didn't say I thought you did it," Amber said. "I said her family. You made it clear last night that you aren't her family. Or is there something you aren't telling me?"

"I was never unfaithful to my wife," Grayson said. "But as for whether there's something I'm not telling you, of course there is. You can't expect to walk in here and have us tell you everything."

"No, you're right," Amber said. "I didn't mean to imply otherwise. I just don't understand why you're getting upset if you aren't sure you know Holly."

"Yeah, maybe I shouldn't get upset," Grayson said, "but I keep thinking that your Holly and my Holly might be the same person. I know my Holly's family very well and they wouldn't do anything to harm her."

"Then it can't be the same person. My Holly was afraid someone was coming to get her and she didn't trust anybody. She didn't want her family to find her," Amber said.

"Then why did she trust you?" Grayson asked.

"Maybe she didn't, but she needed a place to stay. It's hard to be on the run when you're trying to raise a child. She had to trust someone and I was convenient."

"Did Holly seem a little strange to you?" Grayson stirred his coffee with a teaspoon. The spoon clanged loudly against the side with each pass.

"She was interesting. I'll tell you that much. It would be better if we didn't talk about it in front of Lizi."

"Why not?" Lizi asked. "I want to hear about her too."

"Maybe you're right." Grayson downed the rest of his coffee and stood up. "I have some work I need to do at the office. We can talk about this some other time."

"Can I go with you?" Lizi looked eagerly at Grayson. More coaching by Amber, no doubt, or was it? Lizi really seemed eager to go.

"You won't like it, there's nothing for you to do there."

"But I want to see where you work," Lizi said.

Grayson looked at Amber.

She shrugged her shoulders. "It's fine with me, if you don't mind taking her."

"Do you want to go too?"

"Grayson, can I talk to you alone?" Fox asked before Amber had a chance to answer.

They stepped out of the kitchen far enough that Amber and Lizi wouldn't be able to hear them.

"Are you sure you want to take Amber to work with you?" Fox asked.

"You don't have anything to worry about. It's Saturday. There's not much going on that she'd see or overhear. It might be good to have her there in case Lizi gets tired of watching me work."

"That wasn't what I was thinking. If she gets you alone, there's nothing to keep her from claiming you did something inappropriate. Then where will we be?"

"I don't think she's the type to do that."

"You won't know until it's too late."

"She either believes what she says or she's thought this thing out too well to pull something like that. If she planned to do that, she would have just found a way to do it instead of showing up here. I think her plans center around Lizi and she's going to stick with them."

Grayson left Fox standing there. He went back and said something to Lizi and Amber before the three of them left together. Fox went back to the kitchen, put a couple of biscuits on a plate to take up to Fiona, hoping that Fiona would like Amber's cooking better than she liked everyone else's.

She was awake, but still in bed when Fox entered the room. "Don't you think you should get up and at least try to participate in the rest of the world?"

"Is it worth it?" She asked.

"Yes," he said. He knew what he said was true, but sometimes he'd felt the same as his wife.

Fiona rolled over and sat up in bed.

"I brought you something to eat." He held the plate out to her.

"You shouldn't have gone to so much trouble. You know I never feel like eating much." She took the plate and set it on her lap. She tore off a small piece and took a bite.

"Is it good?"

"You didn't make these."

"No."

"Is Maggie here already?" Fiona looked confused. "I thought today was her day off."

"Amber made them."

Fiona looked even more puzzled and then an expression of recognition crossed her face. "You didn't put our guests to work, did you?"

"She volunteered and she knows her way around a kitchen."

Fiona broke off a larger piece and stuffed in her mouth. "It reminds me of eating breakfast at my grandmother's house. You remember how she always made the best biscuits."

"I'm not sure these are as good as hers were." Fox stuck a piece in his mouth.

"Maybe not, but they are good." Fiona took another bite. "I should go down and get to know this woman shouldn't I?"

"Grayson took her and Lizi to work with him this morning."

"Then he decided they were telling the truth?" Fiona bit into the second biscuit.

"I'm not sure what he thinks. You seemed pretty sure about them last night."

"I may have been premature in my judgment."

"Why do you say that?"

"Last night, I thought I'd slip into their room and try to get another look at the girl. It was too dark to see her face, but I heard part of what they said. It sounded like Amber is planning on blackmailing Grayson so he will marry her."

Chapter Nine

During the ride to the office, Amber sat in the passenger seat taking in what little scenery was there. They were on the freeway for a while and then they were on a four lane street. They hadn't gone far on it when she heard Grayson turn on the signal light and they were in a parking lot in front of a three-story building covered with stone and dark glass. Behind it was a shorter metal building that spread out wider. There were only five cars in the parking lot. Grayson pulled into a parking space near the front door that had his name on it. One space closer to the door was Fox's.

Amber and Lizi followed him to the front door where he waved a badge in front of the reader and pulled on the glass door. Once they were inside, Amber could see a receptionist's desk and a few chairs along one wall, but there was no receptionist. On the far side of the room was another door with another badge reader, but Grayson walked over to the receptionist's desk.

"You're supposed to have visitor's badges." He looked over the desk and then he walked around to the other side. He pulled on the handles of some of the drawers, but all were locked. He reached into his pocket and pulled out a set of keys.

He started to look through them, but then he put them back. "Oh, forget it. You're with me. I'm not sure where she keeps them anyway."

Grayson walked over to the next door and held his badge up to the reader near the door. Amber heard a soft pop and Grayson pulled on the handle. The door opened and he held it until Amber and Lizi stepped through.

He pointed to the left. "My office is through there, but I'll give you the five cent tour first."

He walked down the hall the other direction. Pointing at an open door across the hall, he said, "That's our main conference room and training room."

Amber looked inside. She saw only a few blinking lights in the dark room. Grayson touched a panel on the wall and the lights came on, revealing a large table with chairs around it. He touched the panel again and the room went dark.

They walked past a few offices on their right. Amber could see names next to the doors, but Grayson didn't mention them. At the next door on the left, Grayson slipped a key in the lock and turned the handle. The first thing Amber noticed were the computer monitors showing various different images. When the lights flickered on, she could see circuit boards lying on tables with cables connecting them to the machines.

"What's this?" she asked.

"This is the demonstration room," Grayson said. "I'd show you how all this stuff works, but I don't know how to run the equipment. Some things are best left to the experts."

"This is all the stuff you make?"

"Most of it," he said. "But we don't have all the stuff that's being made at our other facilities here. It's kind of impressive, isn't it?"

"If you say so," Amber said.

Grayson picked up one of the boards. "This is one of our newest products. We're making it for a company that makes farm equipment."

"Interesting," Amber said. She could see that Grayson was excited, but to her it just looked like a piece of computer equipment.

Grayson must have gotten the idea. He put the board down. "On with the tour."

They went down another hall. Grayson pointed out the restrooms. Just past them was a small break room with a door going outside. "If you smoke, outside that door is the designated area, but you'll have to have someone let you back in, since you don't have a badge."

"I don't smoke," Amber said.

"There's the exercise room," he said, pointing to another door.

Amber couldn't see inside, but she could hear a treadmill running. "People come in to work out on a Saturday?"

"Yeah, a few people do. That way they don't have to pay for a gym membership," Grayson said. "The really cool thing is that we make the computer that goes in the treadmill in there. We swap it out when we make changes, so it gives us a real world test."

Again, Amber didn't share his enthusiasm.

Down another hallway, he pointed out another set of restrooms and the elevator. They walked past labs hidden behind closed doors that Grayson didn't open. He pointed out a large room full of cubicles. "The two floors above us look a lot like that. We have fewer labs and more cubicles upstairs. Dad was talking about investing in better looking cubicles, but then the accident happened. A lot of stuff got put on hold after that."

"What accident?" Amber asked.

Grayson looked at her inquisitively. "I assumed you knew," he said. "I'll tell you about it some other time."

Was that because he didn't trust her?

"All of this is cubicles, except for a few offices," he said as they entered a larger room. He spoke to someone hidden by the maze of cubical walls, but the walls were too tall for Amber to see much.

He led them through the maze and came out on the other side. They stepped out into another hall. "Back here is the main break room."

By this time, Amber was confused and wasn't sure how to get back to where they started, but Grayson seemed to know exactly where he was. He let them look through the glass windows into the manufacturing building, but he wouldn't let them go inside, saying they weren't dressed for it. There weren't any workers in there, but Amber could see the unfinished product on tables, ready for the workers to continue their tasks on Monday morning.

At last, Grayson led them back to the front of the building. He made one turn and then another. He made one more turn that Amber didn't remember making and they were once more in the main hallway. This time he held his badge up to the reader next to the big glass doors.

They entered a large open space with large cushy looking furniture on one side and a secretary's desk on the other. Around the sides of this space were several doors. Some of them bore name tags. Grayson pointed to two that were clearly marked as another set of restrooms.

"Executive washrooms," he said. "That came with the building. I wouldn't have put them here since we aren't that far from the restrooms down the hall."

Grayson opened the door that bore his name. He stepped aside to reveal another spacious room, well lit with large windows.

"And here's my office. Make yourself at home," he said, pointing toward a couch that sat against the wall. He went to sit in the big leather chair behind the desk.

Amber took a seat on the brown sofa and sunk into its pliable leather. "This is very comfortable."

"It'd better be," Grayson said without looking up from the computer he had just turned on. Grayson looked at his watch. "I really need to get this work done, if I'm going to make it back to my parent's house in time to meet with the lawyers."

"Is this how you normally spend your Saturdays, coming in to work and then meeting with lawyers?" Amber watched as Grayson brought up a spreadsheet on his computer and pulled some papers out of his desk.

"Meeting with lawyers—not so frequent—but coming in to work? Yeah, I'm here a lot and it's more than ever with Dad doing so little. I'm here so much I should probably get a house close by and get rid of my condo over in The Tower."

"You live in a tower?" Lizi's eyes got wider as she looked at Grayson.

"Yeah, it's downtown," Grayson said. "There was a tornado that ripped most of the windows out a few years ago. They put the windows back in it and converted it in to condos. I liked the novelty of it. It's just the kind of place my wife would've liked."

He looked thoughtful.

"I've got to get to work," he said, turning away.

"Why are you meeting with lawyers?" Amber asked.

"To figure out what we're going to do about the two of you. Y'all waltzing in like this is costing us plenty of money."

She hadn't thought they'd bring in lawyers. "I'm sorry."

"Don't worry about it," Grayson said. "We're paying them to do something all the time anyway. If it wasn't this, it'd be something else."

"I didn't mean for this to cost you anything."

"Let me ask you something." Grayson typed a figure into the spreadsheet. "How much would it take to make you go away? If I wrote a check for fifty thousand, would that be enough?"

It took a moment for Amber to understand what he was saying, but not Lizi.

"Daddy," Lizi said, hurrying from the window to stand near Grayson's chair, "Don't you want me?"

Grayson didn't even look at Lizi, but stared straight at Amber without blinking.

"I don't want your money," Amber said. She would have loved if she could've taken the fifty thousand and disappeared with Lizi, but that wouldn't be the right thing for Lizi. Besides, Amber didn't do that anymore. There'd been a time when she would've taken it. It reminded her of that old woman and brought back the smell of that musky old house.

"Let me at least give you something," the woman said. "I was afraid my son was alone when he died. He was all I had left, you know."

"Yes, ma'am, he told me," Amber lied, "But I don't want your money."

"Do you like quilts?" the woman asked. "I've got more quilts than I know what to do with."

At the time, the woman's words were music to Amber's ears. The woman took her into one of the bedrooms, opened a chest and pulled out several quilts. "Pick one out and take it with you."

Amber walked out with one of the most beautiful quilts she had ever seen. She didn't wait long before she took it to a woman she knew bought quilts and within a few minutes had a five thousand dollar check in hand.

The old woman died shortly after that. Amber wondered what she must have thought when she met her son in heaven and he told her that he'd never met Amber.

Grayson opened a drawer of his desk and pulled out a large checkbook, with three checks on each page. "How about seventy-five—no, let's make it an even one hundred thousand. If you're careful, that should last you a while."

She dropped her face into her hands then rubbed her temples with the tips of her fingers. "Do you really have so much money you can offer me a hundred thousand, just like that?"

"Yeah," Grayson said. "Do you want me to write the check or not?"

"Maybe I should let you get back to work. I need to visit the lady's room." Amber stood and walked to the door. She put her hand on the knob and turned back. "Do you mind if I wonder around the office?"

"That's fine." Grayson put the checkbook back in the drawer. "Just make sure the outer office door is unlocked, so you can get back in."

Amber crossed the vast space of the outer office to the women's restroom. She stood at the sink for some time, running cool water over her hands and splashing it on her face. She had just passed up the biggest offer she'd received in her life. He wouldn't make that offer again.

She thought about The Tower. Holly would've liked the name of the building. She would have talked for hours about the strange people who lived there. Amber wondered if Holly's daughter would be living there.

After leaving the restroom, Amber stepped out into the main hallway. She walked the direction they had before, but this time she punched the button on the elevator and rode to the third floor. It was nothing special to look at, just some offices and cubicles. She saw a small conference room or two. She wandered through the maze of cubicles and wondered what people did here during the week. Aside from several meaningless charts, most of what the cubicles told her was a little about the person's family or which school the inhabitant attended. One was covered in purple with fat lizards scattered throughout.

"Did you need something?" A young woman came up from behind Amber, slid past her and sat behind the small desk.

"No, I was just walking around and I noticed your stuff."

"Yeah, I was getting tired of looking at my computer screen too. It's good to see I'm not the only one who had to work today." The woman typed something on the keyboard and then leaned back in her chair.

"Oh, I'm not working," Amber said. "Grayson brought me. He had some work he needed to do."

"Grayson's here?" The woman looked concerned. "Do you know what he's working on?"

"No, I just know he needed to get some work done."

"My boss wanted me to finish this report for him. I was supposed to send it to Grayson's secretary yesterday. I figured that meant nothing would happen until Monday morning, but if he's here..."

"I don't think he's getting much done. My daughter's in there pestering him," Amber said, slipping into her old habit. It was always easier to refer to Lizi as her daughter because people asked fewer questions. "I should probably go make sure she isn't making him pull out his hair."

"He'll do fine. All the kids love him."

Amber wasn't going to tell her that she was also concerned about Lizi.

"Since you're a friend of his, would you mind if I ask you something?" the woman asked. "Do you know how Fox is doing? Everyone's worried about him."

If this woman was worried, she was probably more of a friend than Amber was. "He seems okay to me."

"He used to be so much fun, but now no one ever sees him. I heard that he came in the other day, but with me sitting up here, I wouldn't know." The woman pulled the plastic from the top of a microwavable meal and Amber could smell the very strong scent of cooked tomatoes.

"I don't know him that well." Amber backed out of the cube to get away from the smell. "We just met yesterday."

"To be honest, I don't know him except seeing him in the hall a few times, at a few meetings and at the Christmas party, but he seemed like a lot of fun. Then that accident happened."

The woman used a plastic fork and knife to cut into a chunk of ground beef in the tomato sauce.

"What accident?" Amber knew something had happened, but hoped this woman could tell her more.

"You probably heard about it. It was all over the news. About a year ago, it happened on the traffic circle. I'm not sure if someone didn't yield or what, but it killed Fox's son-in-law, and the grandkids." The woman looked at Amber like she expected her to say something.

"I'm from St. Louis. I didn't know anything about it." Amber wished the woman could tell her more.

"There were rumors that they were going to sell the company after that. Everyone was worried about their jobs, but then Grayson started running things. If you ask me, he knows more about what he's doing than Fox does." The woman took another bite of meat. "I probably shouldn't have said that, should I? Since you're like a friend of the family and all."

Amber decided that she shouldn't get any more rumors started than she already had. She left the woman to finish her meal. She walked around until she found the elevator. From there, she easily made it back to Grayson's office.

When she opened the door of his office, Grayson and Lizi looked like they hadn't moved in all the time she had been gone. Grayson was still hard at work. Lizi was leaning with her elbows propped on the desk, looking very much interested in what Grayson was doing. Grayson looked up briefly, looked at his watch and then went back to work. Lizi was playing her part well, but Amber wondered if this time it might have been better for Lizi to just act like herself.

She beckoned to Lizi and then stepped back out into the outer office. Lizi came through the door a few seconds later.

"I see what you're trying to do," Amber whispered, "but you don't have to pretend to be so interested. Children aren't supposed to be interested in spreadsheets."

"But…"

"We just have to wait for them to do whatever tests they want to do. You don't have to pretend to be his daughter."

"So what should I do?"

"Just act normal."

"I was acting normal."

"Just be yourself. If he takes you in, you aren't going to be able to put on an act the whole time."

"If he takes us in," Lizi said emphatically.

The door to Grayson's office opened and Amber didn't have time to correct her.

"Are y'all ready?" he asked. "I let the time get away from me."

Amber hoped Lizi understood what she had tried to tell her.

Chapter Ten

The clock chimed fifteen minutes after one and Grayson still hadn't arrived. He hadn't called either. Fox hoped the phone would ring and Grayson would tell him why he was late, but Fox also feared it would ring. He imagined a voice on the other end telling him that there'd been an accident, this time, taking his oldest son and the last grandchild. He couldn't bear the thought of losing another one.

"Fox, you know that this woman is likely after money or she's here to harm the family's reputation." It was Alex Cooper who spoke, the most senior of the three lawyers Grayson had assembled. He was also the family attorney, while the other two focused on business law.

"I'm aware of that." Fox paced back and forth as the three men sat watching him. "But we can't afford any mistakes. If Lizi is Grayson's, we want her back with us, no matter what that woman's motives are."

"There'll have to be a paternity test. It won't be too much trouble to get a court order, if she refuses."

"She's already agreed to it. But if she changes her mind, I don't want this thing going to court. If there's even the slightest chance that we could come across like we're trying to take this woman's child away from her..." Fox didn't finish his thought. He looked at the sunbathed street through the window.

"There isn't that big of a risk. She admits the child isn't hers. Besides, we ought to be able to keep this out of the media."

"It's already been in the media," Fox said.

"I mean more than it already has. Right now, those reporters may just be mildly interested. If it becomes a scandal, there'll be no stopping the damage to your family and your company. But we can keep that from happening."

Fox had heard similar claims before and then had spent thousands of dollars cleaning up the mess. "We've still got to get the details of that merger worked out and I'm afraid that this thing will mess that up."

"You're tying our hands. The only thing I can tell you is that we can attempt to verify that this woman is who she says she is. Maybe we'll find something in her past that we can use. Who knows, we might find proof that she's lying."

"If that's what you think you ought to do," Fox said, "y'all do that."

"It could take a while, even longer than the results of a paternity test. I don't know what your plans are for her staying here."

Fox hadn't given that much thought either.

"They came from St. Louis," Fox said. "There's got to be someone who knows her up there. She says she worked a diner that burned down. That shouldn't be too hard to find. I hate to bring up Victoria's death again, but maybe there's a way to find out where Victoria was before that and see if she knew Amber. It's been a long time, but someone ought to remember something."

"We'll find someone who can tell us something, but it could get expensive. Maybe it would be better to just pay this woman off."

"Unless she doesn't want money," Fox said. "That's what worries me. There's no telling what we'd have to do if she's not looking for money. People like that are the most dangerous of all."

"If so, she may be very dangerous," Grayson said, coming into the room. "I offered her a hundred thousand dollars to disappear. She turned me down. I don't think she gave it a second thought."

"It's about time you showed up!" Fox knew his son wouldn't understand the relief he felt seeing him walk into the room, so he showed him anger instead.

"Did y'all already come to a decision without me?"

"We thought it might be better to learn more about Amber before we do anything else."

"I can agree with that," Grayson said, and then to the two business lawyers he said, "Before y'all leave, I'd like to discuss one of our suppliers with you."

Fox decided to leave the room. Grayson could explain what they discussed later, if he needed to, but he had been away from the day to day business operation for so long that they would have to waste time bringing him up to speed if he stayed. He walked past the kitchen. He saw Lizi once more seated at the breakfast bar and Amber standing at the stove with her back to him. She looked innocent enough, but so did a snake until it decided to bite.

"Hey Grandpa," Lizi said, smiling at him, "do you want a grilled cheese sandwich?"

Amber turned around. "I'd be happy to fix you one, if you want one."

"No, I've already eaten."

But he sat with them while they ate. Neither of them had much to say. Fox just enjoyed spending the time with his granddaughter. He knew he was setting himself up for disappointment if it turned out she wasn't who they claimed she was, but having a granddaughter for a few days only to find out she wasn't was better than having no grandchildren at all.

Through the window, Fox saw Fiona in the pool. She had avoided the pool since the day of the accident. Who could blame her for that? She was in the pool when Fox had returned with Grayson and they told her what had happened. Grayson often tried persuading her to continue her daily swims. Fox told him he was wasting his time; things would never be the same again. But there she was, slowly swimming the length of the pool.

As he opened the door to go join her, Fox noticed the thermometer. *Ninety-eight,* not triple digits yet, but it was still warm outside. He walked over to the end of the pool and waited for his wife to reach him.

"What are you doing out here in this hot weather?" Fox crouched down so Fiona wouldn't have to look so far up as she treaded water near the edge of the pool.

"The water feels fine. I decided I needed the exercise." Fiona pulled herself out of the water and sat on the edge of the pool. "I didn't realize how out of shape I am. I think it's time for me to go back to doing this more often."

"Are you sure you want to do that?" Fox handed Fiona her towel.

"I've got to get exercise somehow," she said as she began to towel off.

He stopped himself from mentioning the accident.

"How did your meeting go?" She stood up. "Do we still have house guests?"

"For now," Fox said. "I told Alex to see what he can find on Amber. Once we start looking, I'm not sure what we'll find."

"What about Lizi?" Fiona sat in one of the chairs next to the pool. "How are we going to know if she's Grayson's daughter or not?"

"They can do tests for that."

"Wouldn't it be nice if we could just take their word for it?" Fiona closed her eyes and turned her face to the sun. "What would be the harm? It'll be nice to have a granddaughter again."

"Well, for one thing, there's a lot at stake here. If this turns out to be true, we're not sure how Jack Abrams will take it. He may think we've been lying to him and back out of the merger." That reminded Fox that he should call Celia. She would want to know what was happening as much as anyone and Grayson would forget to call. He always got so busy with work. With Lizi and Amber showing up, he would forget how to treat a woman.

Fox went back inside and dialed Celia's number. He told her their plans.

"If there's anything I can do to help let me know," she said. "I know of a guy up there that's supposed to be really good about finding people who don't want to be found, but you might not like him. He has a questionable reputation. And he's a little strange. When you talk to him on the phone, you would think he's part of a big firm, but someone told me he works out of his mother's basement."

"Maybe we should hold off on that." As touchy as things were, Fox didn't want someone who couldn't be trusted brought in on this, even if it did come at Celia's suggestion. "Let's see what Alex comes up with first and then we'll consider other options."

"I'm not suggesting you need to do anything right away, but..."

"I know what you're saying," Fox said. "I don't want to have to do something like this. But Fiona overheard her talking about blackmailing Grayson to force him to marry her. I'll do what I can first, but I'll keep your guy in mind."

"If you need help with that, let me know. You'll keep me informed, won't you? Dad's really upset about all this. And if she's trying to blackmail Grayson, he's really going to be upset about that."

Fox assured her that she would be one of the first to know if there were any developments. He was glad to have Celia as an ally. He knew her loyalties lay with her father, but rather than just getting upset about it, she wanted to know what was going on before passing judgment.

Chapter Eleven

The shelves were stocked, but she couldn't find what she needed. Amber scanned the pantry shelves, looking for flour. The canister was almost empty. She spotted it above her head. In the kitchen behind her, Lizi was at the stove, watching the pancakes cook on a griddle. Fox sat at the breakfast bar with a coffee cup in hand and the Sunday paper in front of him. As Amber refilled the canister, she heard someone close a cabinet door and then pick up the coffee pot.

"Good morning, Lizi," Grayson said. Amber could hear the faint sound as he filled his mug with coffee.

"Good morning, Daddy."

From the doorway, Amber watched as Lizi turned away from the stove and gave him a big hug, causing him to spill coffee on the counter.

He returned the hug, but Amber still worried that Lizi would push him too far. He'd made it clear that he wasn't Lizi's father. With Lizi treating him like he was, he might think Amber was coaching her. That would be ironic if they called her down for coaching Lizi on the one time she wasn't coaching her at all.

Lizi let go and went back to the pancakes. Grayson cleaned up the mess before he went to join his father.

"What are your plans for church? I don't suppose you want to leave them alone in the house." Grayson spoke softly, but Amber could still hear.

"I suppose we'll go to church like we normally do," Fox spoke more loudly. "You can stay here."

Lizi turned toward them. "Grandpa, can we go to church with you?"

Fox was silent for a few moments. "I suppose so."

Amber stepped out of the pantry.

"We'd like to go to church somewhere, even if it isn't with you." Amber wasn't sure why Fox was reluctant for them to go to church with him. "Maybe there's a church that will send a bus out to pick us up."

Grayson rested his hand on his Dad's shoulder. "Actually, I was hoping y'all would go to church with me. But if y'all want to go to Dad's church, that's fine too."

"That'll work too," Amber said, "but I thought it sounded like you weren't going."

"I try to go every week. We just didn't want you left alone in the house."

"I understand," Amber said. If it had been her house, she wouldn't have trusted a stranger alone there either. "What time do we need to be ready?"

"We need to leave at least by nine."

"You won't have to worry about us making you late."

They were ready even before Grayson and by nine they were on the freeway headed to church.

"Your dad doesn't like me very much," Amber said as they rode along.

"No, I would say not," Grayson said, switching lanes to get around a slower car. "He's afraid of what you might be trying to pull."

"And just what am I trying to pull?"

"I wouldn't worry about it. He got it in his head that you're trying to use blackmail to get me to marry you." Grayson eased off the gas to let another driver switch lanes in front of him. "You aren't, are you?"

"I wouldn't do that," Amber said, remembering the conversation she'd had with Lizi in what she thought was the privacy of their room. If Fox was in the habit of standing in doorways and listening to private conversations, she didn't want Lizi around him, but there wasn't much she could do. These people either knew Lizi's family or they didn't.

"I didn't think so," Grayson said. "But it isn't like you have much to work with. My life is an open book. I've got nothing to hide."

"You might be surprised," Amber said. "Everyone has secrets they don't let other people to know."

"Just what kind of secrets do you think I have?" Grayson asked. "Should I be worried that you'll go digging into my past?"

"No, I won't do that." Amber turned her head and looked out the window. "All I really want it what's best for Lizi."

"But you've had her all these years without looking for her family?"

"You wouldn't understand." Amber kept looking out the window.

"No, I suppose not," Grayson said. "I eat kids for lunch. What would I know about wanting a kid of my own?"

"Will I have to find my Sunday school class by myself?" Lizi asked from the back seat.

"Of course not, we'll find someone who can tell us where you're supposed to go." Grayson looked back at her for a moment and then looked back at the road.

"Are there very many kids my age?"

"I don't know. I'm sure there's several," Grayson said. "To tell you the truth, I haven't paid much attention to how many kids there are."

They rode in silence until they reached the church. Amber used the time to think about her new role in Lizi's life. She wasn't sure what would happen next. She just knew that things were changing and she hated that feeling. But after Grayson parked the car, she got out and pushed those thoughts aside.

"Shall I tell everyone I'm your future wife?" she asked with a smile as they approached the front entrance. She thought to make light of what Fox had overheard. Grayson didn't think it was funny. He frowned the whole way from the car to the front entrance.

"Good morning, Grayson," Bob said, extending his hand. Bob waited a moment for Grayson to explain the other two.

"I'm Amber Mills," she said, extending her own hand. "This is my daughter, Lizi. We're staying with Grayson's parents and he was kind enough to bring us to church."

"Glad to have y'all. I'm Bob and this is my wife Jillian. Where y'all from?"

"St. Louis, but we may be moving down here. We'll see how things work out."

Grayson appeared more relaxed after Amber introduced herself. She told herself to avoid saying things that would make Grayson uncomfortable. These were his friends; he wouldn't want them to think poorly of him.

"What grade are you in?" Jillian asked Lizi.

"I'll be in the sixth grade next year."

"You can come with me and I'll show you where your class is."

Lizi looked at Amber.

"Try to stay out of trouble," Amber said.

"I will." Lizi followed after Jillian.

"Just what kind of trouble do you think she would get into?" Grayson asked.

"It's better if you don't know." Amber walked toward the front door like she knew where she was going. Grayson quickened his pace to catch up.

Just inside the door, more people greeted Amber. One of them handed her a bulletin. She repeated her story and stepped out of the way.

"Where to?" she asked, when Grayson caught up to her.

"This way." Grayson led the way down the hall. Along the way they met several of Grayson's friends who had more time to ask probing questions about why Amber was with Grayson. For most, the answer Amber gave Bob and Jillian was satisfactory, but one woman—a woman old enough to be Amber's great-grandmother—believed there was something more.

"It's about time Grayson found someone." She held onto her cane tightly as she looked Amber over carefully.

"I'm staying with his parents." Amber tried her now well-rehearsed speech.

"You aren't into breast enhancements and that stuff, are you?" The woman looked at Amber's chest, which was just below eye level, as if to make sure.

"No ma'am." She tried to hide her laugher. "I'm happy with the way God made me."

"Good for you." The woman repositioned her cane and leaned heavily on it. "If you ask me, it's that surgery that did Grayson's wife in."

"You knew his wife?" Amber wondered if this woman could tell her more than she'd learned from Grayson and his family.

"Knew her? I taught her in Sunday school." The woman looked off to the side. "Of course that was before she showed up with Grayson on her arm. And before—" Her voice drifted off to nothing. "O well, that's in the past. I've got to get to class or they'll start without me." The woman turned and walked into a classroom where several other elderly women were already seated.

"What did she mean about your wife having surgery?" Amber asked.

"She was never happy about how she looked, but now isn't the time to talk about that."

Amber took that to mean he didn't want to talk about it at all. He led her down the hall to the room where his class met.

The rest of the morning went without a hitch. There were plenty of inquisitive stares from Grayson's good friends and one uncomfortable encounter after the preaching service. Amber and Lizi were standing off to the side waiting as Grayson talked to some of his friends. Amber noticed a woman who was watching them closely. The woman looked as if she couldn't quite decide what to do and then she approached them with courage.

The woman introduced herself and then said, "We have some clothes that people donated for a fund raiser. If you would like to look through them to see if there's anything you can wear, I'd be happy to show you where they are."

Amber looked at the woman for a moment, taking in what she said. "I appreciate the offer, but I can't afford to spend money on clothes right now."

"No, that wasn't what I meant," the woman said. "You could have the clothes, if you need them."

"Excuse me," Grayson said to his friends and walked over to Amber.

"Are you sure?" Amber asked. "We really would appreciate that."

"That won't be necessary," Grayson said.

"I just thought…" the woman began and then turned and walked away.

"What did you do that for?" Amber asked. "If you haven't noticed, Lizi needs new clothes and this is the best dress I own. Maggie would like to burn the rest."

"Let's talk about this somewhere else." Grayson walked toward the door, trusting that Amber and Lizi would follow.

"Did I do something wrong?" Amber asked, catching up to him before he reached the asphalt. "She offered. I wasn't begging."

"No, you didn't do anything wrong," Grayson said. "People donate to help people who don't have much money to buy clothes."

"I don't know if you've noticed, but I fit that description."

"Yeah, I've noticed," Grayson said. "But it doesn't look right with you staying with my family and then taking clothes from the church."

"I wasn't trying to steal from anyone."

"No, that wasn't what I meant." Grayson opened the door for her and waited for her to get in. "I'll find some time to take you shopping tomorrow and we'll let that be the end of it."

"Oh I see," Amber said. "You're worried about what the people at church will think of you."

"No, of course not!" Grayson said much too quickly.

Amber didn't believe him. She started to tell him as much, but Grayson pushed the door shut.

She waited until he got in on the other side.

"Do you really think people would think less of you if…"

"No," Grayson said before she could finish. "Most of them don't have any idea what kind of money I make."

"How much do you make?" Lizi asked from the back seat. "Is it a lot?"

"It's enough," Grayson said. "It's enough I can afford to buy y'all some new clothes. Holly would've wanted it that way."

Amber wanted to question him about that, but something in the tone of his voice told her that she shouldn't.

Chapter Twelve

Fox answered the phone.

"Is Grayson there?" Celia's voice sounded worried from the other end of the line. "His secretary said he isn't at work and he isn't answering his cell phone."

"He took Amber and Lizi shopping." Fox shifted the phone to his other ear. "Did you need something?"

"He missed a meeting with Dad. They were supposed to talk about the Oklahoma City facility."

"I can talk to him about it," Fox said. "If y'all are just looking for a decision, Grayson will go with whatever I decide."

"No, it's a little late for that," Celia said. "Dad was pretty steamed when Grayson didn't show up. I probably shouldn't repeat what he said, but he's a little concerned that y'all aren't serious about this merger."

"Of course we're serious about it!" Fox said. "I'll call your father and apologize for Grayson."

"Maybe it'd be better if you didn't," Celia said. "Give him some time to cool off. And it'd be better if it came from Grayson."

"I'll talk to Grayson and make sure he smooths things over."

"I thought you might," Celia said. "I'm a little worried about all this. We thought this merger would be beneficial to both companies. Were we wrong?"

"No, you weren't wrong," Fox said, but he wasn't about to tell her just how much they had riding on the merger—not until the paperwork was signed. With all that the merger would bring with it, the thing that interested them the most was that it brought with it a team of experienced software engineers who could go to work right away on some of the new products. You could hire an individual off the street and you might get someone good and you might get someone who was laid off because he didn't know what he was doing. With the merger, they would have a team with proven success and the processes already in place to do the work. It looked like it would save them millions.

"This thing with Amber and Lizi, is that going away soon?" Celia asked. "I mean, should we be concerned?"

"It looks like it'll be an ongoing thing," Fox said. "There's a strong possibility that Grayson will want to take Lizi in. If she's Holly's kid, anyway." Fox still didn't feel comfortable about telling Celia who Holly was, but it was best that she understood that Lizi would be around for a while.

"Yeah, I know him well enough to understand that," Celia said. "But what about Amber? I assume she'll be out of the picture as soon as you know what's going on with Lizi?"

"That may not be a safe assumption," Fox said. "Fiona overheard her talking about finding a way to get Grayson to marry her."

"But he won't do that, right?"

"I would say no," Fox said, "But he isn't really avoiding her either. He took her to the office on Saturday and to church on Sunday and then shopping today. He says it's nothing to worry about, but from what Fiona said, Amber is looking for marriage no matter what it takes to make it happen."

"Do you think there's really anything she can do?"

"Let's just say that I wouldn't underestimate her," Fox said. "If you want to marry Grayson, you'd better consider her a serious challenger. If she gets her way..."

"I know what I want," Celia said, "but are you okay with that? I mean, maybe I'm as much of an interloper as she is."

"She can't be trusted," Fox said. "All I can say is that you'd make a better addition to the family than she would."

"Of course, I think the same thing," Celia said with a laugh. "But I'm not sure I'm in any position to do anything about it. They're sleeping under the same roof and going to the same church. How's a girl supposed to compete with that? If I try, I'll just come across as jealous."

"I'll see what I can do about it," Fox said, "but you've got to promise me that you'll do what you can to keep your father from walking away from this merger."

"I'll do my best." Celia changed the subject. "Has Alex found out anything?"

"Not likely. He wouldn't have done much this weekend and I haven't talked to him today."

"That seems awfully convenient for Amber. She isn't taking weekends off."

"I'll call Alex and make sure he knows how urgent this is." Fox thought Celia seemed satisfied with that, but he knew she wouldn't stay that way for long with Amber trying to edge into her territory. He ought to talk to Grayson too, just to make sure he wasn't letting Amber pull him in.

Alex didn't seem surprised to receive a call from Fox, but he wasn't very helpful either. "I've got people looking into to it. We've found some things, but nothing I'd recommend taking action on until we know more."

"Tell me what you've got." Even a little information was better than none at all.

"Keep in mind that we haven't been able to verify much of this," Alex said. The sound of papers rustling came through the line. "We've found birth records for an Elizabeth Jacobs up there that would be about the right age, but it's incomplete and it was filed more than five years after the date of birth."

"What does that mean?"

"Like I said, we need to look into this more," Alex said. "But what I would guess is that Amber needed a birth certificate to get Elizabeth in school or something. You might ask her. The birth certificate has her name in the section for the delivering physician or midwife. But the rest of it is hardly filled out at all. The mother's name is given as Holly, with no maiden name or middle initial. For the father's name, it just gives the last name as Jacobs."

"Why would they let her by with that? Wouldn't someone have questioned it?"

"What good would it do?" Alex asked. "She could've made up information to put in there. Maybe they thought it was better to leave it blank than to put in false information."

"But wouldn't someone think it was odd that she was raising a kid that wasn't her own?"

"Maybe, but if she was taking good care of her, I don't see why anyone would think anything about, much less want to do anything about it. I suppose the state might have had some issue with it, but what could they have done other than take Elizabeth away from Amber and place her in foster care. I don't know about you, but I don't see the logic of doing that."

"So, you think Amber provided her with a good environment to grow up in?"

"That all depends on what you call a good environment."

Fox heard more papers rustling. Alex wouldn't be rushed.

"She was named in a few lawsuits and get this," Alex said, pausing for a moment, "one of them involved falsifying birth records. In another, the plaintiffs accused her of convincing their father to put her in his will under false pretenses."

"So she could be trying to do that again." Fox liked what he heard.

"Let's not jump to conclusions just yet. The court sided with her in both cases. At best we have a place to start. But it might be a good idea to get a copy of that birth certificate she showed you. I'm sure it's fake, so it might provide some leverage."

When Fox put down the phone, he climbed the stairs and walked down the hall until he came to the room where Amber and Lizi were staying. He opened the door and walked in, telling himself that he had no reason to feel guilty about violating their privacy. It was his house.

He looked around the room. There wasn't much to tell him anything about the occupants—a book one of them had brought up from the library, a Bible on the nightstand. He picked it up. It looked new. The gold on the edge of the pages still looked crisp. He opened the cover and looked at the inscription. "Given to Amber Mills." It listed a date a few months earlier and gave the name of a Baptist church in St. Louis. Fox wondered if she'd somehow found out Grayson was a Baptist and wanted him to think she was too. Fox wrote the name of the church down anyway. Someone at the church might know her. He went around to the other side of the bed and saw another Bible that looked similar to the first. It lay on the floor. The inscription was identical, right down to the date and Bible verse, "Study to show thyself approved, a workman that needeth not to be ashamed, rightly dividing the word of truth," except here the name was Elizabeth Mills. Did Baptists see anything wrong with joining the church with the wrong name? He'd have to ask Grayson.

Fox looked out the window to make sure the three of them hadn't return from shopping—not that it would do much good since Grayson usually parked in back. Fox stepped into the bathroom and looked around. There wasn't much out of place there either. Maggie would have put most of it back in order or had a maid do it as they made their way through the house. He didn't trust them, but the house was too big for Maggie to clean alone. As long as Maggie kept an eye on them they couldn't do too much harm.

A tube of toothpaste lay next to the sink. It looked new, so Maggie had probably given them that. An old hairbrush lay next to it. It clearly belonged to them. But the hair clip beside it looked familiar. He picked it up and ran his fingers over the translucent blue plastic and the pink flower glued to it. He could still see his granddaughter pull it from her hair and hand it to him only a couple of minutes before her death. He slipped it into his pocket. He couldn't fault Lizi for wanting it, but she couldn't understand its significance. Just by touching it he felt like he'd disturbed a grave.

In the closet he found more of their stuff. A few clothes hung on one of the bars and a few were folded neatly on the shelf. The two bags on the floor looked more interesting. He picked up the smaller bag and rummaged through it—a couple of books, a game of some sort, a deck of cards, little more. It didn't look like anything from the house. He put the small bag down and opened the larger bag. He pulled out a worn blanket and set it aside. Even with all its holes, it looked clean. There were several folders with papers in them and a photo album, along with less important things. He put the folders aside and opened the album. Most of the pictures were of Lizi—her baby pictures, her as a toddler, her first day of school. Amber appeared in a few. The earliest photos showed the image of a woman who could've been Victoria, but she looked different. He wasn't sure what it was. Amber was sure to claim it was Holly, whether it was or not. It would be hard to prove otherwise. He put down the album and picked up the folders.

Plastic bags rustled just outside the door. They were back. He had to move quickly or they would find him looking through their things.

"Mr. Jacobs! I didn't know you were in here." Maggie stopped in the doorway. "They just got back a few minutes ago."

Fox began stuffing everything back in the bag.

"Do you want me to do that? What'll they think if they find you in here?"

"That's alright. I've got it." Fox pulled the zipper closed. As he left the room, he remembered that he hadn't put the blanket back in the bag, but it was too late to do anything about it. Amber was making her way toward him with more bags.

She carried bags with both arms. If she saw him come out of the room, she didn't show any sign that it bothered her.

"It looks like Grayson will be selling stock to pay his bills this month," Fox said dryly.

Amber stopped and looked at him. "I told him we didn't need all this stuff. He bought so much I can probably go two weeks without wearing the same outfit twice. I assumed he had the money or he wouldn't have bought it. He should've told me he would have to sell stock."

Silly woman. She looked like she was genuinely concerned. Knowing Grayson, he probably wouldn't even notice that what they'd spent was missing from his bank account.

"I wouldn't worry about it." Fox left her standing there looking worried and went downstairs, where he found Grayson at the pool table racking the balls. Lizi watched him, holding a cue stick in her hand like she didn't know what to do with it.

"Grandpa, do you want to play? There's another stick over there." Lizi pointed to the three still in the rack.

"Pool's a two person game, Lizi." Grayson moved the cue ball into place.

"Do you want to play the winner?" Lizi asked.

"No, Grayson proved he was better than me a long time ago." Fox doubted Lizi had a chance of winning unless Grayson let her. He stood and watched to see how his son would play it.

Grayson let her break. Her first attempt weakly scattered the balls. None fell in the pockets.

"Here, let me show you," Grayson said, taking his turn. One ball clunked against the cue ball before it rolled into a pocket, but Grayson missed the next. Fox knew it was intentional.

Lizi took another shot and the cue ball missed its intended target. Grayson sent a ball toward a corner, but it stopped short. The game would last a long time if he kept this up. Fox decided it would be a good time to try calling the church in St. Louis.

After finding the number on the Internet, Fox dialed the number and waited for someone to pick up. It rang a few times and then a recorded voice gave some information about the church before saying, "our office hours are nine to five Tuesday through Friday. If you need to speak with our pastor you may call..." Fox put down the phone, knowing the pastor would just tell him that he would have to speak to the secretary when she got to work on Tuesday if he wanted to know who was on the church roll. He decided to see how the game progressed.

Lizi sunk the eight ball.

"You did good," Grayson said.

"You let me win."

"I—," Grayson began but didn't finish. He stood there looking like he didn't know what to say—a trap he had set for himself. "I'll tell you what. Let's play again and I'll play to win this time."

"How will I know?" Lizi asked. "You didn't before."

"You'll know when he beats you," Fox said, but Lizi ignored his comment.

She reached into her pocket and pulled out a dollar coin. The golden coin clanked against the table as she set it down.

"Are you willing to bet a dollar that you'll win?"

"Lizi! Put your money away," Amber said, coming into the room. "What did I tell you about gambling?"

"I thought you were talking about cards." Lizi picked up the coin and slipped it into her pocket.

"I meant everything—cards, pool or anything else," Amber said. "Now come help me fix supper."

"That's Maggie's job," Fox said.

"She has something she needs to do. I told her I'd fix supper. I hope I didn't overstep my bounds." Amber said, putting her arm around Lizi and guiding her toward the kitchen. "She hasn't left yet, if you want her to fix supper instead."

"No, that's alright, but she should have told me." Fox could tell that Amber wouldn't be easy to get rid of. It was so easy for her to step in and take control without anyone realizing what she'd done.

Chapter Thirteen

Tuesday afternoon, Amber wiped the wet rag across the counter. She could smell the lemony sent from the dish soap. Something hard bumped under her hand. It looked like something had dried from a spoon that had been lying there. She wiped the spot a little harder until it went away.

"Miss Mills, don't do that," Maggie said, coming back into the room, "That's my job. You'll get your new clothes all messed up."

Amber looked down at her jeans and blouse. They were still unspotted. Maggie was right; she didn't want to mess them up. Maybe Grayson could sell them and get part of his money back. She knew she couldn't afford to pay him, so she would wear only what she needed and leave the tags on the rest. Although she didn't see him as the type to carry it all back to the store.

"I just thought I'd lend a hand, so I wouldn't feel like such a freeloader around here." Amber dropped the rag in the sink.

"If you're feeling guilty, then maybe you shouldn't be here." Maggie picked up the rag and wiped the counter that Amber had just finished wiping. "But if you're going to be a guest in this house then you ought to act like one instead of trying to take my job. I can't afford to lose it."

"I'm not trying to take your job. You let me help you yesterday."

"I know, but I really need to be doing the job I'm paid to do."

"I'm sorry," Amber said. "I wasn't trying to cause you trouble. It's just that I don't feel comfortable sitting around here with nothing to do. There's no telling when they'll decide what they're going to do about Lizi."

Maggie grunted and went on working. Amber left her and went to join Lizi in the game room. It was no surprise to find her at the pool table. Aside from Maggie, it seemed like they had the large house to themselves. Fiona had said she felt tired after her morning swim and wanted to lie down. Fox was off somewhere—maybe with Fiona. Grayson had left for work early that morning, saying that he needed to get caught up after taking so much time off the day before.

Lizi dropped one ball in a pocket, then another and then another. The fourth shot, the six-ball, didn't fall. The cue ball rolled to a stop in a perfect position to drop the nine-ball in a corner pocket.

"That wouldn't have been very good in a game," Amber said, pointing to the nine-ball. "You don't want to make it so easy for your opponent." It wasn't that Amber cared if Lizi was good at the game as much as she just wanted her to learn to think ahead. Maybe chess would be a better game to teach her.

"I thought it would go in." Lizi repositioned herself behind the cue ball and shot again. This time the six-ball fell. She dropped the eight-ball in the side pocket and began pulling the balls out. "Do you want to play?"

"You aren't going to try to take money from me, like you did Grayson, are you?" Amber selected one of the cues.

"He didn't mind." Lizi tapped the cue ball. Most of the balls rolled around the table and came to rest, but one ball fell in a pocket.

"It's hard to be certain. We don't want him thinking you're a pool hustler. We don't want him to get too worried about what he's getting himself into when he takes you in." Amber aimed at a ball near the corner after Lizi missed a shot.

"Us," Lizi said as she watched Amber.

"What was that?" Amber asked after the ball fell in the pocket.

"You said 'takes *you* in'. Don't you mean 'takes *us* in'?" Lizi put her stick behind her neck and rested it on her shoulders.

"No, Lizi, we've already talked about this." Amber took aim on another ball. "I know it isn't the way we'd like things to be, but he can give you a lot more than I ever could. You seemed okay with it before."

"I don't want to stay with him if you don't stay too." Lizi looked at Amber with a worried look on her face.

"I told you I won't be far away," Amber said. "There's got to be some kind of work around here. But if you're sure you don't want to stay with him—" Amber missed a shot. "Maybe you're right. I was sure he was your father, but since he isn't, it might be better if we just left. Is that what you want?"

Lizi shrugged. "Are you sure he isn't my Daddy?"

"If he is, would you want to stay then?" Amber asked.

"Yeah," Lizi said, "but I want you to stay too."

"So, you like him," Amber said.

"Yeah, yesterday was fun."

"You know that he isn't going to be able to do what he did yesterday all the time." Amber had enjoyed spending the day with Grayson too, but she had also seen how he looked at his BlackBerry, only to resolutely put it aside. "He's a very busy man and he spends a lot of time working."

"I know," Lizi said, lining up her shot. "But I still like him. If I pray, do you think God will make him my Daddy?"

"I don't think it works that way," Amber said, "but you can try. You heard what they said as well as I did. I don't think there's any possibility that he and your mother had a child together."

"I'm still going to pray for it." With her left hand, Lizi fingered something hanging from a chain around her neck. It hadn't been there before.

"What's this?" Amber reached for the piece of gold. When she held it in her hand she could see the charm was a little fairy with golden wings holding an emerald in her hands. Small jewels adorned her head like a wreath of flowers. They looked real. "Where'd you get this?"

"Grayson gave it to me. Can I keep it?" Lizi looked at Amber with hope in her eyes. "He said he had it made for his wife. Doesn't that mean he has to be my father?"

"Yes, you can keep it as long as he doesn't want it back, but try not to read too much into it. And don't lose; it looks expensive. There's any number of reasons why he might have decided to give it to you," Amber said, running her fingers over the charm. "Interesting—"

"What is?" Lizi took the charm from her and tried to hold it to where she could see it without removing the chain.

"I was just remembering how Holly used to talk about your father." Amber stared out the window, but saw nothing, only Holly sitting in their living room, with Lizi in her lap. "She used to say he was the prince of the fairies. She said the fairies visited because he told them to. I wonder if Grayson gave her jewelry like this."

"We could ask him."

"No, we'd better not."

Amber didn't see Grayson until he came through the door at a quarter to ten that evening. Amber sat on a couch reading a book by the light of a lamp. He looked tired, but it could have been the dim lighting.

"I came this close to going home and sleeping in my own bed tonight." Grayson held his thumb and index finger about an inch apart to show her. "But I had dinner with Celia and now I'm under orders to make sure you haven't murdered my parents with an ax or something. You haven't, have you?"

"No, I couldn't find one."

"You wouldn't," Grayson said. "I don't think they have one. I've never seen it if they do. So, what have you been doing instead?"

"I've been reading most of the evening." Amber put a bookmark between the pages and closed the book.

"Where is everybody?" Grayson sat down in a chair, leaned his head back and spread his legs out in front of him.

"Your parents went to bed about an hour ago. I sent Lizi up to take a bath." Amber put the book on the table next the couch. "Did you enjoy your evening?"

"Not really," Grayson said. "Would you believe we spent the whole evening talking about you?"

"I can't believe I'm that interesting."

"Celia seems to think so."

Grayson looked at Amber. "I should have asked sooner, but when were you saved?"

"Last Easter," Amber said, remembering the events of the day. "I took Lizi to see an Easter program and we both accepted Christ afterward. Actually, that's not quite right. We went for another reason, but it happened to be Easter."

"So, it hasn't been that long ago."

"Just a few months."

"That's good." He leaned his head back and closed his eyes.

"I wonder if my life would be different if I'd done that sooner," she said.

"Sure it would."

"Makes me wish I had."

Grayson straightened up in his chair. "Tell me about Victoria."

"I'm sorry?" Amber asked. "I didn't know Victoria."

"Of course you didn't," Grayson said. "I'm tired. I meant Holly. Tell me about Holly."

"What do you want to know?"

"Everything," he said. "How did the two of you meet?"

"You want the long version or the short version?"

"Whatever you'll give me."

"Okay," Amber said. "It was a dark and stormy night..."

"No, be serious," Grayson said. "I'm too tired for foolishness."

"I'm not exactly joking," Amber said. "It really was a stormy night. I was working in this all night diner and she came in and sat down at one of the booths. Her hair was dripping wet, her dress was soaked, and she was very pregnant. I went over to take her order and she told me she didn't have any money but wondered if it would be okay if she sat there until the rain stopped. Of course, I let her sit there. Most of the tables were empty and I didn't feel right turning away a pregnant woman. If my boss had been there, I would've gotten in trouble, but he was never there at night."

"Is that the same diner that burned down?" Grayson asked.

"No, this one closed for a different reason." Amber decided against telling him it closed after the authorities found marijuana growing in the owner's attic.

"Keep going. How'd y'all become friends?"

"It rained all night and she was still there when I got off my shift." Amber ran her middle finger along the seam of the leather couch. "I told her she could stay at my place if she didn't have anywhere else to go."

"Just like that?" Grayson's disbelief showed on his face. "Just like that, you offered to let a perfect stranger stay with you?"

"Well, yeah," Amber said. "It seemed like the right thing to do. I'd seen a big bruise on her neck and I figured she was trying to hide from a boyfriend or something. It wasn't like there was much she could steal from me and she wasn't on drugs."

"How could you tell?"

"I've seen enough people on drugs to know the difference."

"How long did she stay there?" Grayson leaned back in his chair.

"It was kind of off and on part of the time, but she was there until she died. She was scared of so many things. I thought she might have been scared of her husband. It was hard to tell because she almost never called people by their real names. She had a nickname for everyone. There at the last, I wouldn't see her for several days at a time. Lizi wasn't very old and I had to take care of her when Holly wasn't there. I was afraid to let Holly take care of her by herself. There's no telling what she might have done."

"What was her nickname for Lizi's father? Grayson asked.

"She always called him the prince of fairies." Amber could still visualize how Holly's face would light up when she spoke of him. "It was really odd. Sometimes I thought she was afraid of him, but she never said anything bad about him. At least not until the last. She showed me newspaper article about someone who'd died in a car and she said the prince of fairies did it."

"Are you sure she said the *prince of fairies*?" Grayson moved forward in his chair.

"Yeah, why?"

"Nothing," Grayson said. "It just sounds interesting."

"Yeah, I thought so too. She would come back with bruises and I'd ask if her husband did it. She would say, 'no, not the Prince of Fairies, he loves me.'"

"You must have had a hard time putting up with Holly," Grayson said.

"Not really. Holly was only there for a couple of years. It made life interesting."

"My wife Victoria made my life interesting for a while too, but I didn't enjoy it all that much. I planned to spend my life with her and then everything went crazy. I guess I wasn't cut out for married life."

"Celia seems to think you are."

"I could do worse and it would make Dad happy," Grayson signed. "I figure I'll marry her eventually. The only thing is, with Dad more or less retired, Steve too busy spending money to pay attention to business, and Abby still mourning her husband, all I have time for is to keep the business running. I don't have time to be a proper husband."

"I don't guess you have time for Lizi either."

"I'll make time for Lizi," he said. "Somehow—I just hope she's who you say she is."

At that point, Amber was supposed to reassure him that she was, but she was beginning to feel that she couldn't be sure of anything.

"Can't you get someone to help you at work?"

"I could, but with this merger going on, we've implemented a hiring freeze," Grayson said. "We'll be eliminating several duplicate positions between the two companies. I don't want to lay off more people than I just have to."

"Could I be of some help? Maybe you wouldn't have to work so hard and you could spend more time with Lizi."

"Didn't I just tell you that I can't hire someone right now?"

"You wouldn't have to pay me. All I'm doing is sitting around waiting for you to decide what you're going to do with Lizi. I might as well be doing something useful."

"Yeah, that's probably not fair to you and her, but there's just so much stuff going on right now. Dad and the lawyers are looking into it. If I weren't afraid it would get me in some kind of legal trouble, I'd be half tempted to just claim she's my daughter and be done with it."

"Even though you say that she couldn't be? And what if you found out later that she isn't who I think she is?"

"That's why you're still sitting around here doing nothing. But as far as you helping at work, there isn't much I could have you do that would really help," Grayson said. "It isn't that I don't appreciate the offer, but most of what I do is making decisions and other people do the real work. What keeps me busy is keeping up with everyone else."

"It must be fun being in charge."

"I enjoy what I do, if that's what you mean," Grayson said.

"Just keep in mind that I'm bored out of my mind if you need any help manning the magic eight ball or whatever it is you use to make decisions."

Chapter Fourteen

"Yeah, I know Amber." Bill Krueger's voice sounded trustworthy enough over the phone, though Fox knew only that he pastored a church in St. Louis.

"I need you to verify some information." Fox leaned back in the leather chair behind the desk. "That is if you have a little time."

"O, I've got time. Amber asked if she could list me as a reference. I'll tell you, you won't find a harder working woman. But I've got to ask, where is the 817 area code? I don't recognize it."

"Fort Worth, but sir—"

"Fort Worth? What's she doing looking for a job in Fort Worth? We were hoping she'd find something up here. They just joined our church not that long ago. I guess that explains where they were on Sunday. I was thinking about driving over to see if they were alright."

"I wasn't calling because of a job." Fox didn't want to lie to a preacher, though he wondered if he'd be more forthcoming if he thought he was talking to a potential employer.

"I'm sorry, I just assumed. What can I do for you?"

Fox wondered if he could get the information he needed without telling the pastor the whole story, but decided to trust the other man wasn't part of some scheme Amber had cooked up. "Amber and Lizi showed up on my doorstep the other day. I mean that quite literally, they just showed up and made the claim that Lizi is my son's daughter."

Fox expected the other man to respond to that, but there was only silence on the other end of the line.

"We've never seen this woman or the girl before and we're trying to figure out if there's any truth to what she's been telling us. My fear is that she's just trying to get money."

"I don't know if I can be any help to you there or not," Bill said. "In the time since they joined the church, I haven't had any reason to think she's lied about anything."

"So you think she's telling the truth?"

"Well, I'd like to think so," Bill said, "but I can't tell you that she's always been honest with me either. If she wanted to pull off some kind of scam, she would know how to do it. We've even had her talk to some of our senior citizens about how recognize a scam. She's a pretty good speaker."

"So she just volunteered to talk about that kind of stuff?" Fox knew enough about scams to give a talk on it, but that wasn't the same as trying to scam someone.

"Not exactly," Bill said. "The first time she and Lizi showed up at church, she had a sob story that she wanted us to hear, but it was almost time to start the service, so I told her that if she'd wait we'd see what we could do. She and Lizi sat on the back pew through the whole service. We get to the invitation and here they come. I get my little speech ready about having them wait until after we dismiss. I figured the rest of the church wouldn't want to wait while I listened to their story. They get up to the front and they tell me they want to be saved. Of course I kneel with them right there and tell them all about it. They didn't even ask for money after that. I've about decided to make all the beggars sit through a preaching service. It might do them some good."

Fox swapped ears with the phone, swiveled around in his chair and looked out the window. It was hardly proof that Amber was a con artist. It didn't take much to ask a church for money. "Do you think she might have done that just to convince you to give her even more money? Have you given her any money at all?"

"We have, but as much help as she's been in here at church, I really don't think we've given her enough money to make it worth her while. We would have paid a lot more than that if we'd hired her to do the work. But it seems to me that Amber ought to know who the father of her child is. If he's never met her, I think she's smart enough not to try to make that claim."

"Actually, she says Lizi isn't hers. She says my son's wife had her before she died."

"Could be possible," Bill said. "We assumed that Lizi is hers, but it is strange that Lizi calls her Amber all the time. If Amber says Lizi is your granddaughter, then I suspect she believes she is."

"That's actually good news," Fox said. "We're still looking into that and should be able to get some tests done that will verify it one way or the other. But we think Amber's trying to force my son to marry her. My wife heard her talking to Lizi and we're pretty sure she's looking for some way to blackmail him."

Silence came from the other end of the line for several moments. Fox waited for a response.

"Well," the pastor finally said, "it does sound a little strange, but I know Amber and I would be surprised if she tried."

"My son isn't a poor man. I'm sure that has a lot to do with it."

"Maybe it would do some good if I talked to her."

"I would appreciate it if you would, but I'm not sure I want her knowing I talked to you." Fox could see Amber talking to her pastor and then running off with Lizi. "She isn't here right now anyway."

"It's up to you, but I think I should talk to her. Is this a good number if I call back later?"

"It's fine," Fox assured him. "I'll pay you if you can make this problem go away."

"I don't want your money. I'm more interested in what's going on with Amber." Bill sounded surprised that Fox would even offer.

"Perhaps I said that wrong," Fox said, "But I'm sure there's something that you or your church could use some extra money for."

"Always," Bill said, "but our people are always willing to give when we need it. I'm not sure I'd feel right taking your money for talking to her."

"You're a good man," Fox said.

"I really would like to talk to Amber. Do you know when I can reach her?"

"She should be around this evening."

"I'll call then."

Until then, Fox would have to wait. That wasn't something he wanted to do. He poured a glass of tea and went outside to sit by the pool. He sat there soaking in the morning sun and listening to the burble of the water fountain. He had noticed a wet towel draped over one of the chairs. At least Fiona was getting more exercise. Maybe time did heal all wounds.

The fast click of heels on concrete disturbed Fox's thoughts. He looked back toward the house to see Celia coming toward him. Behind her, he saw the door open and Maggie came out carrying a tray with a pitcher of tea and more glasses.

"Celia! We weren't expecting you." Fox stood up to greet her.

"I tried calling you, but it just went to voice mail." Celia slipped into one of the empty chairs.

"You probably tried calling while I was on the phone with Amber's pastor in St. Louis." Fox sat back down in his own chair.

Celia relaxed a little and crossed her arms. "Did you find out anything?"

"A little." Fox stirred his tea with his spoon. "I won't say it's anything concrete, but I learned enough to know that she can't be trusted."

"But that's not unexpected," Celia said.

"No," Fox said, "But it could be good news anyway. If her own pastor doesn't trust her, it shouldn't be too hard to find something to hold over her head. In any case, her pastor plans on calling to talk to her."

"Yeah, that is good news," Celia said. "She'll have a lot harder time finding something that'll make Grayson feel like he has to marry her."

"I just hope that doesn't mean she's been lying about who Lizi is."

"You mean that she's Holly's kid?" Celia asked.

"Would you like some tea, Miss Abrams?" Maggie put the tray on the table next to Fox.

Celia nodded and Maggie poured tea in a glass.

"I called Grayson at work and Amber answered the phone. You can tell me if I'm over reacting, but what is she doing in his office answering his phone?"

"You'll have to ask him," Fox said. He didn't like seeing the tension between Celia and Grayson. "He had some things he thought she might be able help him with at work."

"Just what kind of things does he do that a waitress would know anything about?"

"That's what I asked," Fox said, "but he didn't think it was a problem. If you're worried, why don't you go over there and see what he has her doing."

"You know," Celia said, "I may just do that. If he's show-ing her any of the data we gave y'all on Dad's company…"

"I'm sure he wouldn't do that," Fox said, though he had the same fears. The last thing he needed was Jack Abrams su-ing them for showing someone like Amber information that she shouldn't see.

Celia opened her purse and pulled out a few business cards. She looked through them and selected one.

"I think you should call this guy," she said, handing the card to Fox. "He'll find a lot more information about Amber than what your lawyers ever will."

Celia's heels clicked even faster as she made her way back toward the house. Then Fox heard her start her car and speed away. It wouldn't take her long to reach the office.

He looked at the card Celia had handed him. "Xander X – Private Investigator" It listed St. Louis, Memphis and Chicago. The card looked professional enough, but a business card couldn't tell you much. It was still too early to give up on what-ever Alex was trying, but bringing in another person wouldn't harm anything. A private investigator might not have the same legal concerns a lawyer would and might be able to look in places a lawyer couldn't.

"Xander X, Private Investigator," a woman's voice an-swered the phone. "How may I direct your call?"

"I might be interested in hiring Xander to do some work for me and I'm looking for more information."

"What's the nature of the work?" the voice asked.

"I need some background information on a woman from St. Louis. It may be hard to find anything. She may have used some assumed names."

"Let me redirect your call to Mr. X. Is it alright if I put you on hold?"

Fox assured her it was and heard the sounds of Jazz music mixed with the faint sound of a clothes dryer as he waited for

Xander to answer the phone. The music came to an abrupt stop a couple of minutes later.

"Sorry about the wait," Xander said. "What can I do for you?"

Fox explained the situation as much as he dared.

"I think we can help you out," Xander said. "It may take a few days, but we'll find the information you're looking for. Before we get started, I do need to know if this information will be used in court."

"Probably not," Fox said. "I don't think this will ever go to court if we find the right information. I'm just looking for a way to convince Amber to disappear."

"In that case, I'm sure we can handle it. We're sure to find something."

"This does need to be discreet," Fox said.

"We can handle that," Xander said. "I'll be in touch with you when we find something and you don't have to worry about paying me anything unless we do."

"I'll be looking forward to your call," Fox said.

"Before you go," Xander said, "if you don't mind me asking, how did you hear about me."

"A business acquaintance, Celia Abrams, gave me your card."

"Ah, yes, I remember Celia," Xander said. "Come to think of it, I think I've seen your name before, but that must have been for another client. But we'll see what we can find out about Amber and get back to you in a few days."

Fox hoped that Xander and his people were as competent as Xander seemed to think they were.

Chapter Fifteen

The endless rows of numbers bled together as Amber stared at the spreadsheet. As far as she could tell, they were just numbers. They didn't seem that important, but Grayson had made her sign a piece of paper saying she wouldn't divulge the information before the IT guy had given her a login account on the laptop in front of her. "Just something to keep the lawyers happy," Grayson had said, but he hadn't asked Lizi to sign anything when he sat her down at his computer to play games and went off to a meeting.

"See if you can create some graphs that show these numbers better," Grayson said before he left. He picked up a stack of binders, and then put a couple back on the desk. "I probably won't need these, but if the phone rings, would you answer it, I'll probably be calling to ask you to bring these down to the conference room. Sandra will catch the rest.

Amber reclined on the couch with the laptop in front of her. She'd removed her shoes and they lay in the floor next to her. An older man with glasses said he would bring her a small table to work at, but Amber didn't wait; the couch was comfortable. Grayson's first suggestion was for her to use Fox's office, but then changed his mind. She asked if they could set her up in an empty cubical.

"No, this is stuff I don't want out of this office," Grayson said. Amber wondered if he was more concerned about letting her out of his sight, but then he ran off to a meeting.

She also wondered if he really expected her to know what she was doing. There wasn't much hope, but she gave it her best and worked undisturbed except for the one phone call. She picked up the binders as she picked up the phone, believing Grayson would tell her he needed them, but Celia was on the other end.

"Where's Grayson?"

"He's in a meeting," Amber said, dropping the binders back on the desk.

"Who is this? I thought I called his office phone."

"You did. This is Amber. I'm in his office."

Silence followed by more silence.

"Put Grayson on the phone. It's important."

"I can't. I told you he's in a meeting."

"Then let me speak to whoever is in there with you."

Amber thought about arguing with her, but instead she handed the phone to Lizi. "Here, talk to Celia."

"Hello?" Lizi said softly into the phone. She listened for a moment. "This is Lizi."

She handed the phone back to Amber. "She hung up."

"She'll call back," Amber said, but she hadn't called back. And Grayson hadn't returned from his meeting. Amber just kept looking at figures that didn't make sense and kept trying to do what Grayson had asked her to. It was a good thing he wasn't paying her or he would have fired her for not accomplishing anything. She picked a couple of columns and made a little bar chart. She picked a couple more and drew another. She was just playing. It didn't tell her much, other than sales were declining and expenses were increasing—that much was obvious.

"That looks pretty good," Grayson said, coming through the door behind her.

"But you're losing money." Amber pointed to the graph.

"Yeah, I can see that—that department anyway. I was talking about what you did." He pointed at one of the columns. "Can you make a line graph out of that column? I'll need it this afternoon. Then I'll take y'all to lunch."

"You don't have to do that," Amber said, "Don't you have things you need to get done."

"You've already done what I planned on doing during lunch." He pointed to the charts. "I've got time, if we don't take too long. Besides, we've got to eat sometime, don't we? And isn't it like the ox that treads the corn?"

"How would I know?" Amber asked. "But thanks for calling me an ox."

"That's not what I meant," Grayson said.

"What did you mean?" Lizi looked up from her game.

"It's in the Bible," Grayson said.

"Really?"

"Get up and we'll find it online," Grayson said. Lizi stood up and let him have his chair.

Amber took a moment to just watch Grayson and Lizi together. It wasn't hard to imagine that Grayson really was her father. She could almost imagine that Holly had planned this, that she had known they would get along so well, but Holly had also predicted that the elves would go to war with the dwarves and that hadn't happened. Or if they had, Amber hadn't seen them.

"At least let me tell him you're here," Sandra's voice carried through the door that swung open once more behind Amber.

"What are you two up to?" Celia's voice sounded loud in Amber's ear.

"I'm helping Lizi find something," he said. "The three of us were about to go to lunch. You wanna come?"

"Of course I'll go," Celia said. "But I thought we might go over those sales figures during lunch."

"Amber's just finishing up some stuff on those," Grayson said. "But let's put that off until after lunch so the rest of my team can go over them with us."

"That's fine, if that's what you want to do," Celia said. "Is she looking at the figures from Dad's company?"

"No, I haven't shown her any of that."

It wasn't clear that Grayson understood Celia didn't want her looking at those figures, but it was obvious to Amber. Amber finished tweaking the last graph and saved the file.

"I'm ready whenever you guys are," Amber said, standing up.

"Let me finish showing this to Lizi and then we'll go." Grayson turned back to the computer. "That meeting is scheduled for one o'clock."

They all rode in Grayson's car to the restaurant. Amber and Lizi rode in the back. Amber was glad she didn't have to spend another minute looking at a spreadsheet she didn't understand.

When they arrived at the restaurant, Celia pointed to a help wanted sign on the door. "Amber, maybe you should put an application in here."

Grayson held the door for them to walk through.

"Yeah, I might do that," Amber said. It was more upscale than anywhere she'd worked before. She could hope that would mean bigger tips. And if Lizi ended up staying with Grayson, it would keep her closer to her.

During the meal, Celia dominated the conversation. Mostly she talked about things she wanted to buy. Grayson seemed to understand.

"How do you keep up with all that?" Amber asked when Celia excused herself for a few minutes.

"I don't," Grayson said. "With Celia, it helps to nod your head and say 'uh huh' a lot. I was thinking about the one o'clock meeting. I didn't agree to anything I'll regret did I?"

"Not unless you mean the new car you said you'd buy for her," Amber said dryly.

Grayson looked at her with a worried expression on his face.

"I'm kidding," Amber said.

Grayson laughed. "Yeah, so am I. I'm not that out of it."

The smile lasted a moment, but his mind was somewhere else. "I've got some more spreadsheets I'd like you to look at this afternoon, if you still want to help."

"I'm not sure I understood what I looked at this morning." Amber didn't want him disappointed in her work.

"You did what I asked you to." Grayson idly scraped his plate with his fork. "I wouldn't expect you to understand it all first thing. No one else understands them either. That's why I'm the one messing with them. If there's something you don't understand, I'd be happy to go over it with you after I finish with the meetings."

"All I've ever been is a waitress," Amber said.

"That's no problem. It isn't like we're paying you any-thing." Grayson handed his credit card to the waiter.

"Aren't you though?" Amber couldn't help but think about the roof over their heads at night and the food they ate at every meal. Then there were the new clothes she and Lizi wore.

"No," Grayson said, looking at his watch. "What is taking Celia so long?"

"Are you going to be late for your meeting?" Amber asked.

"They won't start without us, but I was hoping to show you something before we went back."

"Are you going to show us your condo?" Lizi asked, stick-ing her finger in her soda, pulling it out and sucking off the liquid.

"No, it was something else, but it can wait until another day. I hope she's feeling okay."

The waiter returned with Grayson's credit card. Celia came back from the restroom several minutes later, looking fine. It was after one o'clock by the time they got back to the office.

Amber spent most of the afternoon doing the same thing she'd done that morning. Lizi got bored with the game she was playing and began browsing shelves that lined the walls of Grayson's office.

"I don't think you'll find anything interesting over there," Amber said, referring to the serious looking hardback books.

Lizi pulled out a book and held it up. "This one looks interesting."

It was one of very few novels. On the cover, a man held a sword up proudly and a woman in a long red dress and a cone shaped hat looked lovingly at him.

Lizi stretched out on the floor, opened the cover and began reading. Amber finished what Grayson had asked her to do with the spreadsheet and put the laptop aside. At least the figures on this spreadsheet looked better. Instead of everything going downhill, costs were rising, but so were sales. She walked over to the window and watched the traffic on street.

She turned around when she heard the door open. Grayson stepped through the door with two men and a woman behind him. He looked tired.

"Did you finish with that spreadsheet?" He never lost eye contact with Amber as he walked around his desk.

"Yes," she said, wondering if he thought she was wasting time staring out the window.

"Good." He sat down in his chair, looking relieved. "Did you save it to the network drive?"

Amber nodded.

With an open hand, Grayson gestured toward Lizi. "The girl on the floor is my daughter, Lizi."

Lizi looked up at the mention of her name and then went back to reading. Hearing Grayson call Lizi his daughter gave Amber a strange feeling. She wondered if it was a slip of the tongue, if he'd just said that to answer unasked questions, or if he really believed it. In many ways, it was that last possibility that scared her the most.

"This is—"Grayson motioned toward Amber and paused, as if looking for the right words. "This is Amber."

It was too much to expect Grayson to call Lizi his daughter and then call her Lizi's mother. If Lizi were his, he wouldn't let people think that anyone other than Victoria was her mother. That was okay. She didn't care if people thought she was just one of his employees.

After several minutes of talking, partly about the spread-sheet Amber had been working with, the three strangers and Grayson stood up. He shook hands with each and walked them to the door of his office, which he held open until they walked through. He went back to his computer, looked at his e-mail for a few minutes, responded to one or two then logged off and pushed his chair back.

"I'm ready to get out of this place. How 'bout y'all?" Grayson picked up a folder, stuffed it into his laptop bag, and then stood up, taking the bag with him.

"Can I bring this?" Lizi asked, showing Grayson the book.

"Sure," he said and then turned to look at Amber. "I really appreciate your help today."

"I'm happy to help, but I'm not sure I was all that helpful." She hadn't done anything he couldn't have easily done himself.

"It got those three on the way back to the airport a little faster. That's worth something." Grayson opened the door and waited for Amber and Lizi to collect their things. "I'm leaving earlier. That's not a bad thing either."

"You called Lizi your daughter," Amber said.

"Yeah, I guess I did," Grayson said. "Does that bother you?"

"No, why should it?" Amber asked. "I wouldn't have come if I didn't think you were her father."

"So then, there's really no harm in me saying she is, wheth-er she is or not."

"No, I don't guess."

Grayson led them out to his car. He looked at his watch. "We might still have time."

"Time for what?" Lizi asked as they got in the car.

"Time to show you what I wanted you to see after lunch." He drove a couple blocks down the street and pulled into the parking lot of another building that was smaller than the one they'd just left. There were several workers walking out to their cars for the drive home. He pulled into one of the empty spac-es.

"We used to have our offices here," Grayson said. "We were just leasing it at the time, but I bought the building after my wife—after what happened to my wife."

Amber could hear the catch in his voice, but her curiosity got the better of her. "Why would you buy a building that you don't need?"

"You'll see," he said. He voice was stronger.

They followed him to the front door of the building. He pushed a button beside the door.

"Can I help you, sir?" A woman's voice came through the speaker.

"We're here to see, the lobby." Grayson said.

"I'm sorry, I didn't catch the name," the voice said. "Who do you need to see? What company are you with?"

"We're just here to see the lobby," Grayson said.

The door opened and woman held it for them. "Come in. Who was it you said you needed to see?"

"We're not here to see anyone," Grayson said. "I just want-ed to show these two the lobby."

The woman looked puzzled, but she let them walk through the door.

Inside, Amber could see a large mural. Even without seeing a signature or anyone telling her, she recognized the artist. The landscape with a castle in the distance and fairies in the trees didn't seem to fit with the business, but the artistry was unmistakable. "Holly did this, didn't she?"

"Yeah," Grayson said. "My wife wanted her to do this."

"And you bought the building so someone wouldn't paint over it."

Grayson didn't answer.

"I'm sorry, sir," the receptionist said. "I didn't realize you owned the building or I would've let you in right away."

"No, that's alright," Grayson said. "I don't come so often I'd expect you to know. I just wanted Lizi to see it. Her mother painted it."

"A lot of people comment on it," the receptionist said. "I can tell you that much."

"I've got a couple more of her pieces at home," Grayson said.

"Really? Can we go see them?" Lizi asked.

"If Amber doesn't mind. I've got some things I need to do there anyway."

They walked back to Grayson's car. He opened the rear door for Lizi, keeping Amber from getting in before Lizi's door was closed. He put his hand on the front passenger door to open it, but first he said, "You and I both know that Holly didn't paint that mural."

Amber looked at him in surprise, trying to figure out what kind of game he was playing. "If she didn't paint it, who did? I've seen her work. I'm no art expert, but I know her work when I see it."

Grayson opened the door. "Just checking."

"You were trying to trick me," Amber said.

"You thought I wouldn't?" Grayson asked. "I don't know if this means Lizi is Holly's daughter, but you've proven you knew Holly."

"Is that supposed to make me relax?"

"Is that what you need to do?" Grayson closed her door before she could respond.

When they reached Grayson's condo, he let them inside. "We had a house in the country when Victoria was alive. I kept it for several years after that, but I finally decided to move in here. It's closer to work."

"Did the fairies live in the trees at your house?" Lizi asked.

"Fairies and elves and everything else I'm afraid. They were all there, but they aren't here." A look of sadness crossed Grayson's face, but he turned and walked toward the kitchen, leaving the other two to look around.

"I like it," Lizi said, rushing from room to room.

Amber counted three bedrooms in the nicely decorated condo. It looked very spacious. After looking around, Amber thought Grayson looked busy, so she sat in one of the chairs and waited. She caught Lizi standing in front of the two pictures her mother had painted, just staring at them.

It went on like that for several minutes. Amber wondered what the girl was thinking. Perhaps she was wishing her mother was there instead of Amber.

When they got back to Fox's house, Lizi asked Grayson to play pool. Amber watched for a while, but Maggie came in to tell her that she had a phone call.

"Who?" Amber asked. She couldn't think of any of her friends who knew where she was.

"I don't know," Maggie said. "Do you want to take it in your room?"

Amber went upstairs and picked up the phone. It seemed odd to hear Bill Krueger on the other end of the line.

"Just what have you gotten yourself into?" he asked after talking for a while.

"I probably should've told someone," Amber said. "I'm not sure you'd understand."

"Try me," Bill said. "It might do you good to talk about it. I already know some of it. What's this about you telling someone that Lizi is his daughter?"

Amber didn't need to ask where he had heard that. She lay back on the bed.

"How much do you know?"

"I'm not sure," Bill said. "I only know what Fox Jacobs was able to tell me."

"Lizi isn't my daughter," Amber said. "Her mother was a friend of mine, but she died when Lizi was very young."

Bill made some sort of noise to let her know he understood.

"I didn't try very hard to find her family until a few months ago. I thought I had it figured out that Lizi's father was this guy in Fort Worth."

"You're not so sure now?" Bill asked.

"No, I'm not sure of anything," Amber said. "All I had to go on was what Holly said, but she wasn't right in the head. I figured drugs had messed her up or something. It wouldn't have mattered, but I lost my job and when started having trouble finding enough money to take care of Lizi, I figured she'd be better off with her real family. These people have plenty of money."

"Why didn't you tell us?" Bill asked. "We would've found a way to help you."

"It didn't seem right," Amber said. What more could she tell him? "Before I was saved, I was always conning someone and asking you for help seemed like it was just the same thing. Now I'm not sure what to do."

"Have you been telling them the truth?"

"Mostly," Amber said. "I goofed up on some of that. I didn't think they'd believe the truth."

"Are you trying to blackmail someone to marry you?" Bill asked.

"No, of course not!" Amber said. "Where would you get that idea?"

"That's what Fox said."

"I can't imagine where he'd get that idea," Amber said. "I never said anything about marrying Grayson. Could he have just made it up to see how you'd respond? Grayson doesn't seem to think I'm trying anything. If anything, we seem to be getting along pretty well. Lizi and I went to eat with him and his girlfriend today. And then he took us to see a mural her mother painted."

"Yeah, I suppose he could've just been trying to get a reaction from me," Bill said. "But I'd be careful. If he thinks you're trying something crooked, he'll try to stop you."

"There's nothing to stop," Amber said. "And I'm sure I've got to see this thing through, at least until they've proven to themselves that Lizi is Holly's daughter. Then maybe they'll tell me who Holly's family is."

"Wouldn't it be better for the two of you to just come home until then?"

"What home?" Amber asked. "I sold the house and practically everything else to pay the bills. I don't even have enough money to buy train tickets."

"I think we can find enough money to cover that and there's probably a church member or two who wouldn't mind giving you a room for a while."

"The Jacobs are better able to take care of us. What's the difference between staying with them and staying with people from church?"

"Trust," Bill said. "They might be more likely to believe you if you aren't asking them for money."

Amber wondered if Bill was right and she considered telling them they would be leaving when she went downstairs. They might be glad to see her leave, but she couldn't imagine they'd let her leave with Lizi, not with Grayson calling her his daughter. But maybe that didn't mean anything.

She found Lizi and Grayson playing pool and Fox standing off to one side watching. They all seemed to be enjoying themselves. She could discuss leaving some other time. It wouldn't hurt to wait a little longer.

Lizi sunk the eight-ball.

"Good for you," Amber said, reaching over to rub the girl's back.

"You might not be cheering for her if you knew what happens if she wins," Grayson said. "It involves you."

"Lizi, you know what I said about gambling."

"I'm not gambling. I just wanted to make sure he didn't go easy on me."

"You taught her well," Grayson said as he set up the balls again. "She's quite the little pool hustler."

"You could have refused," Lizi said.

"Yeah, I know," he said. "You did say the best of five didn't you?"

"Not that it'll matter. You might as well pay up now."

"I could still win," Grayson said. "You'll be showing me what's in your diary before the night's over."

Amber wondered what Lizi thought was valuable enough to risk letting someone see her diary.

Chapter Sixteen

Lizi and Grayson were selecting their cues when Fox walked in.

"How do I know you won't let me win like you did last time?" Lizi asked.

"You've got my word," Grayson said.

"We need an incentive to make you play right."

"You know Amber doesn't like you gambling," Grayson said. "I don't want you gambling either."

"I'm not talking about gambling," Lizi said, "just a little something—like a prize."

"Just what did you have in mind?"

"I don't know," Lizi said. "How about, if you win, I'll let you read my diary? What will you do if I win?"

"I can't think of anything," Grayson said. "What is it that you want?"

"You've got to come up with something."

"Okay, if you win, I'll take you to…"

"I don't want to go." Lizi stopped Grayson midsentence.

"You don't even know what I was going to say."

"Doesn't matter," Lizi said, "But I bet Amber would like to go."

"She would, would she?" Grayson looked thoughtful. "Okay, if you win, you want me to take Amber..."

"On a date," Lizi said after Grayson paused.

"That wasn't what I was going to say, but okay," Grayson said. "If you win, I'll take Amber on a date. Does that make you happy?"

"You have to kiss her," Lizi said. "And you have to do it in front of Celia."

"You really are trying to get me in trouble," Grayson said.

Lizi's setup was obvious. Fox figured Grayson would back down.

"I offered to let you read my diary," Lizi said.

"That's fair," Grayson said. "I guess. But I don't know what's in your diary. I have a pretty good idea what'll happen if I do what you want."

So did Fox, but he wasn't worried, Grayson was very good at pool. Then again, maybe he was a little worried. Celia would be very unhappy and that was the last thing they needed right then. Grayson had better not throw the game like he had before.

The first shot to drop was Grayson's as were the second and third.

"You are pretty good," Lizi said as she watched the cue ball hit one side of the table, then the other, before it lightly tapped a ball near a corner. The ball rolled toward the pocket and stopped just short of it.

Lizi eyed the table for a moment, and then dropped three shots. She lined up to take a shot that looked like the wrong angle. The cue ball hit one ball, and then hit another. One dropped in the side pocket and the other dropped in the corner. Fortunately, so did the cue ball.

"Oops," she said and stepped away from the table.

"Who taught you to shoot like that?" Grayson asked, looking for his next shot.

"Amber, but it wasn't supposed to do that," she said. "It was sort of an accident."

Grayson made a couple more shots and Lizi took her turn again. She dropped the remaining balls and finally dropped the eight-ball at about the same time as Amber entered the room.

"Good for you!" Amber rubbed Lizi's shoulder as she spoke.

"You might not be cheering for her if you knew what happens if she wins," Grayson said. "It involves you."

"Lizi, you know what I said about gambling."

"I'm not gambling. I just wanted to make sure he didn't go easy on me."

"You taught her well." Grayson said. "She's quite the little pool hustler."

"You could have refused," Lizi said.

"Yeah, I know," he said. "You did say the best of five didn't you?"

"Not that it'll matter. You might as well pay up now."

"I could still win," Grayson said. "You'll be showing me what's in your diary before the night's over."

Amber sat down on a stool and watched the game. She seemed quiet, deep in thought, as if worried about something. Maybe that meant her talk with her pastor had done some good.

When Lizi started to take a shot during the second game, Amber spoke up. "Are you sure you want to take that shot?"

"Yeah," Lizi said, "why not?"

"Think about what it'll look like afterward," Amber said. "You won't have a good shot."

Amber suggested a different angle.

"Hey! No fair, helping her like that," Grayson said.

Lizi repositioned herself for the angle which Fox thought looked more difficult than the first, but the ball fell and the cue ball rolled to a position that gave Lizi a perfect shot.

The second game went to Lizi. The closest Grayson came to winning was in the third game. They each had one more ball to sink before sinking the eight-ball. Grayson's ball stood in the way of a direct shot. Lizi looked at one angle and then another.

"I don't have a shot," she said.

"Sure you do," Amber said, "just keep it legal."

"No helping her," Grayson said.

"All I did was tell her she still has a shot. She still has to make it."

Lizi raised the cue to a high angle above the cue ball and gave it a good thump. The white ball rose a few inches in to the air, landed on the other side of Grayson's ball and then rolled until it tapped the other ball and came to a stop. The other ball fell in a pocket. Lizi dropped the eight ball easily.

"That's three," Lizi said. "When are you paying up?"

"Soon," Grayson said, looking over toward Amber, "but not right now."

"There won't be any paying up," Amber said. "Lizi, you had your fun, let's just leave it at that."

"That's not fair," Lizi said.

"Phew! That was close." Grayson exaggerate the motion of wiping his forehead.

Fox could imagine Celia's reaction. "Were you going to give Celia fair warning?"

"Somehow, I don't think that was what Lizi had in mind," Grayson said. "Besides, it'd be easier to apologize than to convince her it's okay."

"Grayson, there's something that I think I need to tell you." Amber looked more withdrawn than Fox had ever seen her.

"Maybe you should save it for our date," Grayson said sarcastically.

"What date?"

Grayson looked embarrassed. "I kind of thought you knew. Lizi made me promise to take you on a date it I lost."

"And—" Lizi began.

"And we'll worry about the rest later," Grayson said.

"I already said the bet was off," Amber said.

"You aren't trying to make me go back on a promise are you?" Grayson asked. "I knew what I was risking before we started the game."

"But you didn't know how well Lizi could play," Amber said. "You can't be expected to honor a bet when you didn't know who you were up against. Besides, I don't want you encouraging Lizi to gamble."

"We already decided it wasn't gambling," Grayson said. "It was all in good fun."

"It's still gambling."

"What if it were just a trade?" Grayson asked. "What if Lizi let me read her diary, even though I lost?"

Amber laughed. "She wouldn't do that."

"Yes, I would," Lizi said. "Let me go get it."

"No, don't do that," Grayson said. "I'm not going to read your diary unless you want me to."

"It doesn't matter anyway," Amber said. "It still doesn't make it right."

"How could having a meal together at a nice restaurant be the wrong thing to do?"

"That wasn't what I meant. I just don't want anyone thinking I'm doing something I shouldn't."

"I don't think there's any risk of that. What was it you needed to tell me?"

"Somehow, it doesn't seem like the right time to tell you anymore."

Grayson looked thoughtful. "Maybe I should follow my daughter's lead and play you for your secret."

"Some secrets are too important to rest on the outcome of a game," Amber said.

"Chicken," Grayson laughed. "You're afraid I'll beat you."

"It's not that. Set it up, I'll play, but not to determine what secrets I reveal."

Chapter Seventeen

Amber looked at herself in the mirror one more time. She didn't know why she felt so nervous. It wasn't even a real date. Maybe that was what made her the most nervous. She didn't know how Grayson expected her to act. If it'd been a real date, she could've just focused on spending time with someone she liked, but with this she wasn't sure if Grayson thought it was just one big joke or if he was just trying to get through it because he'd told Lizi he would. Or maybe he thought she'd put Lizi up to it. Under normal circumstances, there wasn't any reason to be uncomfortable spending a couple of hours with Grayson when they'd spent nearly the whole day together on Friday and then stayed up past mid-night talking. He had wanted to hear about Holly.

"How do I look?" Amber asked, turning to Lizi, who was sitting beside her.

"Pretty," Lizi said.

"Do you think so?" Amber asked, looking at her reflection again. It just looked like her own face with a little more makeup than usual. All of it bought by Grayson. She hoped he wasn't disappointed he'd spent the money. She stood up and walked toward the door.

Grayson was downstairs, looking very relaxed, watching a television show.

"Are you ready?" he asked, turning off the television.

"We don't have to go right now, if you want to finish what you're watching."

Grayson stood up, took her by the arm and said, "You look very nice. I would much rather spend the time with you."

If Grayson felt bad about being forced into this, he didn't show any sign of it. Lizi's face was beaming. Only Amber felt bad. She deserved it too. She'd taught Lizi every trick she knew.

They rode in silence until they reached downtown. Amber was too deep in her own thoughts to talk and Grayson didn't seem to mind, or she didn't pay attention when he spoke. He pulled up in front of one of the hotels.

"There's a place in here that will be quiet—unless you want to go somewhere else." Grayson put the car in park.

"I'm sure this is will be fine, but I have to ask, isn't a first date a little early to take a girl to a hotel?" She meant it to be funny, but the words came out wrong. Grayson didn't laugh.

A young man opened the door for her. "Do y'all have luggage?"

"No, we're just here to eat," Grayson said, getting out of the other side of the car. He came around the car and handed the key to the young man.

The automatic sliding door swooshed open as they approached and they walked into a spacious area with several couches and chairs. A desk for the bellhops sat off to the side. The front desk lay on the far side of the room. Two or three people appeared to be checking in. Grayson led the way through the room like he knew where he wanted to go. He led the way up a wide stairway, around a turn and through the entrance of the restaurant.

"Do you come here often?" Amber asked.

"I would say so. It's just a short walk from where I live."

A man showed them to a table near a window. Only they and another couple were there.

"It'll get busier later on," Grayson said, as he picked up the menu. "We're here early. I don't want to keep you out too late and have you sleeping through church tomorrow."

"I didn't embarrass you too much last Sunday?" Amber looked at her own menu.

"That's funny," Grayson said, still looking at his menu.

"What is?" Nothing on the menu looked particularly funny.

"I just realized; you've only been here a little over a week. It seems like it's been longer."

"Have we made it that stressful for you?" Amber put the menu down and took a drink of water. The cold water felt refreshing.

"No, it's not that." Grayson put his own menu on the table. "It's just that so much has happened. I've probably spent more time with you this week than I have with Celia in all the time I've known her."

"I can't believe that." Amber could guess that Celia wouldn't let him by with that.

"I'm sure I exaggerated a little, but I have seen quite a lot of you this week—enough that I think I know a few things about you."

"That's a scary thought," Amber said, thinking about the things she hadn't told him.

"Why do you say that?"

A woman dressed in a white blouse and a black skirt came to take their order. Amber hoped the interruption gave Grayson time to forget what they had been discussing. The woman walked away.

"You were going to tell me why it's scary for me to know about you." Grayson hadn't been so easily distracted.

"Was I?" Amber sipped her water.

"I sure thought you were."

"There's a lot you don't know about me. I've been arrested, uh—" She paused and tried to think. "Let's just say I've been arrested a few times."

"I know," Grayson said, resting his elbows on the table and interlacing his fingers. "Alex told me it was seven."

"Really?" Amber did a mental count of each time. "I guess you're right. I thought it was eight. Maybe that one time wasn't considered an arrest."

"And every time you were accused of taking money under false pretenses, right?" Grayson asked. "But you didn't stay in jail very long."

"I guess they all were for that, but they never had enough evidence." Amber ran her finger along the top edge of her glass. "I guess you could say that I'm good at what I do. Funny thing is, I don't have a dime from it."

"What happened to it?" Grayson still looked more concerned for her than he looked disgusted at what she had told him.

"Part of it went to pay the lawyer. I went to court a few times. A lot of it paid for Lizi's medical bills. She wasn't well when she was a baby. Holly had some expenses too. The rest just disappeared." Amber leaned back as their server put salad bowls in front of them.

"You don't have to tell me all this," Grayson said, when the woman left.

"Yes, I do," Amber said, picking up her salad fork. "I want you to know what kind of background Lizi and I have."

"Tell me about Holly." Grayson took a bite of salad. Amber looked at her own bowl. It looked like any other salad, but it gave her time to think.

"She was strange," Amber said. "But a lot of fun. She had these imaginary friends. At least, that's what I thought they were. She saw fairies and elves. One time she saw a thirty foot tall troll coming down the Interstate. She was afraid of most of them, but other than that, she seemed relatively sane."

"Relative to what?"

"I don't know, but she was my friend." Amber watched a city bus roll past on the street below them. "She would sometimes pretend to be different people. She said it was to confuse the elves. It was hard to take her seriously. She pretended to be me once. That was really weird. I told her not to do it again."

"Did she listen?"

"Yes," she said, "at least she didn't do it around me."

"One time, she showed me a newspaper article about an accident and said, 'The Princess is dead.'"

"Are you sure she said 'the Princess'?"

"Yeah, I think so," Amber said.

"I'm sure you're probably right about what she said," Grayson said. "It does seem to fit, in a weird sort of way."

"Holly clipped all the newspaper articles about that woman."

"So, did I," Grayson said, seeming distracted for the first time in a few minutes. "I've still got them. I used to keep them out all the time, but after I moved, I didn't even pull them out of the box. They're stuffed away in a closet. I should probably throw them out. Especially now that I know that woman wasn't who I thought she was. It's hard to get over losing your spouse."

"Who did you think she was?"

"I thought she was Victoria. That's what the police thought too."

"But she wasn't?"

"No, that would be impossible. That is, if what you've been telling us is true. It makes me wonder just what Victoria got herself into."

"Do you miss her?" Amber thought Grayson looked almost vulnerable.

"Not as much as I did." Grayson came out of his deep thoughts. "What about the medical bills you said Lizi had? Holly must have gotten over her fear of doctors."

"Hardly," Amber said, thinking back to the many visits to the doctor. "She always had me take her. She wasn't afraid anyone would take her from me."

"The story you tell seems to work out so conveniently with what I'm expecting you to say," Grayson said.

"Then you don't believe me."

"That's not what I said. What do you say we change the subject for a while?"

Changing the subject turned into a few minutes of silence. It gave Amber time to eat her salad. When the server returned with their main course, Grayson began to talk more, but he didn't mention anything about the previous conversation. He didn't give her any hint of what he had been thinking about it until they returned to Fox's house.

"Looks like Celia's here," Grayson said pointing to a car on the driveway. He drove through the archway under the second floor leading to the garage and parked the car.

"There's something I'd like to know," Amber said. "If Lizi is Holly's kid, does she have family that will take care of her?"

"Holly didn't have family," Grayson said. "If what you say is true, you're probably the closest friend she ever had. Other than Victoria, of course."

"But what about Lizi."

"Lizi will be taken care of. Whatever happens, I promise that Lizi will be taken care of. But let's not discuss that just yet." Grayson looked her directly in the eye as he spoke. "Things are complicated and I need time to think. Besides, can you imagine how Mom would react if we walk in and tell her that Lizi isn't her granddaughter? I was beginning to think she would waste away to nothing. She was looking more like a ghost than my mother, but the two of you show up and already she's starting to get a tan and she isn't spending all day in bed. Don't ruin that."

Grayson opened his door and Amber did the same. They both walked toward the house.

"Oh!" Grayson said, stopping in his tracks. "There was one more thing that I have to do as part of the deal with my daughter. I don't want you getting too upset with me when we get inside."

"What thing?" Amber asked. She wasn't sure if he had called Lizi his daughter to remind Amber that she still had to go through with her act or whether he had gotten into the habit of thinking of her that way.

"You'll see," he said. "It'll make Lizi happy."

"That's what I'm afraid of."

They walked into the room where Fox, Fiona, Celia and Lizi sat. Grayson grabbed Amber by the shoulders and turned her toward him.

"Don't read too much into this," Grayson whispered. He kissed Amber on the lips.

It was very brief, but when Amber looked at the others in the room, Lizi looked happy while Celia looked furious. Celia walked across the room, slapped Grayson in the face and made a beeline to the front door.

"Maybe you should go talk to her," Fox said. He looked worried, but Fiona was laughing.

"I'll let her cool off first." Then to Amber he said, "Just to let you know, that was part of Lizi's deal."

"You didn't have to tell her that!" Lizi's grin disappeared to be replaced by an angry scowl. She ran out of the room and up the stairs.

Amber found her sprawled out across the bed in their room, crying. She sat on the edge of the bed and rubbed the girl's back. "What's wrong honey?"

Lizi held out her arm, revealing a small bandage. "They're going to make us go away and it's all my fault."

"What happened?" Amber asked, looking at the bandage.

"They took blood and now they're going to use it to prove Grayson isn't my Dad. I shouldn't have made him take you on a date. Now we'll have to leave."

"It doesn't matter what they find out," Amber said. "It's going to work out."

"Does that mean we're leaving?"

"Not yet," Amber said. "Grayson's mulling it over, so for now, we'll just keep doing what we're doing. But let's keep our bags packed in case things don't go well."

Chapter Eighteen

Fox looked at the document on his screen carefully. The handwriting looked like the sample of Amber's handwriting he held in his hand. Xander had been true to his word.

> *As you are aware, I have raised your daughter as my own for many years at my own expense. After giving it considerable thought, I have decided that I deserve some form of compensation. I will return your daughter to you, as we agreed, but please bring twenty-five thousand dollars cash.*

"Is this real?" Fox asked.

"It looks real, doesn't it?" Xander asked.

"Yeah, but looking real and being real are two different things."

"Look," Xander said. "You said you wanted something that would keep Amber from making any claims on your granddaughter. With her record, this will do the trick."

"But we can't use it in court," Fox said.

"When you hired us, I asked if that was important," Xander said. "We looked under every rock we could find and I can tell you right now that either Amber is a lot better at covering up her actions than I think she is or she isn't as crooked as her record seems to indicate."

"I'm just afraid that she's going to realize that this is fake she'll call my bluff," Fox said.

"It's your call," Xander said, "but if it were me, I'd show her the note and tell her to leave. Threaten her with prison time. You do that and she'll leave for sure."

"Have you got anything else? This may not help much." It was worth showing to Amber, just to see how she would respond, but it only raised doubts. It didn't prove anything. The paternity test would come back soon and tell them if Lizi was Grayson's. What Fox needed was a way to get rid of Amber before Grayson did something stupid. Weeks had slipped away since the time Amber and Lizi showed up. It seemed like Grayson was always with them. Then there were those late night conversations and those discussions between Amber and Grayson that ended as soon as Fox walked into the room.

"There is one other thing." Xander said. "Let me send it to you. You'll get an e-mail in a few seconds."

The few seconds turned into a minute, but when he got it, Fox open the e-mail and the image attached to it. The image of a car parked on a street appeared on the screen.

"It's nothing but a car." Fox looked at it closely, but he saw nothing important.

"That's what the police said, but there's an old woman who is convinced the owner of that car had something to do with Victoria's accident. The old woman was in the neighborhood watch. She says she saw that car. I wouldn't have brought it up, if the car wasn't Amber's. I think it's worth looking into. The police wouldn't have known there was a connection. You never know—I think Amber might have killed Victoria to get her kid or something."

"Since they knew each other, maybe they were both there for the same reason." Even with all her failings, Fox didn't see Amber as a coldblooded killer.

"I'm just saying it's worth looking into."

"Keep looking," Fox said. "If nothing else, we might learn more about what happened to Victoria."

Fox printed off a copy of what Xander sent him and went looking for Amber. He saw Maggie scolding one of the maids for not vacuuming under a couch.

"Have you seen Amber?" he asked.

"They're all out by the pool," she said and went back to instructing the woman on how to properly vacuum a floor.

Lizi and Fiona were the only ones in the pool. They were tossing a ball back and forth. Amber sat in one of the chairs with a book open in front of her. Grayson sat at a table with his laptop.

"Amber, can I have a word with you?" Fox asked.

She put her book down. "Sure. What do you need?"

"Alone," Fox said.

Amber followed him back toward the house. It was only when they were away from the others that he showed her the note."

"What is this?" She asked.

"Isn't that your handwriting?"

"It looks like it," she said, "But I didn't write it. I don't know these people. Even if I did, I wouldn't be so stupid as to write this. It doesn't even make sense."

"That's what you'd like me to believe," Fox said.

"Believe what you like," Amber said, "I didn't write this."

"Someone with your handwriting did and the people who you tried to con will say they recognize you."

"Okay, so you've got enough money to buy some people off," Amber said. "I get that, but why? What is it you think I can give you? I don't have any money. What is it that you want?"

"I want you away from my son," Fox said. "And I want you away from my granddaughter. I've seen how you've been using her to manipulate my son. You can't seriously think that you can come into my house and mess with my family without me doing something about it."

"I never meant to hurt anyone."

"You wanted to force my son to marry you."

"I never…"

"Fiona heard you talking about it."

"But…"

"I can call the police right now," Fox said. "Is that what you want? Maybe you can think of a better way to handle this."

Fox reminded himself that Amber was skilled at lying. If he didn't get rid of her now, she would be part of the family before he knew it and the merger with Jack Abram's company would never take place. She would've resorted to blackmail to woo Grayson, if she could've found a way.

"Okay, I can see I've overstayed my welcome. I'll leave," she said. "Let me get Lizi and we'll leave."

"Lizi stays here," Fox said.

"You can't do that," Amber said.

"I think I can," Fox said. "Would you like me to show this nice little letter to the police?"

"And what happens if you find out Lizi isn't Holly's daughter?"

"You should've thought about that before you messed with me," Fox said.

"Fine," she said. "But don't think I'm happy about this."

She turned and walked back to the pool.

"Lizi, come inside for a few minutes," Amber called out, "I need to talk to you."

"Do I have to?" Lizi whined, but when Amber gave her a look that Fox didn't catch, Lizi said, "Oh" and hurriedly swam to the side of the pool. She grabbed a towel and dried herself as she ran after Amber.

Fox followed them inside, but he waited downstairs. He wouldn't give Amber the opportunity to disappear with Lizi. Amber and Lizi came downstairs a few minutes later. They were both crying. They clung to each other for some time and then Amber disappeared out the front door. Fox made sure it was locked behind her. He wasn't happy about doing it, but it had to be done.

He kept his eye on Lizi, fearing she would follow after Amber, but she ran out the back of the house still bawling. Grayson quickly went to the girl. He held her tight and she tried to say something through her tears.

"What's wrong, honey?" Grayson kept asking.

It took a while for him to understand the words, "she left."

"What do you mean she left?" Grayson asked, still holding the crying girl.

"She said to give you this," Lizi said, her sobs lessening.

Grayson held the paper out to where he could read it without letting go of Lizi. He folded it in half, as it had been before, when he finished.

"Come on, she can't have gotten far on foot. Let's go see if we can find her.

Lizi quit crying and went with Grayson to his car.

"What did the note say?" Fox yelled after them, but they didn't take time to respond.

Fox went upstairs to the room where Amber and Lizi had been staying. The smaller of their two bags lay on the bed with a few odds and ends beside it. He went in the closet and saw all the clothes Grayson had paid for still hanging in their place, but the larger bag and the clothes Amber brought with her were gone.

Grayson and Lizi returned a couple of hours later. Neither looked very happy. They would get over it when they realized they were better off without someone like Amber. She would be like a member of the family who wasn't really part of the family—just in the way.

"Did she come back?" Grayson asked.

Fiona shook her head.

"We looked everywhere," Grayson said.

"What did the note say?" Fox asked.

"I don't think she wants you to know," he said. "She did say I could take better care of Lizi than she could."

Fox assumed that meant she hadn't explained the true reason for her departure. That was good. He knew he'd done the right thing, but he wasn't sure all the rest of the family would see it that way.

Grayson and Lizi spent the rest of the day sitting around waiting to answer a phone that would never ring or a doorbell that would never chime. Around six o'clock, Grayson stood up and said, "Come on Lizi, let's go get your things. I'm going to take you home."

Lizi didn't say anything, but got up off the couch and walked slowly toward the stairs.

"What do you mean you're taking her home?" Fox asked. "I thought we decided it would be better if they stayed here until we got things sorted out."

"Lizi is my daughter," Grayson said. "She's going to be moving into my place sometime. It might as well be tonight."

"What if Amber was lying?" Fox asked.

"She wasn't," Grayson said. "She knew too much to be lying."

Chapter Nineteen

"Where are we going?" Lizi asked as Amber pulled their bags out of the closet.

"*We* aren't going anywhere," Amber said, pulling the things Lizi would need out of the larger bag. "*I'm* leaving you with Grayson. He'll take care of you, but something's come up. I can't stay here."

Always let the mark think he's winning. Amber's father hadn't taught her much, but he'd taught her that and she tried to live by it. But Fox wasn't a mark—he just thought he was. And maybe he really was winning. She couldn't stay there if he didn't want her there. Amber knew that paper was forged. She wasn't sure that Fox would risk presenting it in court, but it was clear that he intended to make things go his way. Leaving was the best option, though she hated leaving Lizi behind. It wasn't unexpected. It was too great of a risk to take Lizi with her. She could never win a kidnapping case. Her only choice was to retreat. Lizi would be safe. That was the most important thing.

"But I don't want to stay here by myself."

"I know, but it isn't safe for me to stay. I still think Grayson may be your father. You should be with him." Amber knew her voice sounded surer than she in fact was. All she had to go on was what Holly had told her and Grayson frequently calling Lizi his daughter. The one thing she could be sure of was that she could trust him to take care of Lizi.

"But I want to be with you." The tears started to form in Lizi's eyes.

"None of that, now," Amber said as she quickly changed out of the clothes Grayson bought for her. She didn't want anyone to say she had stolen anything. "I'll be back to see you sometime soon, but I have to leave now."

"Why?" Lizi put her arms around her, keeping her from packing her things.

Amber wasn't sure what to tell Lizi. She wouldn't believe her if she told her it was for her own good. She wasn't sure it was wise to blame it on Fox. It would give Lizi reason to hate the man and Amber didn't want that. They would get the results of the test back and they would know all the truth they needed to know. They would have their proof that Lizi was Holly's. If that also meant Lizi was also Grayson's Amber had no idea, but Amber thought Grayson would take care of her.

She sat down to write a note:

> *Grayson, I know the test results will tell you for sure, but Lizi really is Holly's daughter. I don't know what kind of relationship you and Holly had but I believe you must have loved her in some way. Even if Lizi isn't yours, I'm holding you to your promise to take care of her. I'll be watching. I know you must be wondering why I would abandon Lizi. If there was any other way, I wouldn't. I love her as if she were my own. Maybe you already know what happened. I hope you aren't part of this. Ask Fox to explain.*

She tried to think of what else to say. She couldn't take enough time to say much more, so Amber put the pen down, folded the paper in half and handed it to Lizi. "Give this to Grayson after I leave."

Lizi again threw her arms around Amber. "I don't want you to leave."

Amber held Lizi tight for a few moments then kissed her on the forehead and said, "That's enough of that. I've got to get out of here."

When Amber reached the front door with her bag, she held the girl back with her hand as she told Lizi to stay inside. If she hadn't, she was sure Fox would've prevented the girl from going. The moment the huge door closed behind her, the tears flowed unhindered down Amber's face. They made it hard to see. Lizi wouldn't understand why this had to be done.

She hadn't gotten more than a few houses away when she caught a glimpse of Grayson's car coming from his parent's driveway. She was glad to see he'd come looking for her. That meant he hadn't been involved with what his father had done. But she couldn't let him see her. She ducked down behind a gardener's truck. Amber saw Grayson and Lizi as they drove past. She couldn't go back until she knew how to handle Fox. Grayson would want to know why she left and she wouldn't be able to tell him. Let Fox come up with some kind of explanation.

The gardeners were putting their equipment away. When they climbed into the cab, Amber climbed into their trailer and lay as flat as she could. She hoped they were on their way out. She didn't care where they went as long as they got her outside the fence and away from this place. The smell of gasoline and fresh cut grass filled her nose. Something sharp jabbed her in the leg. It wasn't a very comfortable ride and she felt every bounce, but the trailer was soon traveling along the freeway. The wind sucked Amber's breath away and helped dry her tears.

The driver pulled off the freeway and onto a side street. When he stopped for a red light, Amber climbed out of the trailer. She didn't know where she was, but figured that if she could find a bus stop she could get downtown eventually—

maybe to the train station. But that wouldn't do her any good. What little money she had would be wasted on a ticket back to St. Louis. She wanted to go home, but the house belonged to someone else now. There were people from church who might put her up for a while, but she couldn't do anything if she went back to St. Louis. She had to stay near Lizi. What she needed was time to think about her next move. Her mistake was that she hadn't thought she needed a plan. All she could do now was to try to make the best of it.

The first thing she needed was a roof over her head and then she would start looking for a job. She found a sign for a bus stop and while she waited for a bus to appear, she began searching through her bag. The ID badge Grayson had someone make for her was still there. If she had remembered it before she left she would have left it behind, but it gave her an idea. She could spend a night at the office and no one would notice.

She didn't even have to ride the bus; the office wasn't far from where she'd gotten out. There wasn't a receptionist on duty when she walked in. The building looked completely deserted, but she knew some of the employees worked at odd hours and she'd seen a couple of cars in the parking lot. She didn't want to risk anyone seeing her. She ran her badge across the reader for the executive office suite.

Once inside, Amber hid her bag in a corner of Steve's office. If he showed up, he wouldn't notice an extra bag next to his golf bag, just behind a large canoe paddle. She figured if she was careful she could hide there all day, if she had to, but there were only certain times when she could enter or leave the office unseen. She couldn't stay there long, just long enough to find a job and a place to live.

She went into Grayson's office after she dumped her stuff. She felt more comfortable in there. Her laptop—the one Grayson had let her use—lay where she'd left it. She needed something to pass the time. She tried looking for a job online. After doing that for a while, she opened the file she had been work-ing on when she left that afternoon. If Grayson hadn't wanted to leave early, she would have finished what she'd been doing. She went to work plugging in the last of the numbers. Grayson wouldn't remember how far she had gotten, so when he found it completed he wouldn't think anything about it.

When she finished, she stood at the window and watched the light fade. Amber hadn't felt so alone in a long time. There'd always been someone to talk to. She was either work-ing or Lizi was around. There was always someone she could call, but not now. She turned on the television hidden behind a cabinet door in Grayson's office. Nothing interested her, so she sat at Grayson's desk and started looking through some of the papers he had left there. She didn't mean to be nosy, but she couldn't help but want to know what he had been working on.

Several of the papers had the name Jack Abrams on them. These had something to do with the merger. It was probably something she wasn't supposed to be looking at. She saw a shiny black folder. She opened it and saw even more papers with Jack Abrams Inc. on them. Grayson hadn't shown her any of these and she told herself there was a good reason for it, but her boredom and curiosity got the better of her. She decided to check the shared folder on the network to see if there was any-thing there with his name on it.

Amid the other files and folders Grayson had shown her, she found some files with Jack's name. One spreadsheet looked like it had a lot of the same information the others did, but it didn't match the layout Grayson wanted for the other data. Some of the macros Grayson liked to use wouldn't work properly. Amber copied the data onto another tab and started rearranging it—just to see what would happen. The way Gray-son had explained it, the macros gave him a quick indication of how well different departments were doing and what they needed to correct the problem. She didn't figure it would take long to satisfy her curiosity and she didn't have anything else to do. It was two hours later when she had her answer. If what the spreadsheet said was right, Jack Abrams had been losing money but would be highly profitable within a few months. Even her untrained eye could tell her why Grayson and Fox were so anxious for the merger to go through.

Amber put everything back in its place and left Grayson's office. Back in Steve's office, she pulled the worn blanket out of her bag and curled up on his couch. It wasn't as nice as the bed she had been sleeping in, but she'd slept on worse. She just needed to get out of there before anyone showed up for work the next day.

When she woke the next morning, the sun still hadn't risen. She went to the executive washroom and took a shower. She worried someone might notice an extra wet towel, but she hoped it would only be the cleaning crew. It couldn't be helped. If she was going to look for a job, she wanted to shower first. She finished quickly, and hid her things in Steve's office. He had so much junk in there that even in the unlikely event he showed up at work, he wouldn't notice. It was still too early for much to be open, but she didn't know how long she dared stay at the office.

All that day, Amber made her way into all the places that looked like they might hire someone with her experience. They all asked for a number where she could be reached. She told them she didn't have a phone or a permanent address and asked if it would be okay to check back with them. A few were kind enough to say that they really weren't interested and she shouldn't waste her time checking with them. The earliest any of the others suggested for her to check with them was Monday. She had hoped she wouldn't have to wait so long. It wouldn't take her long to run out of money and the more nights she slept in Steve's office, the more likely that she would be discovered. Even if she wasn't discovered, she feared Fox would have her badge deactivated. Just thinking about that made her wonder if she'd made a mistake by leaving her stuff in Steve's office.

When she got back to the office, she met someone coming out the front door. She didn't remember meeting him, but he smiled as if he might know her. He held the door open for her. "You're going the wrong direction for a Friday."

"I know," she said. "I left something behind."

She saw someone down the hall when she opened the second door, but no one was in the executive suite. It looked like she would be safe for another night, maybe even the whole weekend.

Chapter Twenty

The outside of the chicken looked dry and hard as Fox sawed through it with a steak knife. They should have gone to a restaurant to eat Sunday dinner, but Fiona wanted to cook and she wanted Grayson and Lizi to come. Maybe it was time to hire someone to cook on Maggie's days off. A full-time chef would be the way to go. What was money for if you couldn't have a good meal on Sunday?

Lizi took a couple of bites of her chicken and after chewing a long time spit it out into her napkin. Fox tried not to laugh. He watched Grayson to see if he would say anything, but Grayson was too busy sawing through his own chicken. He would take a bite and then a sip of tea. He would take another bite and another sip of tea.

Lizi pushed the dry chicken to one side of her plate. She stuck her fork into the rubbery mashed potatoes and took a bite. Like her father, she took a drink from her glass and took another bite. She swallowed and took another drink from her glass. She repeated this process until the potatoes on her plate were gone and she went to work on the blackened green beans.

"Can I be excused?" Lizi pushed back from the table.

"Eat some more of your chicken," Grayson said.

"I'm not hungry."

"You will be if you don't eat. Now sit back down and eat."

"You can't make me. You aren't my father!" Lizi slammed her chair back up against the table, sloshing tea from the glasses onto the table cloth. She ran across the room and threw herself on one of the couches on the other side of the big open area.

"Lizi, come back here!" Grayson quickly pushed his own chair back, dropped his napkin beside his plate and walked over to where the girl had her face buried in one of the throw pillows. He sat down next to her on the couch. "How do you know I'm not your father?"

She said something into the pillow that Fox couldn't make out.

Grayson said something then stood up and returned to the table. He put his napkin back in his lap, picked up his knife and began sawing through his chicken.

"Did she believe you?" Fox asked.

"No," Grayson said, "Maybe when the results from that test come back..."

"That shouldn't be long now," Fox said. The lab had had it several days. "It'll be good to know if Amber was telling the truth."

"I already know," Grayson said. "At least, I'm ninety-five percent certain."

"She just misses Amber," Fiona said, pushing the last of her chicken to one side. "I think I cooked the chicken too long. You can't expect her to take it very well when the only mother she's known leaves her with a stranger."

"I still don't get that," Grayson said. "Why would she just leave like that? She said to ask you. What is it that you haven't told me?"

"Your father did what was best for all of us," Fiona said. "It'll be hard on Lizi for a while, but he did what he had to do."

"Okay, but what was it that you did?" Grayson asked.

"Amber isn't the kind of woman you need to be messing with," Fox said.

"Is this still about her trying to blackmail me? I told you she hadn't tried anything."

"No, she didn't have to," Fox said. "She was having Lizi do it for her. You don't really think it was Lizi's idea for you to take Amber on a date, do you?"

"It was just dinner," Grayson said.

"And a kiss," Fox said. "Celia's still upset about that. And the last time I talked to Jack Abrams..."

"They'll get over it," Grayson said.

"They will now that Amber's out of the picture."

"Sure, that will help, but you still haven't told me what you did. What is it that you said to her that made her leave in such a hurry?"

Fox decided that he had to tell Grayson something. "A private investigator I hired sent me a copy of a ransom note that was written in Amber's handwriting," Fox said. "I just showed it to her and gave her the option of leaving or talking to the police about it."

"What do you mean by a ransom note," Grayson asked. "You mean like she kidnaped someone?"

"No, not exactly," Fox said. He was on the verge of lying to his son. "It was written to someone saying that she'd had their daughter for several years and would give her up for a sum of money."

"She never sent us a note like that," Grayson said.

"It wasn't to us," Fox said. "It was for someone else. It looks like she tried to pull something like what she did with us, but she wanted money."

There, he'd done it. He'd lied to his son. Maybe Amber had tried something like that, but the letter was no proof. He didn't like lying to Grayson, but some things just couldn't be helped.

"I can't believe that's true," Grayson said. "I know she's done some things she shouldn't have..."

"I've still got the letter," Fox said. "You can compare it against her handwriting, if you like."

"No, I don't need to," Grayson said. "It's just hard for me to accept. If she did something like that, I know she must have thought she had a good reason."

"Her leaving like she did tells us something," Fox said. "If she thought she could prove she hadn't done it, don't you think she would've stayed instead of leaving Lizi?"

"I know, but—" Grayson didn't finish his thought. "There're some weird things that've been happening up at the office."

"What kind of weird things?" Fox could tell his son wanted to change the subject.

"Maybe they aren't really weird," Grayson said, "But I went in early the other day because there was some work I needed to do. I get there and open the file I thought I'd been working on and it was already done."

"I'm sure you just forgot you finished," Fox said. "You've been under some stress lately."

"There's more to it than that. There were some other files that I don't think I had looked at and when I went in on Monday they were ready for me. I asked everyone who has access to that folder if they had done it and no one owned up to it. Which—considering what they all think of that spreadsheet— they may be afraid I'll make them do it all the time."

"Must be the elves," Fiona said.

"Maybe we shouldn't mention elves," Grayson said, pointing toward Lizi.

"What about elves?" Lizi pulled herself off the couch and rejoined the others at the table. Her eyes were puffy and red, but she seemed to have forgotten the reason for her tears.

"Don't you remember the story about the cobbler and the elf?" Fiona didn't wait for Lizi to answer. She told her how the cobbler would leave out pairs of unfinished shoes every night and an elf would finish the work for him.

"I don't think elves are coming in at night and finishing my work." Grayson put the last bite of chicken in his mouth and washed it down with iced tea. "It has to be someone with access to the files and I don't think we have any elves with a login account."

"Maybe you should leave food out at night, just to make sure," Fiona said.

"I wouldn't know where to leave it. Some of the people with access aren't even in Texas. There may be a few more people with access than I thought. Or maybe someone did it and just forgot."

Alex called the next day to say the test results had come back.

"So what do they say?" Fox asked impatiently.

"I haven't looked at them yet," Alex said. "I thought Grayson should be the first to look at them, but I work for you, so I'll let you make that decision."

"You're probably right," Fox said, giving up on Alex reading off the results over the phone. "I'll talk to Grayson, but what do you say we meet over at Grayson's place at seven o'clock tonight?"

That night, Alex was waiting for the elevator when Fox arrived, so when Lizi opened the door she opened it for both of them. She stood to one side to let them in. "Grayson, there's people here to see you," she yelled as she closed the door. She didn't follow them into the living room, but went to her own room and closed the door.

Alex sat down on the couch and put his briefcase on the coffee table. He pulled out a thick envelope and closed the case as Grayson came into the room. "You can read this as well as I can," he said, pulling the pages from the envelope and handing them to Grayson.

Grayson bent the pages backwards along the fold to straighten them. He looked at the cover page for a few moments and then looked even more briefly at the pages below. "Well, that's that," he said and handed them to Fox.

Fox looked at the cover letter. It had the name and address of the lab across the top. Then after a statement that looked like legalese with comments about how inaccurate their test procedure might be, they stated, "we have determined that there is a paternal match between the two samples submitted."

"Are we sure this is right?" Fox asked, thumbing through the rest of the pages. The rest gave the details of what the lab had done and their results, but he kept looking back at that first page.

"I thought you would be happy," Grayson said. "We have proof that Lizi is your granddaughter."

"I just want us to be sure."

"There aren't any surprises here. Amber knew so much about Holly that I knew she had to have known her. This just tells us that she was telling the truth about Lizi," Grayson said. "I think I need to tell Lizi what we found out."

"Excuse me gentlemen," Alex said, standing up, "if you don't need me any more tonight, I'll be heading home."

"That's fine," Grayson said. He saw Alex out the door before he went to Lizi's room and knocked on her door.

Fox went and stood in the door to watch and listen as Grayson told his daughter about what they had discovered. Grayson sat on the edge of the bed where Lizi lay on her stomach, reading a book.

"Can you take your nose out of the book and talk to me for a few minutes?"

"No," Lizi said, but she put a bookmark between the pages and turned to face Grayson.

"We got the results from that test they did to see if I'm your father or not," Grayson said, holding the papers up.

Lizi put the book down and rolled off the bed, putting her feet over the side to stand up. "I'll start packing my things. Can I take that book with me? I just started it."

"What are you talking about?" Grayson laid the test results on the bed.

"I'll be ready to go when they get here."

"When who gets here?" Grayson asked.

"Isn't social services coming to get me?" Lizi pulled her worn bag out of a drawer.

"No, silly!" Grayson said, laughing with a worried look in his eyes. "The test shows that you're my daughter, so that proves you really are Victoria's kid, like you and Amber said."

"It does?" Lizi asked. "But I'm not Victoria's kid, I'm Holly's. Ask Amber. She'll tell you."

"We can't ask Amber," Grayson said. "We don't know where she is, but the test proves that half of your DNA came from me. The only way for that to happen is if Victoria is your mother."

"I don't believe you," Lizi said. "You're lying. Holly is my mother. When Amber comes back, she'll tell you."

"I don't think she's coming back," Grayson said.

"She has to!" Lizi threw herself on the bed and began crying. Grayson's attempts at comforting her did nothing to dry her tears.

Chapter Twenty-One

Amber never intended to sleep at the office as many nights as she did, but after several days, she still hadn't found work or a better place to sleep. Her badge still worked and her login hadn't been deactivated. Grayson hadn't returned the laptop to the IT guy. Maybe he was letting Lizi use it.

After a couple of weeks, Amber began giving out the number in Fox's office when she applied for a job. Since Fox hardly ever went to work, no one would try to call him there. She only gave it out as an evening phone, hoping that the people she gave it to wouldn't call when other people were around.

One evening while Amber sat behind Fox's big desk waiting for the phone to ring, she heard voices in the outer office. She hit the power button on the computer monitor, fearing someone would open the door and see the computer on. She rushed over to the door and flicked off the lights. On the other side of the door she could hear Lizi's voice.

"Do you think we'll see the elf?" Lizi asked.

That one little word cut at Amber's heart. She wondered if Lizi was beginning to see strange creatures like her mother had. Maybe Grayson would realize she needed help. Amber had often worried that Holly's problem was hereditary, but Grayson had known Holly; he would know what to look for.

"I don't think so," Grayson said. The door to his office closed and Amber couldn't hear more.

She stood there at the door of Fox's office for several minutes with her ear against the crack between the two doors. She feared to go back to what she had been doing until they left.

"Was the elf here?" Lizi asked as they crossed the outer office to the doors.

"I forgot to check," Grayson said. "Remind me and I'll look in the morning, but I'm ready to go home now."

Amber opened the door a crack and looked out. She saw Lizi's blond hair flowing down her back. Grayson and Lizi turned right when they reached the hall and walked toward the exit. Amber stood there for several moments looking at the empty hall through the glass doors.

She turned the light back on and went back to the computer. She made a few more modifications to the file and saved it before she pulled up the document she had found on the network drive named "Whoever you are if you are just looking for something to do you might as well do this.docx." She marked off one more of the items on the list and went on to the next one. She wasn't sure how helpful she really was, but maybe it was enough to pay for the generosity they had extended. Maybe it was worth enough to pay for a long distance phone call. She picked up the phone and dialed.

"Is this a bad time?" she asked when Bill Krueger answered the phone.

"No, not at all," Bill said. "The wife and I were just talking about you. How are you doing?"

"Not so good," Amber said. "I kind of have a problem."

"You told me a little about that the last time we talked."

"It's worse," Amber said. "I left Lizi with Grayson. He's taking care of her, but I don't have a job and I'm down to seventeen dollars and thirty-two cents. I don't exactly have permission to stay where I've been sleeping at night."

"Do you need us to send you money?"

Amber realized how it sounded. "I keep thinking I'll find a job, but no one is interested."

"How much money do you need? We can send it Western-Union. You can probably pick it up tomorrow or the next day."

"I didn't call to ask for money."

"What good is a church if we can't help our own members?"

"I know, but I don't feel right about it."

"Well, if you won't take money, is there something else we can do to help you?"

"Probably not. All I really need is a job."

"We'll keep praying for you," Bill said. He paused for a moment and then asked, "What have you been eating?"

"Not much," Amber said, remembering the cheeseburger she had eaten at noon. She had splurged and ordered a small fries to go with it. "But I'm doing alright."

"At least let us send you enough money for you to eat."

"No, I wouldn't feel right."

"I don't know what else I can offer," Bill said. "Is there a number where I can reach you?"

"As long as you call after seven at night or before seven in the morning." Amber gave him the number on Fox's office phone.

A couple hours later, Amber answered the phone in Fox's office.

"Amber?" the voice on the other end asked.

"Yes?"

"This is Rob Snider."

"O, Grayson's pastor," she said before she stopped to question why Grayson's pastor would be calling her and how he would know to reach her on that phone.

"You know Grayson?" he asked. "I didn't realize you knew him."

"I went to your church with Grayson a few times."

"O, so you **are** that Amber," Rob said. "I just assumed you were someone with the same name. Maybe I should tell you why I'm calling. Your pastor in St. Louis called to ask me if there was anything we could do to help you out. He said you're looking for a job."

"I thought it would be easier to find something."

"Do you know anything about cleaning toilets and vacuuming floors?"

"I know how, if that's what you mean."

"We're looking for a new janitor at church. The guy we had before seems to think that since he's turning seventy-five it's time to quit. It'll have to go through the normal selection process like anyone else we hire at church, but if you're interested, I'm pretty sure you can have the job."

"When do I start?" She knew her excitement was evident in her voice.

"I'll tell you what," the pastor said, "I know you want to start right away, so why don't you come by the church tomorrow morning and you can start learning your responsibilities. We'll make sure you get paid for your time, whether the church decides to hire you or not."

"Does Grayson have to know about this?"

"That depends on how close he pays attention during business meetings," Rob said. "If you're asking if he recommended you—like I said, I didn't quite put two and two together until I called."

"It's not that," Amber said. "It's just that there's been something of a misunderstanding between his family and me. I don't want it to cause a problem."

"For whom?" Rob asked.

"For me," Amber said. "I'm afraid of what his Dad might do."

"Do you need more time to think about it?" Rob asked. "Unless you want to tell me what's going on, I don't know what to tell you."

"No, I really need the money."

"Then we'll see you tomorrow morning?"

"Yeah," Amber said. As she hung up the phone she realized that buying a new bus pass would wipe out the most of her cash. Maybe she could ask for payment at the end of that first day. Being a janitor wasn't like being a waitress. She couldn't expect people to give her a tip.

She went back to work, once more moving through the "if you're looking for something to do" list on the network drive. It seemed like it was getting longer with things that were more difficult. She looked at the next item on the list and decided to skip it. She had already skipped two, but there wasn't much else she could do since she would need more information from other people to do it right. She didn't want to start calling people on the phone.

The phone rang again. She wondered if it would be Rob Snider calling back to say he'd made a mistake and didn't have a job he could offer her after all. She picked it up. It was just someone else calling to say they wouldn't be offering her a job.

When Amber arrived at the church the next morning, things were much quieter than they had been the Sundays she had been there. The large parking lot had only a few cars in it. A few were parked close to the street. She guessed they belonged to carpoolers. Five more sat near a smaller building connect to the main building with a sign that said "office." Amber had never had a hard time finding a church office. She and Lizi had visited quite a few and had walked away with a several thousand dollars, if she totaled it all up. But this time Lizi wasn't there to play the part of the starving child.

Amber pushed the button beside the door and waited. Rob Snider came to the door. He'd replaced his Sunday uniform of a suit coat and tie with something more casual.

"Come on in," he said as he held the door for her. "Let's go see if we can find our elusive janitor."

They found the man in one of the classrooms. He was slowly running a mop over the floor.

"Let me finish this and I'll be right with you," he said.

Amber and the pastor waited as the man took his time finishing the work. It was only then that Rob Snider made the introductions and left Amber with the janitor for him to show her around.

"Just a word of advice," the man said as the pastor disappeared down the hall, "don't ever let them think they can hurry you. If you do, they'll have you running all over the place and you won't get anything done. I never do half the stuff people want me to do. I figure if I wait long enough they'll either change their mind or decide they can do it themselves. I have enough work to do without people adding the stuff they need done to it."

"How much work?" Amber asked.

"Enough—it'll keep you busy all week," the man said. "Just the usual stuff, mop and vacuum the floors, pick up trash, set up chairs. Don't have to mow the lawn—a crew comes and does that, but you'll be responsible for making sure they do it right. Unclog the toilets—whatever needs doing. Let me show you around."

Amber followed him from room to room. He pointed out the closets that held the cleaning supplies and showed her how the electronic locks on the doors to the classrooms and other rooms worked. He showed her where to find the light switches.

"I always hold off on the sanctuary until Friday, or even Saturday if there's an event, so it still needs to be done. Usually, just walk through the rows picking up the trash, run the vacuum over the floor and pull the gum off of the hymn book racks. There ain't much you'll have to do that you wouldn't have to do cleaning your house at home. It's just a lot bigger. You think you can handle that?"

"Sure," Amber said, "I'm sure I'll pick it up right away."

"Good," the man said, unclipping his keys from his belt. He held them out for Amber to take. "The electronic locks are on most of the doors, but any key you might need is on here somewhere. Don't ask me where. If you think you can handle it, I think I'll leave it in your hands and be heading home."

"Wait! You can't mean you're going to quit without showing me how to do this. I thought you were going to train me."

"That's what I've been doing to the past hour. I showed you where everything is. That's all there is to it. You do know how to clean, don't you?"

Amber assured him that she did.

"Then you've got all the basics down."

She walked as far as the door with him and saw him drive away. The keys felt heavy in her hands.

"You didn't tell me he was leaving today," Amber said, walking into Rob's office.

"I didn't know," Rob said. "You don't have to take the job, if you don't want it."

"I need the money."

"Yeah, that much I understand," Rob said, "Have you found a place to live?"

"No, I don't have enough money. I'm down to just a few dollars."

"Let me see what I can come up with. We have a member who may be able to set you up in an efficiency apartment for not a lot of money. I'll see if he'll let you delay the rent payment for a while." Rob picked up the phone and dialed a number.

Chapter Twenty-Two

For the first time in years, Fox was glad to be working. He was at the breakfast bar with a laptop in front of him. In his field of view, just past the laptop's screen, he could see his wife and his granddaughter working in the kitchen. Fiona thought she was teaching their granddaughter to cook, but Fox could tell that Lizi was the better cook. At first, Lizi had tried correcting her grandmother, but now he could tell Lizi was just letting her grandmother talk and doing her own thing. Lizi brought life to the house.

The other thing that made him happy was that he was working on the merger with Jack Abrams Inc. It was going to be good for both sides. When they'd gotten some new data that the accountants hadn't even had a chance to look at, Fox had been eager to see how well it showed them doing. He could plug numbers into a spreadsheet as well as anyone. It was just a revised list of properties owned by Jack Abrams and their estimated values.

When he got to the end of the list and looked at the figure at the bottom, it didn't look right. He couldn't be certain, but he thought he'd seen a report earlier with a higher value. He ran down the list again, comparing what he'd entered with what was on the report. They were all there. Something wasn't right. He dialed Grayson's number.

"What's up Pop?" Grayson asked. "I'm about to board the plane."

"These figures you gave me, are they missing something?"

"No, I don't think so," Grayson said. "I think they just pulled them from public records. It should be every piece of property that is owned by Jack's company."

"I totaled it up and it doesn't seem high enough."

"Maybe you missed something," Grayson said.

"No, I didn't miss anything."

"I wouldn't worry about it," Grayson said. "They're primarily a software company. I wouldn't expect them to own a lot of assets. We'll want to close some of those buildings anyway."

"Yeah, I know, but I thought this figure was higher when we were looking at it before."

"It may have been," Grayson said. "I'll look at it when I get home. Someone may have made a mistake. It happens."

Fox hung up the phone wondering if Grayson thought he was the one who'd made a mistake. He hadn't, but Grayson would have to look at the figures himself before he realized that. Fox wasn't willing to wait the three hours until Grayson was off the plane, much less the days it would be before Grayson had time to run through the figures himself. Fox closed his laptop and gathered his things.

"I leaving," he said, "I may not be home for a few hours."

"Okay," Fiona said. "Where are you going?"

"I've got to talk to someone about the merger."

He didn't go to the office; instead, he drove downtown, where Jack Abrams had his offices. When he got off the elevator, he told the receptionist he wanted to see Jack. She asked him to have a seat while she called Jack's office.

"Someone will be right out," she said.

It was Celia who came to meet him. "Dad's in a meeting. Is there something I can do for you?"

"I have some questions about some figures," Fox said.

"Well, let's take a look," Celia said. "Come on back."

He followed her to her office. It wasn't as spacious as her father's but it was adequate.

"You didn't have to come all the way down here," Celia said. "If you'd called, I would've been happy to drive out there."

"It's good to get away from the house once in a while," Fox said.

"I hear that," Celia said. "Now what are these figures that brought you all the way down here?"

"I've got a report showing all the properties y'all own and when I add up the values it doesn't match what I thought I saw before."

He laid the papers on her desk. She reached across and picked them up. She scanned one sheet and then another. "This isn't something that came from this office."

"No, it's something that our people generated."

She kept turning pages. "Yeah, I don't think we can comment on something that we didn't create. Maybe you should be talking to your people."

"I'm just trying to find out what the discrepancy is," Fox said. "For some reason, the report we had from you doesn't seem to match up with this one and I'm trying to figure out if there's something that wasn't included here."

"That would be my guess," Celia said, "But without having a chance for our people to look over it, I don't feel comfortable saying very much. I'm just noticing here that this does say that these are estimated values. Maybe whoever came up with these figures erred on the low side."

"These may be based on the tax appraisal," Fox said.

"That could be the problem," Celia said, handing the papers back. "I know in some of the places we have property, the tax appraisal is a lot less than what the actual value of the building is."

"Yeah, that could be it," Fox said.

"I'm sorry about the mix up," Celia said, "But this could be better for you. If Dad's company turns out to be worth less, then that just means you'll have a bigger share of the new company."

"I suppose that's true," Fox said. "I just want to make sure we have an accurate estimate."

"We've got plenty of time to figure all that out before we sign the paperwork." Celia leaned back in her chair. "So, is Grayson still getting back tonight?"

"Yeah, he should be in the air now." Fox started putting his stuff back in the bag. "He was just about to board when I talked to him."

"No delays or anything like that?"

"No, I don't think so."

"Then I might stop by his place later on," Celia said. "You must have enjoyed taking care of Lizi while he was away."

"Oh, yeah," Fox said. "I think she's starting to warm up to the idea of having grandparents, but Grayson probably won't be get home until late this evening. Fiona and Lizi are going to fix supper. You're welcome to come eat with us, if you'd like."

"I'd love to," Celia said. "You must be warming up to the idea of having a grandchild again too."

"That's not hard to do," Fox said.

"I hope you don't mind me saying so, but it must have been so hard on you after what happened with your other grandchildren."

"You can't imagine," Fox said. Images of that day flashed through his mind. The sound of children crying. The smell of gasoline, diesel and cement. The sticky feel of blood on his fingers.

"I'm still not sure I understand what happened," Celia said. "I just know there was an accident on the traffic circle."

"I'd rather not talk about it."

"Yeah, you're right. I shouldn't have brought it up. You probably don't even talk about it with your family. Of course, you wouldn't want to discuss it with me."

"I'll never discuss it with my family," Fox said. "We've had enough pain as it is."

"Yeah, there's no reason for you to tell me about it. I'm sure the old newspaper report would tell me what happened."

"It'll tell you as much as any of the rest of the family knows if you really want to know about it." What Fox didn't tell her was that there were some things that the family didn't know and he would never tell them.

"Maybe I'll just let Grayson tell me about it, if he wants to." Celia stood up. "I'll be looking forward to seeing you after while."

Fox left feeling a little better about the figures, but there were still unanswered questions. Whether it answered those questions completely or not, Grayson had a suggestion when he came in. He'd hardly gotten through the front door when he said, "I may know why the figures on that report don't match. That may've been one of those files I left for our elf to work on."

"What do you mean?" Fox asked.

"Let's just say our elf didn't always understand what I needed her to do. She may not have done as thorough of a job as she should've."

"Did you ever figure out who the elf was?" Fox asked. "If you didn't, how do you know it wasn't a saboteur?"

"You'll probably think that's what she was doing when I tell you," Grayson said, "But yes, I talked to one of the IT guys and he was able to tell me which user was editing those files. It was Amber."

Grayson was right. Fox could just see Amber messing with their stuff to get back at him. "But you deactivated her account, right? She won't be able to do it again?"

"It's taken care of," Grayson said. "She won't be sending me marriage proposals through the internal e-mail."

"Now you're just mocking me," Fox said.

"Of course I am, but what I said still might explain why that report doesn't seem to match. She may not have accounted for all of the Jack Abrams properties. I'll have someone look into it."

Chapter Twenty-Three

Most days, the job went about like Amber expected. Some-times people were a little more demanding of her time than they should've been, but most of the time she was free to do her thing with no distractions. She found a broken mp3 player and a set of headphones that someone had thrown in the trash. It was broken beyond repair, but she quickly learned that, if she wore the headphones while she worked, people were less likely to ask for her help doing something else. That worked every day except Sunday.

Sunday wasn't counted as a work day for her, but she was expected to be there early enough to open the doors and to stay late enough to lock up. But no one counted how many hours she worked anyway. It was just $300 a week, two weeks of va-cation a year and she worked until the work was finished, how-ever long that was. She was okay with that, but the thing about Sundays was that there was always someone who wanted something. "Why wasn't my whiteboard cleaned?" "Who erased my whiteboard? Couldn't you see I needed it?" "Why didn't you put the chairs in my classroom back like you found them?"

There wasn't much Amber could do but hide. The storage closet near the balcony made the perfect spot. It was mostly filled with junk—stuff that had once had a useful purpose but no one would use again. No one would miss it unless someone decided to throw it away. In the middle of all that junk was just enough room for a chair. Amber would sit in there and read until time for her Sunday school class to start. Then she'd hide out in there again until the preaching started. Even then, she would find a seat in the very back corner of the balcony.

For all the stuff people asked her to do, it wasn't those people she was hiding from as much as it was two particular people. Those two were there every Sunday. She could look down from the balcony and see the backs of their heads, but Lizi and Grayson never turned to look up at her. Amber longed to go down and sit right next to Lizi. She wondered what Grayson would do if she did. Maybe nothing, but it would cause trouble with Fox if they told him about seeing Amber.

What she needed was a way to see Lizi without Fox realizing she hadn't gone home to St. Louis. At the very least, she needed something that didn't look like she was maneuvering to be a part of Grayson's life. The job at church looked just the opposite. Grayson rarely missed church, so where did she go to get a job? The very church Grayson attended.

It would've been so easy to make life difficult for Fox, but that would just confirm what he feared. It wasn't like he didn't deserve it. She'd never done anything to hurt him and he'd still come up with the letter. She could come up with a letter of her own. He wasn't the only one who could forge handwriting. She wondered what she could say that would make him tremble with fear.

She pushed the thought from her mind and tried to pay attention to the sermon. Rob was preaching away and she didn't have any idea what his topic was. It was probably on forgiveness and he'd aimed right at her, but she hadn't been listening.

The sermon ended and the people disbursed. Amber stayed in her seat in the balcony until she was sure Lizi and Grayson had left. She made her rounds. First, she locked the doors. There were a few people left in the building; they could get out but not come back in. Then she checked every room and every hall, to make sure no one had made a mess that she needed to clean up and to make sure someone wasn't waiting for everyone to leave before they tried stealing something. She'd never done that, but she had some friends who had.

By the time she finished, the only people left in the building were Rob Snider, his wife, Tasha, and a man Amber didn't recognize.

Tasha was standing in the hall outside the pastor's office when Amber came around the corner.

"Rob's counseling with someone," Tasha said. "What are you doing for dinner?"

"I don't have any plans," Amber said.

"Come home with us," Tasha said. "We can get to know each other better."

Amber couldn't say no, but she wasn't sure how much she wanted Tasha knowing about her. "I don't want you to feel like you have to treat me like some charity case."

"No, of course not!" Tasha said. "I just want to get to know you better."

"There's really not that much to know," Amber said.

"Well, see now you have to come home with us," Tasha said. "That's like a challenge. As soon as someone says that, I know there's something interesting that they don't want anyone to know."

For someone who'd accepted the challenge of getting to know Amber's secrets, Tasha didn't try very hard. She hardly spoke at all during the drive to the Sniders' house, which couldn't have been more than five minutes away. Once there, Amber asked if she could help.

"I don't actually cook," Tasha said, pulling something out of the freezer and throwing it in the microwave. "I guess Rob's okay with that; he hasn't left me yet."

"I've never used the microwave very much," Amber said.

"Really? It's a big time saver for us."

"I just don't..." She started to say she didn't like what it did to the food, but stopped herself.

"Yeah, I see how it is," Tasha said. "You already know you're going to hate my cooking and you don't want to hurt my feelings."

"No, it's just that I've worked in restaurants most of my adult life."

"So you're picky about what you eat."

"It's not that," Amber said. "Most of the restaurants I've worked in really weren't all that good, but it was quicker to take a hot meal home than it would've been to throw something in a microwave."

"What do you do now?" Tasha asked. "It's just you, right? It must be a lot of trouble to cook something for just you."

"I don't have a choice," Amber said. "I don't have a lot of money to spend on luxury items."

Tasha laughed.

"What's so funny?" Amber asked.

"I shouldn't have laughed," Tasha said. "It's just a matter of perspective. I've been complaining because the church didn't give us a raise last year and to hear you talk, we're living in the lap of luxury."

"That wasn't what I meant," Amber said.

"No, don't apologize," Tasha said. "I deserved it. You're absolutely right. We would save money if I didn't fix the stuff I do. Here I am complaining when you hardly have anything."

"I'm not complaining," Amber said.

"Exactly," Tasha said. "I'm complaining about having more than you do."

"I've got enough to meet my needs," Amber said.

"Now you're just rubbing it in," Tasha said. "Let's talk about something else before I start feeling guiltier than I already do."

"What do you want to talk about?"

"Tell me what's going on between you and Grayson," Tasha said.

Amber looked at her dumbfounded.

"Oh! A touchy subject," Tasha said. "You don't have to tell me if you don't want, but first you show up with Grayson saying that Lizi is your daughter. Now I haven't seen you anywhere near them and Grayson is saying that Lizi is his daughter. I don't mean to be nosy, but it's a little strange and Grayson isn't talking."

"It's complicated," Amber said.

"Of course it is," Tasha said. "But which is it? Is she your daughter? Is she Grayson's daughter? Is she his and yours—no let's not go there. I don't think Grayson is the type. So what is it?"

"I don't know," Amber said. "I know she isn't mine and she may not be his."

"See? I told you I'd find out something about you that was interesting."

"It's not all that interesting," Amber said. "Her mother died and I raised her."

"Well, it got my attention," Tasha said.

Chapter Twenty-Four

Fox pulled into the church parking lot with Lizi in the seat beside him. A banner near the street bore the words, "Vacation Bible School." A car in front of them came to a stop, blocking the drive. The doors swung open and five kids jumped out. Four of them ran toward the entrance. The fifth went more slowly, first climbing back into the vehicle to get something he had forgotten, only to have his mother tell him to return the prized possession to the back seat. He swung the door closed with a scowl on his face. He walked around the front of the car, dragging his feet with each step.

"You can let me out here," Lizi said as they waited for the mother to watch her son climb the steps.

"No, I'll go inside with you." Fox lifted his foot off the brake, thinking the woman was about to move forward, but quickly put it back when she turned her head to watch her son struggle with the big glass door. "I want to make sure you get to the right place."

"I know where I'm going," Lizi said. "Grayson brought me yesterday."

"When are you going to start calling him Dad?" Fox took his foot off the brake once more. An adult had opened the door for the child and the woman finally moved out of the way. Fox pulled into one of the parking spaces and shut off the engine.

"I never called Amber Mom," she said, unbuckling her seatbelt. "Why shouldn't I keep calling him Grayson?"

"But Amber isn't your mother." Fox unbuckled his own belt. "It makes a difference."

"Grayson doesn't care if I call him Grayson." Lizi slammed the door and headed for the entrance. Fox walked quickly to try to catch up to her. By the time he made it up the steps and through the glass door she was already standing at a table waiting for a woman to sign her in. The woman looked up and eyed him closely.

"Can I help you, sir?"

"I'm her grandfather." Fox pointed at Lizi.

"No, he's not," Lizi said. She left the table with another girl about her age.

The woman's smile faded quickly into a worried look. He could tell she feared he might be some kind of pervert.

"Grayson was busy and asked me to bring her." Fox wasn't sure that Grayson was as busy as he had implied. He suspected that Grayson had asked him to pick her up at the office and take her to Bible School more as an excuse to get him in the office for a few minutes than because he didn't have time to take her.

The woman at the table relaxed a little at the mention of Grayson's name.

"He'll be picking her up afterward."

The woman's smile returned.

"That's good." The woman turned her attention to a brother and sister who had just come in.

Fox looked over in the direction that Lizi and her friend had gone. Another girl had joined them. A door opened near the group and a woman in faded clothes stepped out of a storage closet. She had tied her hair back. She carried a box of cleaning supplies with both hands. She closed the door with her shoulder before she turned to walk down the hall. She looked familiar, but Fox dismissed that thought, since he wouldn't know any of these people. He wondered if she might have been one of the maids who came each week to help clean the house.

She looked at the group of girls and quickly turned around to walk the other way.

"Amber!" Lizi yelled loud enough for everyone to hear. She ran over and threw her arms around the woman with the box. "I didn't think I'd ever see you again."

"Let me put this box down," Amber said. She sat it on a nearby chair before she returned the girl's hug.

This wasn't what Fox had hoped for. He'd gotten her out of the house, but here she was at Grayson's church where she probably saw them every week. Why hadn't Grayson said something? It had been better when she'd been at the house. At least Fox had been able to keep an eye on her. Fox edged through the mass of children toward where the reunion had taken place.

"They got the test back. I guess it says that Grayson's my Dad," Lizi said.

"If that's what it says, then he is," Amber said. "Are you disappointed?"

"I wanted to stay with you." Lizi's tears flowed.

Amber looked up and saw Fox standing there.

"What are you doing here?" she asked, still holding the crying girl.

"I was about to ask you the same thing," Fox said. "I thought you were gone."

"I work here," she said. "My pastor in St. Louis got me this job."

"Of course you're going to tell me that this being Grayson's church is just a coincidence and had nothing to do with it."

"This wasn't my first choice," Amber said. "It's the only job I could find, but you'd better believe I'm going to stay close to Lizi."

"I'm having a real hard time trusting you," Fox said. "I don't want you around my granddaughter. We can get a restraining order if we have to." Fox hoped she didn't see how hollow his threat was. Grayson wouldn't be easily convinced to seek a restraining order.

"Tell him he isn't my grandfather," Lizi said. A flash of anger drove away the tears.

"I can't do that," Amber said. "If Grayson is your dad then I'm afraid you're stuck with him as a grandparent."

"But he's mean," Lizi said.

"There's nothing we can do about that," Amber said. "He can't help being what he is."

By this time, everyone was watching. A man Fox recognized as Grayson's pastor stepped forward and grabbed him on the arm.

"Sir, you're making a scene. Maybe it would be better if you left," the pastor said. "You can discuss this some other time."

Fox started to tell the man he wasn't about to leave Lizi with Amber there, but there were already too many eyes watching. Fox turned around and walked back through the children toward the door. He saw the eyes of the woman at the table staring at him. He walked out the door, down the steps and out to his car. The pastor followed him.

"I'm sorry I had to ask you to leave like that," the pastor said. "It isn't that we don't want you here, but with all these kids around…"

"Don't worry about it," Fox said, opening his car door. "I should've known better than to confront Amber here. She doesn't like me very much."

"Grayson has already told me a little about the situation." The man rested his hand on the car door as Fox sat down. "I can tell you and Amber aren't on the best of terms, but to us she's been an answer to prayer."

"Does Grayson know she's here?" Fox asked.

"You'll have to ask him that," the man said. "I know Amber didn't want him to know. Yesterday, she spent the day avoiding Lizi. Looks like it didn't work so well today."

"I'm sure she knew exactly what she was doing."

"Maybe," the pastor said, staring out across the parking lot. "I think she's trying to do the right thing. She just doesn't seem to know what that is."

When Fox was able to leave, he didn't go home as he had planned. He went back to the office. He found Grayson in his office talking on the phone. Grayson talked to the other person for a few minutes before he put the phone down and turned his attention to his father.

"Did you get her there okay?" Grayson asked.

"Fine," Fox said, "But they kicked me out."

"They what?" Grayson asked. "I'm sure they didn't mean anything by it."

"Well they did," Fox said. "It wouldn't have happened if I hadn't seen Amber."

"You saw who?" Grayson moved forward in his chair. "What was Amber doing there? I thought she must have gone back to St. Louis or something."

"She's the new janitor." Fox said.

"How is she? Is she doing okay?"

"I'm sure she's fine, but it isn't like I had a chance to ask. Your pastor escorted me out before I could ask very much." Fox didn't feel the need to explain the argument.

"I think I'll go find out for myself." Grayson pulled up his schedule on the computer. "It looks like I have a meeting."

"I'm sure she'll still be there when you go pick up Lizi— unless she decides to take her and disappear."

"Probably, but the meeting can wait." He went to the door of his office. "Sandra, I need you to let everyone know we won't be meeting and clear my schedule for the rest of the day."

"Do you think that's wise," Fox asked, wanting to tell his son he had to have the meeting, but already knowing his retort.

"What do I tell Celia?" Sandra asked.

"If she asks, tell her I've got other plans," Grayson said.

"You know she'll be upset."

"If she's upset, she'll be upset with me, not you."

To his father, he said, "Celia made plans for lunch. She decided we could do something since Lizi is at church."

"If I were you, I would do that," Fox said. He could see that Grayson was ignoring Celia again. He had hoped that things would improve with Amber gone.

"But I'm not going to," he said, standing up and gathering his things. "I'm going up to church to talk to Amber. As quickly as she left last time, I don't want her disappearing before I have a chance to talk to her."

Fox watched his son disappear through the door. He could see him making a mistake, but he could do nothing to stop him. It wouldn't be long and Amber would have him in her clutches again.

Chapter Twenty-Five

The redheaded kid on the floor looked at the pizza box Amber held out to him. He reached for a slice and then retracted his hand. "I don't like pepperoni."

"Someone will bring something else around," Amber said, holding the box out to the next boy. He pulled a slice from the box without comment.

"Do you have a key to this closet over here?" a woman behind Amber asked.

Amber turned around. She still couldn't remember the woman's name. She was just a person who'd volunteered for Bible School.

"I'm sure I must," Amber said. She put the pizza box on the floor in the middle of the circle of fourth grade boys. They could help themselves. She reached for her set of keys and found the one that worked in most of the locks when the electronic key didn't. When she slipped it into the lock, it turned and the door opened.

"Can you help me carry one of the tables?" The woman pulled one of the tables from the stack, but waited for Amber to help her carry it.

Amber helped her set it up and returned to the closet to close the door. She went to the table where the pizzas were stacked. She picked up a napkin, opened the first box and grabbed a slice before she even noticed it was sausage pizza. It would do. She'd been distracted all day because of the activity. Someone always needed something, and she still had a floor to mop in another part of the building. She would soon go back to it, but her gaze fell on Lizi, who sat in a circle of girls her age.

Lizi looked up and saw Amber watching her. She stood up, ran over to Amber and hugged her.

"I missed you," Lizi said.

Lizi clung to her for some time, but Amber wasn't about to tell her she should go back to the other girls. A shadow in the corner of her eye told her that someone was standing next to her. She turned and saw that it was Grayson.

"I need to talk to you," he said. "When were you going to tell me you were working here?"

"It just fell in my lap," Amber said. "I had to do something."

"Yeah, it's a shame I couldn't hire you to do what you were doing at the office. I've got all this work at the office that hasn't been getting done without you there to do it." Grayson lifted the lid of one of the pizza boxes and looked inside.

"You must have someone else who can do it," Amber said.

"Of course, but—"

"The elves have been doing it," Lizi interrupted him.

Amber looked at Lizi, hoping for some assurance that the girl was joking, but she looked like she believed what she said.

"Run along," Grayson said. "Amber and I need to talk."

"No!" Lizi held onto Amber more tightly.

"Go on back to your friends," Amber said.

Lizi went back and sat on the floor with the other girls in her age group, but she kept looking at Amber and Grayson.

"Do you think me bringing her down here might have caused that?" Amber kept her voice low, fearing Lizi might hear from across the room.

"Caused what?" Grayson didn't look worried at all. It only made Amber feel worse. He wouldn't help her if he saw nothing wrong.

"Her seeing elves—I wouldn't have brought her down here if I had thought it would cause that."

Grayson looked confused for several seconds and then his expression changed to one of understanding. "She isn't seeing elves. It's just pretend."

"How can you be so sure? Holly saw them before she died."

"I know," Grayson said. "We really need to talk. Let's find someplace where there aren't so many people around."

Amber followed him out of the room where the kids were gathered and down the hall. They hadn't gone halfway down the tile hallway before Amber saw several black marks on the tile.

"I just cleaned this," she said. "Now I'll have to do it all over again."

"It doesn't look that bad," Grayson said, "they're hardly noticeable."

He led her out to the main hallway. He crossed the carpet and opened one of the sanctuary doors. The lights came on as they entered. Grayson walked down the aisle past a few rows of chairs and then pointed to one row. "This should be okay."

Amber sat where he pointed. Grayson sat in one of the chairs in the next row, resting his arm on the back and looking back at her. She waited for him to speak.

"We got the test results," he said at last.

"What did they tell you?" Amber asked.

"They came back a match," Grayson said.

"So, they matched between Holly and Lizi?"

"No, they didn't have a sample for that. There's a match between Lizi and me," Grayson said.

"So you're telling me that you really are Lizi's father."

"I was pretty sure it would come back that way," Grayson said.

"Then you and Holly?"

"Holly was Victoria."

"How can that be?" Amber asked. "I've seen pictures of Victoria and she doesn't look like Holly."

"You must have been looking at some of the early pictures. She went through plastic surgery several times. She never was happy with how she looked. I can't help but wonder if they didn't give her the wrong stuff one of the times they put her under. They say they didn't, but she just wasn't right after that last surgery. That's why I don't think you need to worry about Lizi seeing elves. I just wonder who that woman was we thought was Victoria."

"But I heard her talking about seeing elves at the office."

"My mother got her started on that. She didn't see an elf. There was someone doing some work after hours for a while. Whoever it was would finish a lot of the stuff I needed finished before I got there the next morning. My mother suggested it was like the story of the cobbler and the elf. That got Lizi started. But it stopped the other day. Now I see why. Our elf got herself a paying job."

"You think it was me?"

"Don't try to lie to me, Amber," Grayson said. "I know it was you."

"Yeah, it was me," Amber said. "I hope you don't mind, but I needed a place to sleep for a while, so I borrowed the office."

"You should've heard Dad when he found out about that," Grayson said.

"I wasn't trying to cause any trouble."

"He'll get over it, as long as you stay out of his way," Grayson said.

"That's what I'm trying to do," Amber said. "But I hope you won't make me give up Lizi completely. I've known her her whole life."

"No, I wouldn't do that," Grayson said. "We'll work something out. I don't know what, but we'll work something out. Lizi cries herself to sleep every night because she misses you. I had the police wake me up the other night. I thought she was asleep in her room, but they found her out walking the streets. She was headed for the train station to buy a ticket to St. Louis. She tried to tell them that her parents live up there. She didn't tell them where she lives until CPS showed up."

"Sounds like something she would do," Amber said. "Is there any chance I get to see her more than just here at church?"

"Yeah, of course, but can we talk about it later." Grayson stood up. "And if you get the urge to play elf again, let me know. I've got a ton of stuff that isn't getting done. I still can't pay you. And now, Dad would have a fit if he saw your name on the payroll."

"There's so much to do here that I'm not sure when I could get over there." Amber didn't want to tell him that she wouldn't help him, but it seemed like everyone at church needed her to do something.

"I wasn't being serious," Grayson said. "I wouldn't be comfortable having you work without us paying you something. But if you want to come by the office sometime, I've been taking Lizi to work with me a lot, so if you have any free time at all during the week, come on by.

"I'll keep that in mind."

Amber saw Lizi a few more times that day as she went from one activity to the next with the other children, but she wasn't alone with her until just before the kids went home for the day. Grayson was off talking to one of his friends and Amber was on her hands and knees trying to rub the black marks off the tile when Lizi came out of one of the classrooms. She carried a brightly painted picture frame made from wooden tongue depressors. "This is for you," she said, holding it out to Amber.

"Thank you, it's very pretty," Amber said, rocking back on her heels and reaching out to accept it.

"They told me to make it for my Dad. I told them I didn't have one."

"But you know that Grayson is your father."

"Yeah, but I wanted to make it for you," Lizi said. "Don't you want it?"

"Of course I do," Amber said. "I just wish I had a picture of you to put in it."

"You've got pictures of me."

"Nothing recent," Amber said.

Lizi shrugged. "Can I come live with you again?"

"No," Amber said, "You need to stay with your father."

"But I miss you."

"I know, but you'll still see me. I'll be here every Sunday."

"You weren't here last Sunday."

"Yes, I was," Amber said. "I sat in the balcony, so you couldn't see me, but I'll be here from now on."

"It isn't the same. You won't be there to tell me stories at night."

"There'll have to be some changes," Amber said. "That's just the way it is."

Lizi hesitated and then said, "I know, but I don't like it."

"Are you ready?" Grayson asked, as he walked toward them.

"Yeah." Lizi sounded reluctant. She hugged Amber before she followed her father to the door.

Grayson had already opened the door when Lizi turned around and ran back to Amber.

"Guess what," she said with a smile on her face. "They do have cows in Fort Worth. Grayson's going to take me to see some. You want to come?"

Amber looked at Grayson. He stood there looking at them with the door open.

"There's plenty of room," he said. "I'm sure those black marks will be there again tomorrow."

"Let me put this stuff away," she said, pointing toward the bucket and rag on the floor. She wasn't about to pass up a chance to spend some time with Lizi.

Chapter Twenty-Six

The doors to Fox's office opened and Sandra walked in. Fox had stayed longer at the office than he had in a long time. In part, it was because he hoped Grayson would come back. In part, it was because he needed to understand more about what Grayson had been doing with the business, but he wasn't even sure where to get started.

"I forwarded you an e-mail," Sandra said. "Grayson won't be able to take care of it with him being out on a date. I probably shouldn't call it that. He didn't say it was a date. He took Lizi with him."

"Where did Celia take them off to this time?" Fox asked. "Did they say?"

"Celia?" Sandra asked. "It wasn't Celia. He called me to say that he's taking Amber and Lizi to see the cattle drive and then he's going to take them out to eat. I told him it wouldn't take very long to drive a few cows down the street, so he ought to take them somewhere else while he's goofing off. He said he might."

The e-mail came up and Fox opened it. One of the lawyers had sent it to Grayson. The subject said, "Unpaid Taxes." Sandra left the room and Fox began to skim the message. "I did a records search and found these additional items that are in the Jack Abrams name. All have unpaid taxes associated with them. They appear to be things that Jack intends to include in the merger. If this list is accurate, Jack Abrams Inc. owes significantly more than the value of their physical assets. You will need to decide if it is worth taking on this much debt for the benefit we'll receive."

He didn't have to add up the figures to see that Jack Abrams Inc. was much deeper in debt than any of the previous figures had shown. If these figures were right, just what they owed the government was enough to say that Jack Abrams Inc. was worthless.

Fox dialed Grayson's cell phone. It rang several times, but Grayson didn't answer. He dialed again. Again, Grayson didn't answer, but Fox left a message. "We've got a problem."

Next, he dialed Jack Abrams' number. It would be good to give the man a chance to explain what was going on. Jack listened as Fox explained what he'd seen in the e-mail.

"I just don't see how we can continue with this merger, given what we know now."

When Fox finished, Jack said, "I'm sure there's some kind of misunderstanding. They may have some old data. Give me a few days to look into it and I'll get back to you."

That didn't make Fox feel better about the situation, but he didn't know what else he could do. They needed the experience of Jack's workforce, if they wanted their business to grow. Fox wanted to believe that Jack would be able to show that he wasn't trying to push his debt off on them.

But Fox didn't have to wait days for Jack to answer his concerns. It wasn't two hours later when Celia showed up. She dropped a manila envelope on his desk. "Dad says you want to back out of the merger."

Of course, that wasn't true. He wanted the merger to work, but it never would if it required them to take on very much debt. The new company would never survive.

"That's not exactly what I said."

"You should take a look at that before you back out," Celia said. "I didn't want to have to do this, but my Dad has so much riding on this merger. So, there it is."

Celia sat down in one of the big chairs on the other side of the desk and waited quietly as Fox opened the envelope. What tumbled out were several pictures and typed papers.

"What is this?" Fox asked.

"It's proof," Celia said. "I know what happened last year and I know what it would do to your family if they found out."

"What is it you think you know?" Fox asked. Looking through the pictures, he could see that they were all from the accident.

"I know that you killed your grandchildren," Celia said. "And I know what it would do to your children and Fiona if she found out."

Fox could see Fiona hiding away in her shell once more if she found out what had really happened that day—maybe even worse. Steve—he didn't know what Steve would do, but Donna would be hurt terribly. And Abby would take it the hardest of all. She'd lost both her children and her husband. She would never forgive Fox if she knew that he'd caused it. Fox hadn't yet forgiven himself, but it would do no good for the family to know his part in it. Even Grayson would be hurt if he knew his father's part in the accident. Anyone who saw the pictures and read the statements from the witnesses would realize what he'd done.

"You won't show this to the family, will you?"

"No," Celia said. "I really hate that I had to show you this at all. As soon as the paperwork for the merger is done, I'll burn every copy I have and I'll be glad to do it. I love your family too much to want to hurt them."

"Does your father know about this?" Fox asked.

"No, and I'm not going to tell him," Celia said.

Fox sealed the contents of the envelope and dropped it in his desk, wondering how many copies Celia had made. Even one was too many.

Chapter Twenty-Seven

The three of them sat in a restaurant. Grayson sat across from Amber and Lizi sat next to her.

"If Dad knew you were here, he'd throw a fit. He's not very happy with you." Grayson cut into his steak. "So, Lizi, let's not tell him, okay?"

Lizi nodded her head, but it was more like she was saying she had no intention of telling him anyway.

"I'm not very happy with him either," Amber said. She wasn't about to say what she really thought. The man was Grayson's father and Grayson wouldn't share her frustration, no matter how much his father did to her.

"No, I don't suppose you would be," he said. "But you've got to understand the way he is. He's decided that he wants Celia to be part of the family and he's afraid that you'll get in the way."

"But I never tried to…"

"I know," Grayson said. "Of course, Lizi hasn't helped anything."

"What did I do?" Lizi asked.

"Oh, nothing—nothing at all," Grayson said.

"What is it that you want?" Amber asked. "You and Celia seem like a pretty hot item."

"It's not all that," Grayson said, "but I could do worse. I just want to get past this merger before making any commitments. I don't want marriage to be a condition of the merger."

Amber didn't know what to say to that, but Grayson was ready to change the subject.

After they ate, Grayson drove her back to her apartment. As they approached the building, they could see several police cars parked in the parking lot. When they got closer, they could see a couple of officers talking to a man with a bruised eye and a busted lip. An ambulance sat near the police cars. The paramedics were treating a man with a bloody face.

"This doesn't look like a very safe place to live," Grayson said as he drove between the police cars.

"It's what I can afford," Amber said. "Besides, this stuff doesn't happen every night."

"We need to see if we can find you something better." He parked the car and unbuckled his seatbelt.

"You don't have to see me to my door," Amber said. "I know the way."

"Actually, I've got something for you in the trunk." He hit the button to release the trunk and got out.

Amber walked around to the back of the car with him. In the trunk she saw the clothes he had bought for her, some of which still had the tags on them.

"Before you refuse to take them—I meant for these to be a gift and I still do." He scooped up the plastic bags he had used to protect them, closed the trunk and strolled toward the entrance to the building. Amber and Lizi hurried to catch up.

When Amber opened the door to her apartment and stepped in, the smell of stale smoke greeted her.

"Where do you want these?" Grayson asked.

"Just leave them on the bed. I'll put them away later." Amber pointed toward the bed.

Grayson put the clothes down and Amber expected him to leave so he could get away from the smell, but he sat down on the couch as if he was in no hurry. Lizi threw herself across the foot of the bed, taking up the little space left, so Amber went and sat next to Grayson.

"Tell me one of my mother's stories," Lizi said. "You haven't told me one in a long time."

Amber immediately thought of a story but couldn't remember if Holly had told it to her or if it was one she had made up to keep Lizi satisfied. "The elves and the fairies were fighting," Amber began. As she told the story, she could see Lizi's eyes begin to droop and then close. When she knew Lizi had fallen asleep she quit talking.

"You're just going to stop and not tell me how it ends?" Grayson asked.

"The elves and the fairies kill each other," Amber said, abbreviating the end.

"Figures," Grayson said. "That was Victoria's idea of a happy ending."

"No, actually, she probably ended it by saying the prince of the fairies came and defeated the elves."

"That sounds a little better."

"Can I ask you something? What was Victoria like before she lost it?"

Grayson thought for a moment and then said, "She was a lot of fun. She had this smile. When she looked you in the eye and smiled, you just knew she thought you were the most important person in the world. Anyone who knew her loved her. She took a lot of care with her appearance. I never could convince her she was pretty. She could really tear into you when she was angry though. Would you believe we got into a fight the same night I asked her to marry me?"

Amber waited for him to tell her more.

"She didn't like the ring," Grayson said. "My great-grandmother had this ring and I ended up with it somehow.

It's a real pretty thing and I had this idea that I would give it to Victoria as an engagement ring. She liked it until I told her where it came from. That was my mistake, not realizing a woman wouldn't want a ring some other woman had worn."

"I don't see anything wrong with it."

"You don't have a problem with cleaning toilets either," Grayson said. "That's something I don't think Victoria would have ever done."

"So you won't be giving the ring to Celia either?" Amber asked.

"No, I won't be giving it to Celia. I wouldn't try to give her a ring without taking her to the jeweler and letting her pick the diamond and the setting. But, I haven't made plans to do that."

Amber looked at the clothes on the bed and stood up. "I guess I'd better put these things away if I'm going to have a bed to sleep in."

"Are you saying you're about to throw me out?" Grayson asked.

"No, you can stay longer," Amber said.

"I need to be going anyway. I need to get this girl to bed." He pointed at Lizi. "I would suggest letting her sleep here, but I don't think this neighborhood is very safe."

"No, I don't think it is either."

Lizi sat up on the bed, rubbed her eyes and stood up. With Grayson guiding her from behind, she was able to make it out the door. Amber watched out the window for them to drive away.

Chapter Twenty-Eight

It was late enough to be dark outside when Fox opened the door for Grayson. He didn't see Lizi with him. "Where's Lizi?"

"She's asleep in the car. I won't stay long. I got your message. What's the problem?"

"Nothing," Fox said, "It was just misunderstanding. Celia was able to explain it to where I understood it better."

"Good," Grayson said. "You had me worried. You sounded like it was something bad."

It was bad, but Fox couldn't tell Grayson that. He couldn't tell anyone.

After a Grayson left, Fox went upstairs to bed. Fiona didn't move when he slipped under the sheet. He didn't want to wake her. She seemed to rest better now. She wouldn't if she found out what had really happened the day of the accident.

He began to have dreams about the accident again. He often dreamed of the accident. The cement mixer was coming and he had to get out of the way, but the car wouldn't move. He pressed on the accelerator as hard as he could, but the car wouldn't speed up. This time the dream was different. Celia was there with a camera in her hand.

"Say cheese," she said as she snapped one picture after another.

"Help me get out of the way," he kept yelling at her, but she kept snapping pictures.

"I don't want to do this, but I have to," she was saying.

He woke before the cement mixer crushed the car, but he knew it was coming. Worse, it had really happened. He couldn't get away from it.

Chapter Twenty-Nine

"You're the new janitor, aren't you?" A woman stopped Amber in the hall Sunday morning just as she came out of the classroom where they had met for Bible study.

"That's right," Amber said. She could already tell the woman wanted something.

"One of the toilets won't flush," the woman said.

"Which one?" Amber asked.

"I'll show you," the woman said, turning and walking a short distance down the hall.

"Just tell me which bathroom it's in," Amber said. "I don't have time to take care of it right now."

The woman looked surprised. "I tried to flush it and I don't think any of it went down."

"Did it overflow?"

"No, but it almost did. With it being Sunday, I figured you'd want to take care of it right away. If I'd known you were going to put it off, I wouldn't have bothered to tell you."

"You did the right thing by telling me," Amber said as sweetly as she could muster. "If you hadn't, I probably would-n't have found out until I cleaned the restrooms later in the week, but the worship service is going to start in a few minutes and I'm not dressed to unclog toilets."

The woman didn't look very happy, but it couldn't be helped. Grayson came out of the classroom as the woman walked away.

"Is something wrong?" he asked.

"Not really," she said, "But I'm beginning to hate this job."

"Maybe you won't have to work here very long. Are you looking for another job?"

"When am I supposed to have time?" She asked.

"What are your plans for lunch?" He avoided her question.

"It looks like I'll be unclogging a toilet. After that, I'm free."

"I'm sure Lizi would like to eat lunch with you."

When they got to the sanctuary, Amber saw Lizi had already chosen a seat. She had one of her friends with her. Amber sat next to Lizi. Grayson had several people who wanted to talk to him, but she knew he would join them shortly.

She hadn't been sitting there long when Lizi asked, "What is she doing here?"

Amber turned around to look and saw Celia standing in the aisle talking to Grayson. She couldn't make out what they were saying. The conversation ended quickly and Celia came toward them.

"You don't mind if I sit there." Celia pointed to the seat next to Amber.

Grayson showed up after the music director had asked everyone to greet each other. Everyone was standing and either talking to someone or singing along as they waited to be told they could sit down. By that time, the whole row had filled up except for one empty seat on the other side of Celia.

"I saved you a seat, Grayson," Celia said loudly enough for the people several rows away to hear above the music.

The people in front of them turned around to look at them. Amber noticed the pastor, who was standing to one side on stage, put his hand above his eyes to shield them from the glare of the bright lights. Grayson made his way in front of all the people on that row and stood next to Celia.

Lizi moved closer to Amber and whispered in her ear. "He was going to sit next to you."

"It'll be okay. I'm sure he didn't know Celia would come," Amber whispered back. She wondered if there was a good way to tell Lizi that it wasn't her job to match Grayson up with her. The harder she tried, the less likely he would be interested.

They sat down and Amber saw Celia's arm go up behind Grayson and she began running her fingers through the hair at the back of his neck. Grayson turned and whispered something to her. Celia took her hand down and rested it on his arm. It stayed there for a while, until Grayson pulled his arm away. Celia let her hand fall to his leg. He didn't seem to like that and he gently removed Celia's hand. The hand went back to his neck, with her fingers making their way through his hair. It stayed there until Grayson whispered to Celia again and it went back to his arm. All through the service this went on— from the neck to the arm to the leg and back to the neck again. With all the movement beside her, Amber couldn't keep her mind on what song they were singing or what the preacher was saying.

She paid so much attention to what they were doing that she almost forgot about the clogged toilet, but after the service she went to check on it. She opened the door and she could see water standing in the floor. She had thought she could take care of it quickly, but for this she was going to have to change into her work clothes and get a mop. She hoped Grayson didn't mind waiting.

As she was going to get what she needed, she ran into the woman who had first told her about it.

"I tried flushing that thing again after I talked to you," the woman said. "I figured the third time's the charm, but I think it got a little water on the floor."

"I'm going to take care of it right now," Amber said. She hoped the woman wouldn't go back and try again.

When she put on her old shoes and waded through the water, she could see that someone had tried to stuff too much paper down the toilet. It took her a few minutes to eliminate that problem.

As Amber was beginning to clean up the mess on the floor, Celia opened the door of the restroom and yelled in, "Amber, are you in here?"

Amber came around to where she could see her.

"Grayson sent me to ask how much longer you're going to be." Celia looked at the water that was still standing on the floor. "I sure wouldn't want this job."

"I'm going to tell him you said you would meet us at the restaurant." Celia backed out of the doorway.

"Wait!" Amber said. "I don't have a car."

Celia stuck her head back through the door. "I'm sure there's a bus stop close to there."

"But, it might take an hour to get there."

"Oh, I didn't think of that," Celia said. "I never ride the bus."

"No, I wouldn't think you would."

"Do you mind if we go on ahead without you? It looks like this might take a while."

"No, go on without me."

She didn't hurry as much she had been doing before. She took her time, making sure the whole restroom was clean, all the while feeling sorry for herself. No one cared that she had to work while they were off enjoying themselves.

By the time she finished her task, changed clothes again, waited for several minutes at the bus stop and rode around to the bus stop near her apartment, it was after two o'clock. As she walked across the parking lot, past two men sitting on a car with beer bottles in their hands, she saw a car that looked like

Grayson's. She walked through the front entrance and saw Grayson and Lizi sitting in the lobby.

"How was lunch?" Grayson stood as she approached.

"What lunch?" She made her way to the elevator. "I'm just now getting home. I haven't had time to eat lunch."

"I'm sorry," he said as he and Lizi followed her. "We were going to wait for you, but Celia said you said to go on."

"What else could I say?" Amber mashed the button and the door opened.

He waited for Lizi to step through before he stepped across the threshold.

Amber jabbed the button for the third floor with her finger. "I'm sure Celia enjoyed her time with you better without me around."

"Celia isn't a bad person." Grayson leaned against the wall and rested his weight on the handrail.

"Did I say she was?"

The doors closed and the elevator began to move.

"She's a really good friend," Grayson said, "when you get to know her."

"That was plenty obvious in church this morning."

"Yeah, about that…"

The elevator doors opened and Amber stepped out, avoiding an old man waiting for the elevator. She walked briskly down the hall. Lizi followed her, but Grayson held the door so it wouldn't close before the man could get on. The strong smell of stale smoke greeted her when Amber opened the door. Lizi held the door and waited for Grayson.

Amber opened the refrigerator and looked inside for something to eat.

"You sit down over here and I'll fix your lunch." Grayson pulled out the one chair at the very small table that served as the efficiency apartment's dining room table.

"That's not necessary." Amber pulled the cottage cheese out, along with a package of bologna and the store brand cheese that felt a little like rubber.

"No, I insist." He went and pulled the packages from her hands. "You've been working. You should get to rest."

Too tired to argue, Amber sat in the chair and watched as he pulled a plate from the cabinet. It was the one with the green stripe around it. It didn't match the other two with blue stripes. He pulled out a couple slices of bread, to which he added the bologna and cheese before he smeared the cheap mayonnaise on it. He scooped out cottage cheese and put it beside the sandwich.

"That," he said as he placed it in front of her, "is about the extent of my cooking abilities. So if you want something else, ask Lizi."

"This is fine," Amber said. "Don't you ever cook?"

"Not much," he said. "I usually fail when I try."

Grayson put everything away and leaned up against the counter as he watched her eat. "Pretend that's dinner at a fine restaurant and it doesn't smell so awful in here."

She finished eating and pushed her plate aside.

"There's something I've been meaning to ask you," Grayson said. He walked over to the window and slid it open. The hot air from outside rushed in. "That's a little better. Maybe we can get some of this stale air out of here."

"You were going to ask?" Amber prompted him.

"Oh, nothing important, but Dad was certain you had some dastardly plan to get me to marry you—he still does, actually."

"I told you I didn't," Amber said.

"Yeah, I know, but I'm curious. What would you have done if you had?"

Amber wasn't sure why he was asking. Maybe he was trying to trip her up. Maybe she hadn't convinced him she wasn't trying anything after all. "Don't you think that if I was going to try something I'd try harder than what I have at whatever it is you think I've been doing?"

"Who said I thought you'd been doing anything," Grayson asked. "I was just curious. You must have given it some thought. You wouldn't have to give up Lizi that way."

"I haven't given her up," Amber said. "I just don't see her as often."

"You know what I mean," Grayson said.

"Sure I thought about it," Amber said. "And then I thought about how much I don't want Fox as my father-in-law."

"I would laugh, but I think you might be serious."

"Well, yeah, I'm serious," Amber said. "Anytime I did something he didn't like, he'd go dig something up out of my past or if that didn't work he'd make something up. You know I'm right."

Grayson looked like he was going to disagree, but then he said, "Yeah, in fact, I found some stuff the other day that he dug up about you. Maybe he made it up—I'm not sure. He might not know what to do with it or he didn't want me to see it or he's just waiting for when he needed it."

"Are you going to tell me what it is or do I have to guess?"

"It has to do with the way Victoria died," Grayson said.

"I've got nothing to hide there," Amber said, wondering if that was why Fox hadn't used whatever it was. Maybe he was smart enough to know that it wouldn't work.

"Tell me what happened," Grayson said. "I know what the news reports said, but what really happened?"

"Pretty much what they said, I came home from the store and Holly was in the garage with the car running."

"Dad has a guy who found a witness. She says there's more to it than that. She says you killed Victoria. It sounds very convincing."

"You think I killed her? Of course I didn't!" she said. "There may very well be another witness. I didn't think so, but there could have been. I was so distracted with everything I wasn't trying to find out who had seen what. I've done some rotten things, but I wouldn't kill someone."

"Tell me exactly what happened," Grayson said. "I want you to fill in all the little details. I want to know what happened before you left, what you bought at the store, how you discovered her body and what you did after that."

"I don't remember what I bought," she said. "No, wait. I did buy a gallon of milk. I remember because with all the commotion I forgot to put it away and it went bad."

"Humor me."

"Like I said, we went to the store."

"Did you ask Victoria if she wanted to go?"

"I don't know—probably not. I would have told her I was going. She must have asked me to take Lizi along or I would have left her at home."

"So you go to the store and come back. You open the garage door and there she is?"

"No, I parked on the drive. There was only room for one car and since I drove mine more, I let her park in the garage to get her car out of the way."

"Then what happened?"

"I took Lizi inside and went to unload my car. I didn't think anything about it since I was going to be in and out and Victoria was around someplace. I figured she was in their room."

"You didn't notice the car running in the garage?"

"Not at first. It had a little four cylinder engine and you could push the accelerator to the floor and it still wasn't very loud." Amber took a deep breath. "I was putting everything away in the kitchen and I started to smell the exhaust fumes. That's when I went out to the garage and saw her. Lizi was curled up on the concrete like she had just fallen asleep. I picked her up and tried to wake her, but she wasn't breathing. It was hard to breathe out there. I couldn't help them both. I opened the car door and shut off the engine. I rushed Lizi inside and gave her mouth to mouth. It seemed like forever before she started breathing again. I didn't want to leave her, but I went to see if I could do anything for Holly. I drug her out of the car and I tried, but it was too late. So I put her back in the car, started the engine, locked the door and went to call 911 at the neighbor's house."

"Why would you put her back in the car?"

"It's not like she wasn't dead already, but I figured if she was still in the car with it running when they got there then they'd ignore Lizi. I knew they'd take her away from me if they found out she was Holly's, I mean Victoria's, instead of mine."

"You didn't take Lizi to the doctor to see if she was okay?"

"No, she seemed fine by the time all of the emergency workers got there. I put her in their room. She fell asleep, and that worried me a little, but she was breathing okay. She's fine now. Isn't she?"

"There's nothing wrong with her, as far as I can tell." He looked thoughtful. "You would think it would have some kind of lasting effect."

"Kids are resilient," Amber said.

"How do you explain the bruise on her head?"

"I'm sure she must have gotten it while she was playing or something. What happened ten years ago isn't going to cause a bruise now." Amber wondered if Grayson was just searching for something that proved she had done something wrong. Maybe he was more like his father than she had thought.

"No, no," he said. He looked perturbed. "The medical examiner found a bruise on Victoria's head that could have come from a blunt object and it could have been enough to knock her out."

"I don't know what could have caused it," Amber said. "If anyone mentioned it, I don't remember it."

Grayson looked like he wanted to say something, but the words didn't come out.

"You don't believe me, do you?" Amber asked. "Fox has you convinced that I'm lying to you."

"I just want to understand," Grayson said.

"But your father keeps telling you that I can't be trusted."

"Not in so many words," Grayson said.

"I've told you about my past." She knew she hadn't told him all of it, but enough that he had a good idea of what her life had been like before. "I can't change who I was. I can only tell you that I don't want to be that person anymore."

"I believe you," he said. "But you've got to understand that my father usually knows what he's talking about."

"Usually," Amber said, "But he's sure got it in for me."

Chapter Thirty

Fox opened the glass doors to the executive suite. Sandra was talking on the phone, but she held her hand over the mouth piece and said, "You're in early today."

"Yeah, I've got lots to do," Fox said. More than anything, he expected he would spend the day thinking about why they hadn't backed out of the merger. But it wasn't the business side of things that he feared the most. He'd worried about what Amber would do to weasel her way into the family, just to stay close to Lizi. At least, she had an excuse—it wasn't right, but she had an excuse. Celia and her father had pushed their way in just because their business was about to go under. But their plan would succeed where Amber's had failed.

It was ten o'clock then Grayson walked through the door to Fox's office. "There's no way we can go through with this merger."

Fox had been anticipating this meeting. He knew Grayson would see the same thing he did. It had only been a matter of time. "Why do you say that? We already decided we need this merger if we're going to grow."

Grayson laid a stack of papers on Fox's desk. Even before he picked them up, Fox could tell that they had the same information he'd looked at before. But he flipped through the pages to show Grayson he was looking at them. "What am I supposed to be seeing here?"

"Jack Abrams is deep in debt and he's trying to push that debt off on us."

"Let's not jump to conclusions," Fox said. "He may be able to explain what's going on. Let me talk to him and we'll give him a chance to look into it."

It hurt to argue for Jack Abrams when Fox already knew what the man was up to, but the envelope in the desk was a heavy reminder that he had no choice, not if he wanted to protect his family from his secret.

"I'll give it time," Grayson said, "But I'm going to pull people off the merger and put them back to work on other things."

"No," Fox said, "Keep them working on the merger. We've got to assume it'll work out."

"You're being overly optimistic," Grayson said.

"Don't give up so quickly," Fox said. "I don't think it's too optimistic to think it'll work. This isn't the first time we've run into problems."

Grayson didn't push the issue further, but Fox knew it wasn't over. Unless Jack Abrams came up with a really good explanation, Grayson would be looking at those figures again and he would want to know why Fox felt they should go ahead with the merger. Fox wouldn't have an answer for him. At best, he'd delayed the inevitable. If Celia's silence was dependent on the merger, he was going to have to find a way to make it happen, even if it was against Grayson's better judgment.

But Grayson didn't leave. He sat down across from Fox and stared out the window for a long time. Fox knew he would either leave or he would say something when he was ready.

"We should put a birdfeeder out there," Grayson said.

"It'll just make a mess on the cars," Fox said.

"Yeah, you're probably right." Grayson kept looking out the window. "Maybe in back by the break room—no one parks back there."

"Who is going to keep it filled?"

"We can have maintenance do it," Grayson said. "It wouldn't take them very long."

"If that's what you want to do," Fox said. "I guess that's okay."

Grayson's gaze didn't turn from the window. "I talked to Amber."

"You've seen her several times recently, haven't you? Didn't you take her on another date?"

Grayson turned his head from the window and looked at his father. He looked confused. "No, we didn't go on a date. But I was going to say that I talked to her about how Victoria died. She has this idea that you're digging into her past to get rid of her."

"Well, I am," Fox said. "I might as well admit it."

"I wish you wouldn't," Grayson said. "I don't want Lizi thinking she has to choose between you and Amber."

"Amber isn't a very good influence on her," Fox said. "Just look at some of the stuff she's taught her."

"I'm not saying she's been the best influence on Lizi," Grayson said, "but you've got to admit that Lizi isn't that bad off for the experience. There are a few things I wish she wouldn't do. I just don't think that's a good reason to keep Lizi away from Amber."

Fox could think of plenty of reasons. Amber had a history as a con artist. Maybe she'd changed her spots for a while, but they wouldn't stay that way forever. She'd held onto Lizi for years without any thought of Lizi's family. Just because she'd raised the girl didn't mean she had a right to her. "Aren't you a little worried that she might have killed Victoria?"

"That's what I was going to say," Grayson said. "I talked to her and I don't think she did."

"But…"

"But nothing," Grayson said. "Yeah, there were some people who think they saw something, but look at how many years have passed. It's almost ten years now. You can't trust what people think they remember from that day."

"You can't trust what Amber remembers either," Fox said.

"Okay, so maybe not," Grayson said, "But she ought to know whether she killed Victoria or not. Besides, what's her motive? Do you think she wanted Lizi so much that she would kill Victoria? I don't think so. Just give it a rest, okay? Can you do that?"

"I don't think I should be faulted for trying to protect my family," Fox said.

"If this is a problem, it's my problem," Grayson said. "Can you just let me handle it? If you want to go digging into stuff, why don't you see if you can find that hit and run driver that caused your accident? They never found him, right?"

Grayson had dealt Fox a low blow. The reason they hadn't found the hit and run driver was because there hadn't been one. There'd been another driver on the other side of the cement mixer who'd left the scene of the accident, but maybe he wasn't aware of the accident he barely missed. Maybe he'd been in a hurry and didn't want to be bothered. Whatever had happened, he wasn't at fault. He hadn't forced the cement mixer over, like some of the witnesses had thought. It wouldn't do Fox any good to trace the guy down, but he couldn't tell Grayson that. "I just want my family to be safe and happy."

Grayson may have believed him, but Fox couldn't believe himself. The one thing he'd not done was keep his family safe and happy. All he could hope for now was for them to be less unhappy and to preserve what little family he had left. Of course, he would try to protect Lizi; she was the only future the family had left.

Celia arrived at noon to take Grayson and Lizi to lunch. Fox wondered if she would mention their previous conversation, but she acted no different from normal. It was as if she had forgotten it, but Fox knew better. She would go on acting like she always had, pretending to want what was best for them and all the while she'd position herself for what was best for her. The woman made Amber look like an amateur. He would not let her have her way.

Chapter Thirty-One

Alex scooped up a briefcase and a stack of papers from the guest chair in his office. "Have a seat, if you can find one. You didn't have to come down here. I know how to find your office."

"I'm afraid that wouldn't have worked this time," Fox said. "There're too many listening ears."

"Well that's enough to get my attention," Alex said, going around to the big leather chair behind his desk. He dropped the briefcase and the papers on the floor. "Is something going on that you don't want your employees to know about?"

"There's something going on that my family can't know about," Fox said. "I'm relying on you to keep it between us."

"Of course," Alex said. "It won't leave this office without your permission."

Fox knew that he could expect that from Alex, but was glad of the verbal confirmation.

"You aren't having an affair, are you?" Alex asked.

Fox looked at him in disbelief that he would ask. "No, of course not."

"Good," Alex said, settling back in his chair, "I've heard about too many of those lately. So, what's going on?"

"I've run into a snag with the merger," Fox said.

"You're still going through with it? I thought with some of the message traffic I saw y'all would be backing out of that."

"Yeah, I want to," Fox said, "but there's a problem. Celia won't let me."

"Just what do you mean by 'she won't let me'?" Alex asked. "I didn't think you were so far along that you couldn't back out."

"Under normal circumstances, I would agree but Celia has been digging into the accident. She'll use what she's found out if I don't go through with the merger."

Alex interlaced his fingers. "I wouldn't worry about it. There's not enough there to make a case against you. The eye witness accounts are too different be much good, even in a civil case. I'd be happy to recommend another attorney if you want to talk to someone with more experience with this kind of situation, but I'm sure you don't have anything to worry about. You made a mistake in judgment, but you weren't the only one. The guy in the cement mixer was probably going too fast, not that it was necessarily the cause, but it would raise enough questions that a jury isn't likely to convict. But I don't think there's anyone who wants to pursue it, no matter what Celia thinks she's found."

"It's not a jury I'm worried about," Fox said. "I know a good lawyer would be able to argue against it in court, but I was there. I know what happened. I know I shouldn't have done what I did. Just because the witnesses aren't sure what happened doesn't mean I don't know that I caused the accident."

"I'm just a lawyer," Alex said. "I'm not your psychiatrist or your pastor. Other than to say that you may not remember things quite the way they happened, it's not my place to tell you how to deal with your feelings of guilt. As your friend, I'll tell you that I hope you can find a way to work it out, but as a lawyer, all I can do is talk to you about the law."

"And I don't need you to tell me how to handle it," Fox said. He knew that Alex wouldn't understand anyway. "I'm learning to cope with it. My problem is that if my family learns what I did that day, it'll turn the whole family against me. Maybe that's what I deserve, but I'm afraid of what it'll do to them. I don't think they can handle it. Fiona and Abby are just barely coping as it is. Fiona has gotten better since Lizi showed up, but if she found out the accident was my fault, it wouldn't be good. And Abby—I worry about her as it is. Steve and Donna—well, they're Steve and Donna, but how am I supposed to help my family if they don't want to look at me?"

Fox knew that he didn't really know how his family would react, but he knew a little. It was his own fault for how he'd raised them, but his family didn't take well to people doing them wrong—just like he didn't take well to what Celia had done—or what Amber had done.

He could tell himself that he feared the trouble she would cause Grayson, but the thing that burned him up what that she'd kept Lizi from them all those years. All those years, he should've been able to spend time with his granddaughter. Fiona should've been able to get to do things with her. She should've been at the family gatherings. But because Amber hadn't wanted to bother herself with finding Lizi's family, she'd been missing. That was not something he could take lightly.

Alex would never be able to understand Fox's problem. He was more laid back than Fox, but he understood enough that he tried to offer help. "What kind of solution are you looking for here? Are you looking for a legal solution? Some other kind of solution?"

"I'm looking for whatever will work," Fox said. "I want to be able to back away from that merger without any fear that Celia will tell my family what she thinks happened."

Alex rubbed his eyes with both hands. "There probably isn't a legal solution for that. If there is, it'll take a better lawyer

than me to find it. We could take them to court for some of
what they've tried with the merger, but that won't keep Celia
from saying what she wants about the accident."

"It's not just what she can say about it," Fox said. "She has
pictures and witness statements."

"Sure," Alex said, "but it all amounts to the same thing.
Legally, there isn't much we can do to silence her. Even if we
didn't have the First Amendment to deal with, if she just said
something to one of your children it might cause you all the
same trouble you're trying to avoid. If we could get a gag order—which we can't—people would still wonder what it is that
you're trying to hide. That could be worse for you than if let
your family think she was saying stuff to get back at you for
some reason."

"So, I should be looking for another kind of solution," Fox
said.

"I would think so, yes. Unless..." Alex's voice trailed off.

"Unless what?" Fox asked.

"Unless we can find a way to do to them what they're trying to do to you," Alex said. "With the unpaid taxes and the
other stuff we've seen, I think we can assume that they haven't
been following the law like they should. If we look, we're sure
to find some legal problem that they won't want coming to
light. It would almost be like a trade. We wouldn't say anything as long as they don't say anything."

"It sounds good," Fox said, "but would it work?"

"Who's to say?" Alex asked. "I'm sure that as long as she
thinks you can get them out of whatever financial mess they're
in, she's not going to say a word about the accident to any of
your family. If you call her hand, I'd bet on her telling what she
knows. What we need is something that she doesn't want to
happen more than what they need this merger."

"Like if they were facing jail time," Fox said. He felt strange
talking about people he'd once thought his friends going to jail.

"If we could find something they've done that's illegal then we'd have something to hold over them."

"Yes, but we've got to careful. That could backfire on us. If we find out they're involved in something illegal and don't report it, we could get in all kinds of legal hot water."

"In other words, we shouldn't even go looking for something like that." Fox had the feeling that if Jack Abrams was involved in anything shady, he didn't want to know about it.

"It probably wouldn't do us any good anyway," Alex said. "As long as she has something you value to hold over you, you're going to have a hard time getting her to give it up voluntarily. You're going to need something that scares Celia so much that she won't dare reveal your secret."

"Do you have any idea what that might be?" Fox asked. "I don't know what could possibly scare her that much."

"No," Alex said, "I don't know either, but it's something we could look into. We'll need some time to do it."

"How much time?" Fox wasn't sure how long he could stall, if it came to that. They were getting closer and closer to the point where they'd have to sign the papers or back out. It didn't help that Grayson had to be kept in the dark. Fox had to walk a line between encouraging Grayson enough to keep the process going and finding a way to slow the process enough that they could find a way out of the problem.

"This isn't something I can schedule like a project," Alex said. "It'll take as long as it takes. It could be that we'll start looking and we'll find something in a few hours. Or it could be that it'll take days or weeks to sort through everything and find something useful."

"Or it could be that we find nothing at all," Fox said.

"Yeah, it could be," Alex said, "But I think we've got to try. Besides, I'm confident that there's got to be something. Nobody is completely without fear of something."

"That may be true," Fox said, "But that doesn't mean we'll find it in time."

"But you still want us to look."

"Of course," Fox said. "Let's not leave any stone unturned. And there's a guy I think I'll bring in on this. I've used him before and he turned out to be pretty useful."

"You're talking about the guy who found that information on Amber," Alex said.

"That's the one." Fox could tell that Alex didn't approve. "Like I said, let's not leave any stone unturned. Is there some reason why you think I shouldn't use him?"

"Just my personal reservations," Alex said. "I'm sure it'll work out fine."

Chapter Thirty-Two

Amber made her way between the seats in the sanctuary, walking down one row and then another, looking for any trash that people had left behind. She heard someone come in, but she didn't look up. She spotted a church bulletin someone had wadded up and stuffed in the hymn rack. She dug it out and continued on.

"I'll help you," Tasha Snyder said, moving down from Amber and walking along beside her. "You'd think people would pick up their own trash."

"Or at least keep their gum off the seats." Amber wondered if Tasha had offered to help because she had nothing better to do or if she another motive. She didn't have to guess for long.

"I saw you were sitting with Grayson on Sunday," Tasha said.

"I was sitting with Lizi," Amber said.

"Yeah, and Grayson was on the other side of her. The three of you looked like a nice looking family."

"Grayson's girlfriend was sitting next to him."

"Was she? I didn't notice."

"Are you trying to hint at something?"

"No, not at all," Tasha said. "I'll come right out and say it. I think you ought to marry that guy. It would solve a bunch of problems. Lizi needs a mother. You want to spend more time with her. And I'm not sure how much Grayson makes, but it seems like he makes enough to support all of you."

"Yeah, I'm pretty sure of that," Amber said. She wondered what Tasha would think if she knew just how much of an understatement she'd made.

"Maybe you should grab him while you can."

"It's not that simple," Amber said. "I can't just go tell him that we ought to get married because of Lizi."

"No, that wasn't what I had in mind," Tasha said. She handed Amber the trash she'd found when they finished that section. "But what would be wrong with doing that? Grayson's a sensible guy. I bet he's already thought about it. If you were to encourage him, he might go for it."

"It's complicated," Amber said. "Grayson's father and I aren't on the best of terms right now."

They walked over to the next section to continue their search for trash.

"That's not the ideal situation," Tasha said, "but there are plenty of people who don't get along with their in-laws."

"It's more complicated than that. Grayson's father already thinks I'm trying to force Grayson to marry me. If he found out I asked Grayson to marry me, he would really blow a gasket."

Tasha laughed.

"I didn't mean that to be funny."

"No, I know you didn't," she said, "but I can't imagine someone forcing Grayson to do anything."

"Fox seems to think I would resort to blackmail," Amber said.

"Who would do something like that?"

"I would," Amber said. "At least, I have something of a reputation for that. I wouldn't do that anymore, but a few years ago I might have."

Tasha laughed again. "That's too funny. Just what egregious thing has Grayson done that you could blackmail him with?"

"I don't know," Amber said. "I haven't been looking for anything."

"You wouldn't find anything if you did," Tasha said. "I'm sure Grayson's done some things that he isn't proud of, but you're not going to find something that would force him to marry you. But I'd be surprised if you need to."

"Maybe so, but Fox doesn't see it that way. He doesn't want me involved with his family and he won't stop at anything to keep me away. It's bad enough that I see Lizi and Grayson here at church. He hasn't done anything yet, but he could."

"Like what?" Tasha asked. "Or do I want to know? He can't do anything to you just for spending time with them."

Amber told her all about the note Fox had shown her.

"That's all it took to scare you away?" Tasha asked. "You didn't write it, did you?"

"No, but it looks like my handwriting. Besides, I couldn't stay in his house if he didn't want me there."

"I still don't see why it matters. If you didn't do it, he's got nothing over you."

"And I intend to keep it that way," Amber said. "If this hadn't worked, he would've just kept looking until he found something that would."

"That's one way of looking at it," Tasha said. "It could be that he couldn't find anything, so he made something up."

Amber reached down to pick up a piece of paper and found a woman's hairbrush lying next to it. The paper went in the trash and the hairbrush would go in lost and found.

"The only problem with that," Amber said, "Is that I know there's stuff to be found if he looks hard enough."

"Like what?" Tasha asked. "You don't have to answer that."

"I've done some things," Amber said. "I know how to get things when I want them. I told Grayson about some of that. Like, I claimed to be the girlfriend of this guy that died so that his mother would give me a quilt. Then I went and sold the quilt."

"It's dishonest," Tasha said, "but that's hardly enough to keep you away from Lizi. Can you make restitution? He can't do anything if you there's no one who thinks you owe anything."

"Not likely," Amber said. Her past was like a great fog. It was hard to remember the people she'd encountered and to remember what she'd done to each was even harder. "Where would I come up with that kind of money? And I don't even remember half the people. Someone could come tell me that I did something to them and I might have to take their word for it. That's was scares me about Fox. If he knew how easy it would be for anybody to come up and claim I did something to them, he wouldn't mess with things like that note. He could pay someone to say I did something to them and I might not know whether they were telling the truth or not. And it would be impossible for me to prove they weren't."

Tasha sat down and motioned for Amber to do the same. "Maybe this isn't a good thing, but don't you think that anyone who would try to get their money back would've tried by now? I'm sure the people involved didn't like what happened to them, but if they know who took their money and haven't asked for it back, maybe they don't think it's worth the trouble."

"Yeah, but I was careful. I always went to people who didn't realize what I was doing. I used to get money from churches and they didn't know what hit them." Amber leaned against the seat back, glad to be off her feet for a while.

"I'm sure they knew more than you realized," Tasha said. "We have people come by the church all the time asking for money. They always have some story about needing the money to buy food or to fix their car. When we help people like that, we know that a lot of them aren't going to use the money for what they say they are. But we're not going to ask for the money back if we find out they used it for something else."

"Amateurs," Amber said and didn't miss the look Tasha gave her when she did. "If I were going to ask for money to fix my car, I'd show up with the bill. I can't remember which churches, but there were a couple of churches that gave me more than ten thousand dollars each to pay Lizi's medical bills."

"I'm sure they were happy to do it," Tasha said.

"Sure they were," Amber said, "but I didn't use it to pay medical bills. I didn't owe anything on medical bills at the time."

"We're always careful about that here," Tasha said. "Not that I remember us just giving that much money to a non-member, but I think we would send the money directly to the company instead of giving it to the individual. Even if they weren't trying to scam us, they might be tempted to use the money for something else and then they wouldn't be any better off."

"These churches were the same way. It took some doing," Amber said. As she thought about it, she remembered enjoying the challenge more than the money she'd gotten. "I would take Lizi with me when I'd visit churches. They're always more eager to give when there's a kid there. I would always wait until we were in the pastor's office before I said anything about needing money. If you say something as soon as you get in the door, the person you talk to has to go find someone and they talk each other out of it, so I always asked to see the pastor."

"Sounds sensible," Tasha said, but Amber could tell she didn't know what to say.

"Once you're in the pastor's office, that's when you open your purse and pull out the medical bills. It helps if you have more than one. The first and maybe the second, you pull out you lay on the desk and say someone else is helping you pay those. Then you pull out another one and ask if the church would be able to help. They've all got to look real and the pastor always has to talk to some other people about it, so you let him make a copy and in a few days you get a check in the mail made out to whatever company you listed at the top of the bill."

From the look on Tasha's face, Amber could tell that what she'd described had left a bad taste in the other woman's mouth. She was silent, probably trying to think of Amber the way she had before.

"I still want to say that even though you weren't honest in how you got the money, those churches would still think it was a good thing they helped you," Tasha said after the long pause.

"Why?" Amber asked. "I'm not your soft cuddly beggar who's out of work because he can't pass a drug test."

"I can see that," Tasha said. "But you aren't that person anymore. And I'm sure you used it to help with raising Lizi."

"No," Amber said, "I'm not like that anymore, but I can't change my past. I'm sure that if they could find enough evidence, I could go to jail for part of it."

"You're right," Tasha said, "you can't do anything about your past, but you can let God take care of that." She still looked like she was absorbing what Amber had told her.

"Textbook answer?" Amber asked.

"Yeah, probably, but give me a few days and I'll mean it," Tasha said. "You aren't quite what I expected."

Chapter Thirty-Three

Had Fox heard Amber's conversation with Tasha, he might have found something in it to use against her and been glad of it, but he had put all of that aside to focus on the problem of Celia. Back at home, he closed himself off in his office and locked the door—something he almost never did. He couldn't risk Fiona or Maggie walking in and overhearing his conversation. He picked up the phone and dialed Xander's number.

The phone rang two or three times before a recorded message came on expressing how important his call was and that someone would be able to help him shortly. He must have been on hold for a couple of minutes when he heard a woman's voice asking him how she could direct his call. Within seconds of telling her that he needed to speak to Xander, Xander was on the other end of the line.

"What can we do for you today, Mr. Jacobs?" Xander asked. "Did that note work for you?"

"Yes, it seems to have," Fox said. "She isn't living in the house anymore." He wasn't ready to tell Xander that she was still hanging around. There was time for that later.

"I'm not surprised," Xander said. "I know her type. They just go for the easy money. As soon as you let them know that you aren't going to be an easy mark, they'll back off."

"That seems to be the case," Fox said, "but I called about something else you might be able to help me with."

"Always ready to help whenever I can," Xander said. "What is it you need?"

"I've got a woman who has me over a barrel and things are not going to go well for me if I can't get this thing under control pretty soon."

"Yeah, I've run into several cases like that. The man has an affair with a woman from the office and then she threatens to tell his wife about it."

"No, no! It's nothing like that!" Fox said. "I haven't had an affair."

"Then it's something else," Xander said. "It's all about the same."

"Yeah, it's something else," Fox said, "but I can't tell you what it is."

"That's fine," Xander said. "It's probably best that I don't know. So, who is this woman and how can I take care of it for you?"

"Her name is Celia Abrams."

"I know Celia," Xander said. "I've done some work for her before."

"Is that going to be a problem? I need you to find anything you can that she doesn't want people to know."

"No problem at all," Xander said. "We do what we can for the people who pay the bills. But it might be good if we don't mention this to Celia."

"I have no intention of saying a word about you to Celia."

"That'll make life easier for me," Xander said. "I don't like offending my best customers."

"If this puts you in an uncomfortable position, I should be able to find someone else," Fox said, though he hoped Xander wouldn't take him up on the offer. "I can find someone down here, but you were so helpful last time."

"Oh, no," Xander said. "It won't be a problem at all. I can get a team to work down there right away, if need be, but the way we do things these days, we may be able to find what you need without leaving the office."

"Whatever it takes," Fox said. "I just want it done."

"We'll get it done," Xander said. "But so we're clear on this, do you want us to continue looking for stuff on Amber while we're doing this or can I use some of the resources I had working that to work on this?"

"As far as I'm concerned, this is top priority," Fox said. "I want whatever resources you have focused 100% on this. We'll go back to Amber if we have to, but right now, this is the most important thing."

"Do you want a report on what we've found on Amber?" Xander asked. "Shall we call it the tentative final report?"

"Is there anything you can tell me that's new from last time?" Fox asked.

"Let me see," Xander said.

Fox could hear the click of a mouse and the keys of a keyboard. Several seconds later, Xander came back on the line.

"It says here that we've interviewed several people who know her," Xander said. "The people she's been around most recently speak highly of her. We talked to her pastor and some of the people she goes to church with. We tried to talk to her previous employer, but his attorney won't let him talk to us. We found some people who say they gave her money. There might be something there, if we push it some, but all the ones we found say that they gave it to her because she needed it. We haven't found anyone who said they gave her money and didn't get what she promised. Those are the kind of people we need to find because they're the ones that think she owes them something. These others are just a big waste of time. So, let me know later if you want us to keep looking."

"I'll let you know," Fox said, not wanting to distract Xander from Celia at all. "Should I be concerned that you might have the same problem with Celia? Are you going to find anything other than people who think she's alright?"

"No, I wouldn't be concerned at all," Xander said. "I can't promise what I'll find, but Celia's different from Amber. Celia's the type of person who does things for what it will gain her."

"And Amber isn't?"

"Somewhat, I'm sure," Xander said. "But you've got to appreciate the artistry of what she does."

At this point, Fox began to wonder if Xander had lost it.

"Amber is a true scam artist. She can scam someone and when she's done they don't even know they've been scammed. And that makes me really scared for you. I'm not sure what Amber was trying, but if we don't keep an eye on her, she'll find a way back in and you'll be handing over the keys to the house and the car and everything else."

"Then you don't think we've scared her away."

"No, I'm sure we have, but I wouldn't count on it being for good."

Fox had to weigh the possibility that Xander was right and that Xander was just looking for a reason for Fox to keep paying him money. "I'll keep that in mind. For now, let's just focus on Celia."

In the days that followed, Fox could do little but wait for someone to come up with some answers. Xander was off doing his thing and Alex said he was still looking, but looking was all it was. For all Fox knew, the result of all the looking would be that they would discover there was nothing they could do.

He went to work more, but that was just so he wouldn't sit at home thinking about how bad things were. The problem with being at work was that Grayson expected him to show up at meetings. Grayson had run things fine without him before, but now he all but grabbed him by the arm and dragged him from meeting to meeting.

The thing Fox hated about the meetings was that they were like death knells. In one such meeting, Fox sat at the head of the long table beside Grayson as one of the managers was presenting a chart.

"Our analysis," the manager said, "shows that next year, as a result of the merger, our department is going to need $20 million more than we have budgeted for this year."

Grayson wrote something in his notebook. Without looking up he said, "Yeah, that's not going to happen. We're all going to have to make some tough decisions for next year. We're not going to be able to fund the projects even at the level we funded them this year."

"You know that we're talking about layoffs, if we do that," the manager giving the presentation said. The others were nodding in agreement.

"Yeah, I know," Grayson said.

"Even above the duplicated positions," the manager said. "You can't expect us to absorb all the stuff we're picking up from Jack Abrams and do it on a lower budget."

"I hear you," Grayson said, "But the money just isn't there."

"What about the money that Jack Abrams has? Won't the merger bring in money that we can budget for the new stuff?"

"It's not going to work out that way," Grayson said.

"Then why are we going through with the merger?" the manager asked. "If..."

Grayson interrupted him. "We're not. I want y'all to go back and refigure everything assuming that the merger won't take place. Tomorrow, I want us to meet again and we'll try this again."

"No," Fox said, "That's not what we're going to do. I don't want to see any charts that even hint at the possibility that the merger won't happen."

"But Dad..."

"Don't 'but Dad' me," Fox said. "Am I still the majority owner of this company or not?"

Grayson assured him that he was. In a different setting, Grayson might have pointed out that he wasn't far behind. Here, that good-natured joshing seemed out of place.

"Then we're not sending them back to make charts without the merger taken into account."

"Fine," Grayson said, "But if we go through with the merger, the numbers they've been working with will be incorrect."

"So, let's wait until we get the correct numbers." Fox knew they already had the correct numbers and if he got his way, they wouldn't be going through with the merger, but the last thing he needed was for Celia to see a chart that showed they weren't going through with it.

After the meeting, Grayson followed Fox back to his office. Fox had known better than to hope he wouldn't. Behind the closed door, Grayson was less respectful.

"What are you thinking?" he asked. "We're spending thousands of dollars trying to hammer out the budget for next year and you won't let me send those guys off to do it right. We both know that we can't afford to go through with that merger. Why don't we put an end to it now and be done with it?"

"We can't do that," Fox said. "You're the one who said we needed Jack Abrams' developers."

"And I still think that's a good idea," Grayson said, "but from a business standpoint the merger doesn't make sense anymore. Instead of a merger, maybe we can make an offer to buy those divisions. Even if we made the offer on the high side, we'd be better off than taking on all that debt."

"It's my decision," Fox said.

"It's a bad decision," Grayson said, "and it's devaluing the investment the rest of us have made in the company."

"Just what investment would that be?" Fox asked. "Your mother and I gave you kids the shares you have in the company."

"Yeah, but then I bought most of Steve's shares and part of Abby's. I've worked hard to get this company where it is. It's not just your company anymore."

Fox knew his son was right and would've liked to have told him as much, but he had no choice. It was going to divide the family one way or the other. If the family found out what he'd done, it would drive them all away. If he went through with the merger, it would drive Grayson away for sure and maybe some of the others.

"And once you've finished throwing your weight around, you're going to retire and leave me to clean up the mess," Grayson said. "The only thing is that this mess is too big to clean up."

"You have no idea," Fox said, but he refused to tell Grayson more.

As soon as Grayson left, Fox called Xander. "Please tell me you have something."

"Not just yet," Xander said, "But I've been thinking that we might be able to try something with Celia that's similar to what we did with Amber. I'll need to know more about the kind of trouble she's causing you."

"I'm not comfortable talking about that," Fox said.

"Just tell what you can," Xander said. "I may already know part of it. I imagine it has something to do with this merger. She wants you to go through with it and you want to pull out. Right?"

Fox confirmed Xander's statement.

"I just don't know what she's holding over you."

"It's something that I did that my family doesn't know I'm responsible for."

"The accident?" Xander asked.

"How did you know?" Fox asked.

"It's my job to know," Xander said, "But don't worry. I won't talk to your family. I'm more interested in how we can put a stop to Celia."

Fox did worry. One more person knowing was one more person who could tell the family. On the other hand, since Xander knew, he might be of even greater help.

"Tell me what you can do," Fox said.

"What I would suggest is to fix it so that Celia looks like she's lying," Xander said. "All we have to do is make it look like Celia paid witnesses to say that they saw what she wanted them to see. That way, it won't do her any good to say anything because it'll just look like she made it up. Why, you'll even look less likely to have done whatever she says you did."

It sounded like it would work. Fox had his reservations about what they might have to do to pull it off, but if Xander could do it, it would do the trick.

"So what do you say?" Xander asked. "Do you want me to try that or not?"

"Yeah, go for it," Fox said. "It's no worse than what she's trying to pull."

Chapter Thirty-Four

Thursday morning, not long after she'd gotten to work, Amber found herself trying to communicate with a man who knew very little English. Since she knew no Spanish, she was getting nowhere. She rarely had to speak to the landscaping crew, but she'd received more than a few complaints that the flowerbeds had weeds in them.

"I need you to pull the weeds," she said again, pointing to the flowerbed. The man looked where she pointed, but she got no sense that he intended to do what she said. She wondered if he understood, but didn't want to admit it.

She heard someone speaking in Spanish behind her and turned to see Grayson and Lizi there. Grayson continued to speak to the man. When he stopped, the man was on his knees pulling weeds from the flowerbed.

"He says they'll get it done today and if not, they'll finish it tomorrow," Grayson said.

"Thanks. I was beginning to wonder if he just didn't want to do it."

"No, he was just having trouble understanding you, but it's all good now. Is there anything else you need me to tell him?"

"No," Amber said. "What are you guys doing here?"

"I tried calling," Grayson said. "You need a cell phone. I called the church, but I guess I called before anyone was here or something, so I thought I'd swing by."

"I can't afford one," Amber said.

"Then I'll get you one," Grayson said.

"I'd rather you didn't," Amber said. "What is it you wanted?"

"Can I leave Lizi with you today?"

"Of course," Amber said.

"I've got a meeting this afternoon at another company and I don't figure they'll let me bring her along."

"Not that I'm complaining, but why me and not your parents instead?"

"You make it sound like you wouldn't be my first choice," Grayson said.

"I know you've left her with your parents before."

"Only when they asked," Grayson said. "But the thing is my Dad and I aren't getting along well right now."

"That seems to be going around."

"Maybe so," Grayson said. "At least with you, you understand why Dad doesn't like you. With the stuff going on with me, I think he's gone totally nuts."

"Is it something you want to talk about?"

"Maybe some other time," Grayson said. "I've got to get back to the office so I can get ready for that meeting. But the other thing I was going to say is that Mom hasn't been well since the accident. I don't want her feeling like she has to keep up with Lizi when she isn't feeling well."

"Are you going to pick her up here after your meeting?"

"Yeah," Grayson said, "I don't expect it'll run late. I should be back here before you go home."

"We'll wait on you if you're late," Amber said. There wasn't much else she could say. If she left, that meant taking Lizi with her on the bus to get back to her apartment. By the time they got there, Grayson might have finished his meeting and he wouldn't know where they were. But Amber would enjoy the day with Lizi, even if it meant they stayed at church till midnight.

After Grayson left, Amber went about her tasks with Lizi tagging along behind. At times, Lizi was helpful.

"Grandpa doesn't like Celia," Lizi said.

"How do you know?" Amber asked.

"I heard them talking."

"About what?"

"I don't know," Lizi said, "But Grandpa wasn't very happy. I don't think he's ever happy."

Amber opened a closet door and pulled out a vacuum cleaner. "Maybe he just hasn't had a whole lot to be happy about lately."

"Grandma says it's because the other grandkids died."

"I'm sure she's right," Amber said. "Grief is a powerful thing. Lots of people go through depression after they lose someone. And kids aren't supposed to die before their parents."

"I think it's because he's running out of money."

"What makes you say that?" Amber asked. "He's not about to run out of money." She found an outlet and plugged in the vacuum cleaner. It came to life.

"He and Dad keep talking about it," Lizi said, yelling above the noise of the vacuum cleaner.

"I'm sure you just didn't understand," Amber said. "It's probably just business."

That wasn't good enough for Lizi. "Dad thinks Grandpa is ruining the company."

"Is that what he told you?" Amber ran the vacuum cleaner along the wall.

"I heard him talking to someone else."

"Did they know you were listening?"

Lizi shook her head.

Amber knew she should talk to her about eavesdropping, but she knew where she'd learned it. It wouldn't be easy to tell her not to follow her example. Grayson could tell her, if he ever caught her at it.

"Just because he said it doesn't mean he meant it," Amber said. "He may have just been frustrated."

"Then he's frustrated a lot."

Lizi was a kid and may have misunderstood, but kids often pick up on things that adults don't. It shouldn't have been any of Amber's concern but she wanted what was best for Lizi. If Grayson and Fox were having financial difficulties, that gave her reason to be concerned. She didn't think they would handle being without money very well.

She decided to ask Grayson about it on the way home that evening. It was well after seven when he showed up. With it being so late, he bought their supper. Lizi chose McDonalds. Amber waited until they were all seated at a booth before she broached the subject of his finances.

"Are you having financial difficulties?" She asked, believing it best to just come out and ask him.

Grayson sat there with a fry stuck halfway in his mouth. It took him a moment to decide to chew it before answering her. "No, are you asking because I brought you here? This was where Lizi wanted to go."

"Lizi says you've been talking to people about what Fox is doing. It sounds like you guys could be in some real trouble." Amber didn't try to hide her source because she knew he would guess. "I wouldn't ask, but I'm concerned for Lizi."

"I know you are," Grayson said. "But don't be. Whatever happens, I'll make sure she's taken care of. Even if we lose the company, I can get a job somewhere. It might not pay as much as I'm making now, but she'll have a roof over her head and she won't starve."

"Then you could be losing the company?"

"That is one possibility," Grayson said, "but I don't think that will happen. God will work it out."

"So, you're going to sit back and wait for God to handle it?" Amber asked.

"I'm not going to just do nothing, if that's what you mean," Grayson said. "I'm just saying that in the end it's up to God, but I plan on doing everything I can."

"Is there anything I can do to help?"

Grayson was too polite to laugh. "No, I'm sure there's not—unless you have a couple hundred million dollars lying around to pay the IRS."

"You guy's owe that much in taxes? The IRS lets you by with that?" Amber looked at Grayson in disbelief.

"No," Grayson said, "We don't owe that much—at least not yet. And I don't know why the IRS would let someone by with that. I'm sure they'll do something eventually. That's why, if this merger goes through, we'll have to find the money to pay it down. To tell you the truth, I'm not sure if the government will let us go through with the merger until the taxes are paid."

"Can you do that?" Amber asked. She pictured Grayson going to the bank and withdrawing a bunch of money and taking it down to the IRS.

"No," Grayson said. "Even if we were to sell off every asset Jack Abrams has, we would come up short and that doesn't cover what they owe on their other debts."

"Then why go through with the merger?"

"That's the question we've all been asking," Grayson said. "Everyone except for Dad. He's got it in his head that we have to go through with this thing."

"There's nothing you can do?"

"Nothing but ride it out and hope for the best."

Chapter Thirty-Five

"Tell me you've got good news," Fox said into the phone. He'd called Xander again, but Xander was not one to be rushed.

"We're getting there," Xander said. "This isn't the kind of job you can do in an hour or two. We have to talk to all the witnesses and we've got to convince them that Celia wants to pay them to say what she wants them to say. I'm sure you realize the value of doing this job right."

"Yeah, yeah," Fox said. "I get all that. The problem is that we're getting closer and closer to signing the paperwork and I haven't seen any evidence that you've been doing anything that will help me."

"We've been doing lots of stuff," Xander said. "Would it help if I told you about some of what we've been doing?"

"That might be a good idea," Fox said. He wondered if any of Xander's other clients let him by without some kind of status report.

"Let me bring up the file and refresh my memory," Xander said. Only the clack of the keys came across the phone line for several seconds. "Here we go. There's a woman who was in the lane to the right of the cement mixer. She didn't see what happened on the other side, but she saw the same car that some of the other witnesses thought caused the accident. She says she doesn't think the driver did more than get his tires on the line between the lanes. She doesn't think that was enough to cause the guy in the cement mixer to swerve like he did."

"I know what she saw," Fox said. "I've gone over and over the report. How is that going to help me?"

"Well, what we did is ask her if someone had paid her to say that the driver had stayed in his lane."

"And she told you that no one had," Fox said. "She said the same thing about the accident last year. No one had to pay her to say the guy stayed in his lane."

"But that's just to plant a seed," Xander said. "In a few days, she's going to receive a letter from Celia offering her some money to say that the driver's wheels hadn't even touched the line."

"So you're going to make it look even more like I was at fault," Fox said.

"No, not at all," Xander said. "Her original statement is in the police report. That won't change, but if Celia tries something and we ask this woman if someone paid her to change her statement, she'll say she got a letter from Celia. It doesn't matter if she accepts the payment or not."

"You're sure that this will work?"

"Yes," Xander said. "You agreed to go through with this."

"I know, but I'm getting nervous. It's taking longer than I thought it would."

"These things take time," Xander said.

"Yeah, but you're making me nervous by saying people are going to get letters in a few days. Why haven't they already gotten them?"

"They may have," Xander said. "They've already been mailed. It's just hard to know how long it'll take the postal service to deliver stuff. You wouldn't want to accuse Celia of paying people to lie without knowing they've gotten those letters."

"How long do we have to wait? Is it safe to assume that they'll have gotten these letters a couple of days after you sent them?"

"We could do that," Xander said, "But I prefer confirmation. We'll talk to these people again and see how many of them remember getting the letter. I'll call you after that. Then you can be sure that they'll say Celia tried to pay them."

Waiting was the hardest part for Fox. Even with Grayson being against the merger, his relationship with Celia didn't look like it had changed. He couldn't risk asking Celia what she'd done to keep him interested and with their relationship on such shaky ground, he couldn't talk to Grayson either. It was the worst of all situations. Not only were they facing financial ruin, but Celia was on her way to becoming a member of the family.

One morning, Celia showed up at the office while Grayson was away. She walked in and handed Fox a folder. "I've got some new figures for you. We're not fleecing you as bad as you think we are."

Fox opened the folder and looked at the papers. It was a bunch of numbers. "We'll have to look these over carefully."

"I know," Celia said, "but I can summarize. Some of the property values are higher than what your people came up with."

"How do I know I can trust these figures?"

"You don't," Celia said. "I wouldn't, but they're accurate."

"Have you shown this to Grayson?" Fox asked.

"Not yet. This whole thing's a touchy subject with him."

"You expected otherwise?" Fox closed the folder and laid it aside.

"No," Celia said, "I'm just saying that he and I don't talk about the merger."

"He's not blind, you know. He can see your dad's company isn't worth anything." As he spoke, Fox doubted his own words. It didn't make sense that Grayson would still be with

Celia. Maybe he was blind with love. Maybe he thought Jack Abrams wasn't smart enough to realize how bad off his company was.

"He doesn't know what you know," Celia said. "Besides, it'll all work out."

"No, it won't," Fox said. "I'm not letting you ruin this company, just so you can bail your dad out."

"Oh, you make it sound like I'm a terrible person. What I'm doing isn't as bad as what you did. At least, I haven't killed anyone."

Celia's words stung, as she had meant for them to. As she spoke, Fox could see the faces of his grandchildren peering out from the picture frame on his desk. They all looked like they were happy and smiling, much like they'd been the day of the accident. Why hadn't he thought about what might happen to them? Why hadn't he stopped?

But the sting of her words lasted only a short time because he had a plan and it had already begun. "You won't be able to hurt me."

"It isn't by choice," Celia said. "If you hadn't driven me to it..."

"You still aren't going to hurt me," Fox said. "You can tell my wife. You can tell my family. You can tell anyone you think would care what happened the day of the accident and they won't believe you."

Celia looked at him for some time before saying, "You think I'm bluffing."

"No," Fox said, "I don't think you're bluffing. I just don't care if you're bluffing. No one will believe you."

She took in his words. "It sounds like you're up to something. You think you can beat me at this game. I'm sure you're right. I'm not very good at this. So, what do you think? Should we just forget the whole thing?"

"Just like that, you're going to back down?"

"No," Celia said, "of course not. If this is a game, then what's the point of quitting before all the cards are turned over? You can't think I'll back down just because you say you don't care. You could be bluffing too."

"Suit yourself," Fox said. "Believe me or don't. Tell my family or don't. It'll all amount to the same thing. They aren't going to believe you."

He thought he saw fear in Celia's eyes. It was fleeting, but it was there. It wasn't over yet. She would try something else. She would test his defenses to see how well they would stand, but he was confident that when that time came he would be ready for her. He was beginning to look forward to it. She could try, but she would have no power over him and he would prove it once and for all. She would be gone—she and her father and her father's company.

Celia stood up. "I'm going to give you plenty of time to think about this. It doesn't do me any good if I have to tell your family what you did, but don't think I won't do it. If you're so sure they won't believe me, why don't you go tell them yourself?"

That was one thing that Fox wouldn't and couldn't do. Whatever everyone else thought had happened on that terrible day, he needed his family to believe that it hadn't been his fault, that he hadn't knowingly made a stupid mistake that had cost his grandchildren and his son-in-law their lives. If he told them, they would have no choice but to believe him. It would cost him everything.

"I don't need to tell them," Fox said, "but you're going to have to or you'll just prove that you were bluffing the whole time. I hope you do tell them. When you tell them, I'm going to be right there to show them why you can't be believed. There won't be a merger and you can be sure that Grayson won't want anything to do with you after that."

"You sound confident," Celia said. "I'll give you that much, but there's one thing you're forgetting."

"What's that?" Fox asked.

"I've got the truth on my side. You may be right that they won't believe what I say over what you say, but if they start looking, the truth is there. What happens then? The truth may not be very important to you, but I know it's important to Grayson. He'll look into this. I'm surprise he hasn't already. When he finds out that you've been lying to him…"

"You're one to talk," Fox said. "You've done nothing but lie to us since we started talking about a merger."

"That isn't true," Celia said. "That folder on your desk is truthful. And you came to us. Maybe we made some of the figures look a little more favorable, but we haven't gone to a lot of trouble to hide information from you. Maybe you ought to think about that. Information can mean different things just by the way it's presented. Are you sure you want to risk me presenting certain pieces of information to your family?"

With that, Celia left. It hadn't been the best of encounters, but Fox knew it had been a victory for him, no matter how small it might have been.

Chapter Thirty-Six

If she hadn't seen the car when it pulled into the church parking lot, it might not have been so obvious. While cleaning the glass on one of the side doors, Amber noticed an old car pull into the parking lot. As it went past, she'd noticed that the driver had dark hair, was clean shaven and wore a white shirt. She recognized neither car nor driver. That didn't bother her because there were often people pulling into the parking lot that she didn't know. Some had business at the church and others were looking for a place to park for a few minutes or just a place to turn around. So she didn't think much about it when it parked in the shade of a tree. She went on wiping the glass.

But she took notice when the driver's door opened and a man with a bushy head of red hair and a beard got out. He wore a tie and a tweed jacket. His black shoes stood out against his brown pants and white socks. His Coke bottle glasses were as thick as any she'd ever seen, but she was sure the man hadn't been wearing glasses before.

He closed the car door. He used the key to lock the door and walked to the back of the car. There he made a sharp left turn and walked a straight line at the end of the yellow lines that marked the concrete until he was directly in front of the front entrance to the building. He made a sharp right turn and walked straight across the parking lot. When he got to the curb, he didn't step up on the walkway, but he followed the curb until he reached the wheelchair cutout. Instead of climbing the steps, as most people would do, he walked up the wheelchair ramp, first one way and then the other.

Leaving her cleaning supplies at the side door, Amber hastily walked along the hall until she came to the front entrance. The man had his hands between his face and the glass as he looked at what was inside. His eyebrows looked like two red caterpillars sitting on the rim of his glasses. Amber pushed the other side of the double door open.

"Oh, hi!" the man said. "I was beginning to wonder if anyone was here. I'm Dr. Brad Edwards, professor of psychology."

"I'm pleased to meet you, Dr. Edwards. Is there…"

"No, it's Dr. Brad Edwards," the man under the red mop said. "My father is Dr. Anthony Edwards and my brother is Dr. Jackson Edwards. Call me Dr. Brad Edwards so you won't get us confused."

"I don't think there's any risk of that," Amber said. She tried to focus on the features of this man's face. If this man was trying to play a trick on someone, she hoped it wasn't her; she didn't know who he was. "What can we do for you, Dr. Brad Edwards?"

Dr. Brad Edwards stepped through the door and it closed behind him. "I need to speak to a Miss Amber Mills."

The mention of her own name made Amber wonder even more why this man would show up in disguise. Whoever this man was, he wasn't a professor of psychology. That meant he was looking for information. He had to be someone Fox had hired.

"Why do you need to see her?"

"It's important that that remain between me and her."

"She's around here somewhere," Amber said. "Is she expecting you?"

"No," Dr. Brad Edwards said, "I didn't tell her I was coming."

Amber was looking for some kind of slipup that would tell her whether this guy knew who she was or not. He played ignorant very well.

"I'm Amber Mills," she said. The man showed no sign that he was surprised to hear that. "What can I do for you?"

"You came up in a study I'm doing," Dr. Brad Edwards said. "If you don't mind, I'd like to ask you some questions."

"What kind of study?" Amber asked.

"If I told you that, it might taint the results. I promise I won't make you answer any questions you don't want to."

"That'll be okay—I guess." Amber knew he wouldn't have told her the truth anyway. By letting him ask questions, she might discover what he really wanted to know.

"It's my understanding that you've spent some time in the home of Fox Jacobs."

"That's correct," Amber said.

"Yes, I know it is," Dr. Brad Edwards said. "That was just my way of being polite when I mentioned that I know what has been going on in your life over the past several weeks."

"I see."

"During that time, you also spent some time with Celia Abrams."

"If you could call it that," Amber said. "I encountered her a few times."

"That's good enough for our purposes. During those encounters, what was your impression of her?"

"What kind of impression are you looking for? Do you want me to say that she dresses well? Do you want me to say that she's well spoken?"

"What's your impression of her as a person? Is she someone you would trust? Do you think she would make a good friend? How do you think she would respond if you made her mad?"

"I don't see us ever becoming great friends," Amber said. "As for what she would do if she was mad, I'm not sure, but I suspect she would try to get even."

"What about Fox? How would he respond?"

"He wouldn't let it slide either, but he would take longer coming to a decision on what to do."

"What if he paid someone to do something and that someone decided that it might be better if he didn't give him what he wanted."

Amber got the impression that this man was talking about himself.

"I'm sure he would fire whoever it was. He'd hire someone to look into it and he'd eventually get the lawyers involved. Are you thinking about not doing something Fox wanted you to do?"

"No," Dr. Brad Edwards said. "But as I said before, I can't answer your questions about the study.

The man's beard looked lopsided. And one eyebrow was twisted in a funny sort of way—so much so that Amber had the urge to reach up and stick it back on for the man.

"You're a private investigator, aren't you? Fox hired you to investigate me."

"I'm Dr. Brad Edwards and I'm a professor of psychology. No one hired me."

Amber reached up and pulled the man's wig from his head. She waved it in front of his face.

"Well, if you're going to be that way…" The man pulled off the two pieces of fuzz above his eyes. He gingerly removed the beard. He shoved it all into his coat pocket. He removed the tweed coat and his tie. Just when Amber thought he was done, he pulled out a contact lens case. He took off his glasses and put his contacts in the case. Once he'd put those in the coat, all that was left was the man Amber had seen pull into the parking lot.

"Let me introduce myself," the man said. "I'm Xander X. I've got a card here somewhere." He pulled out a couple of business cards and handed them to Amber.

The card said, "Xander X Investigations" at the top. It gave his name and contact information.

"If you know anyone who needs an investigator, be sure to give them my card."

"What's with the disguise?" Amber asked. "And why are you really here?"

"I need some advice," Xander said. "I knew you wouldn't help me if I told you who I was, so I decided to let one of my associates ask you."

"You call your wig an associate?"

"When you put it that way, it doesn't sound as nice," Xander said. "I like to think of Dr. Brad Edwards as one of my associates."

"Just how many associates do you have?"

"I'm not sure. I've lost count. I don't use all of them as much as others. I use Dr. Brad Edwards quite a bit. You'd be surprised how many people will talk to you if they think you're doing a scientific study."

"No, I probably wouldn't," Amber said. "But next time, you might want to look in a mirror before you bring your associate out."

"I'll keep that in mind," Xander said. "And I can see why you wouldn't be surprised."

"What's that supposed to mean?"

"I did my research. I even know what your handwriting looks like."

"So, you're the one who forged that note."

"Yeah, that was me," Xander said. "I thought it was pretty good."

"Yeah, but you made a mistake. I would've never written a note like that."

"Really? Now see? That's why I wanted to come to you for advice. You're better at this stuff than I am," Xander said, but he couldn't resist a moment of gloating. "Although, it got you out of Fox's house, didn't it?"

"Yes, it did," Amber said. She wasn't about to explain why.

"I've got this problem," Xander said. "If you don't want to help me, that's fine, but at least hear me out."

"I'm listening."

"Fox hired me to do some work for him."

"To investigate me," Amber said.

"Yeah, he did that too, but that's not what I'm doing right now. He hired me to help him with a problem he's having with Celia Abrams. See, she has this information about an accident he was in several months ago and he doesn't want it let out."

"Where did she get the information?"

"She got it from me, but that's not the point."

"Did you forge this stuff or is it real?"

"Some of it might not be completely real," Xander said. "But it would've been if people had taken better pictures. I just don't understand people using cell phones to take pictures all the time. They always turn out so crummy. People need to learn to carry a good camera with them, just in case they see a wreck."

"Yeah, there should be a law," Amber said.

"So here's the thing," Xander said. "Celia hired me to help her and then Fox hired me to help him get rid of the problem that I helped her create."

"That's sounds like a conflict of interest," Amber said.

"It wouldn't have been," Xander said, "But I always fail to take into account how good I am at my job. I did such a good job for Celia that I didn't think anything could mess it up. Then Fox asked for help and I've done such a good job that I don't think Celia's going to be able to use the stuff I did for her. All I have to do is give Fox a report on what I did. He'll be able to use it to put a stop to Celia. I'm just not sure whether I should give the report to Fox or not."

"That sounds like a question of ethics. Why are you asking me?" Amber asked.

"No, I'm not asking about the ethics of it," Xander said. "But I've noticed that you always escape unscathed when you scam someone. I figured you would be the perfect person to ask what I should do if I don't want to either of them to come after me."

"It's a little late to ask that," Amber said. "You should've thought this through before you decided to take the job."

"That's easy for you to say. I've got to work for whoever it is that's paying the bills."

"Who is that?" Amber asked.

"Right now?" Xander asked. "Right now, it is Fox."

"Then shouldn't you be working for Fox?"

"Yeah, but I don't want Celia coming after me. What would you do?"

"I would've stayed out of this mess," Amber said.

"I'm sure you would've, but what if you hadn't? You've got to have some idea of what you would do."

Xander looked so pitiful that Amber felt like she had to give him an answer. She wasn't sure that it would do him any good, but she had to think of something. At least she had the experience to draw on.

"Well, you've got to give Fox what he's paying you for," she said. "If you don't, it'll just make him mad and things won't go well. And then you've got to make Celia think that what you did works out well for her."

Xander looked at her like she'd lost her mind. "You're just telling me that so I'll go away, aren't you."

She assured him she wasn't.

"Then how do I do that? I'm trying to work both sides of this thing."

"I don't know. Maybe you can't. You asked me what I would do and I told you." It was against Amber's better judgment to have told him as much as she had.

"But just like that, you want me to make her think that one of the worst things is something good."

"If you can," Amber said. "If you can't, then I'd say give Fox the information and run. You don't want Celia finding out that you were the one helping him."

"I could do that," Xander said. "I'll give him the information and be out of here before she knows I was involved. Or I might just give him the information and tell Celia what I did. Would that work?"

"It might," Amber said. "As long as Fox doesn't find out you told her."

Chapter Thirty-Seven

The parking lot was full at the Shell station when Fox pulled off the road, but no one was pumping gas from any of the four pumps. He was still close enough to 820 to hear the constant roar of the traffic and yet the station seemed like it was off the beaten path. He'd driven past this place many times when he crossed Lake Worth, but he'd never gotten off the freeway to see what was over here.

He found one parking space in back near a tree. It was tight enough that he couldn't open his door all the way. He could just imagine someone coming back to their car and putting a big dent in his. He locked the doors and walked to the entrance to the small building.

The first thing he noticed when he got inside was the people. They were largely a mass of people, but they'd formed something resembling a line and were giving their orders to a woman with a pad. She was tearing off these orders and passing them to another woman who was sweating over the grill in back.

Away from the activity at the counter, the building had dark wooden tables and a hodgepodge of chairs. Shelves and cases with snack food and sodas, as well as other things you might find at most gas stations lined the walls. All of the tables were taken. Fox scanned the room looking for the man he was to meet, though he didn't know what he looked like.

Fox's eye fell on a man sitting at a table by himself. The man beckoned for Fox to come over. Fox wove through the people waiting for their food and sat down across from the man.

Xander pushed a red basket with a hamburger and fries in it across the table. "I went ahead and ordered for you. I knew you wouldn't want to wait for your food."

Fox looked at the burger. It was much bigger than he needed. "When you said you wanted to meet here, I wasn't expecting so many people."

"I wasn't either," Xander said. "But what can you expect? I'm not from around here. How was I supposed to know that a place like this would be so busy?"

Fox picked up the burger and bit into it. It was thick and juicy, loaded with grease.

"Well, the food's good anyway," Xander said.

Fox would've preferred less grease, but he couldn't complain about the taste. "Did you bring it?"

"Of course I did." Xander pulled a folder from under the table and laid it next to Fox.

Fox pulled a napkin from the dispenser and wiped his hands. He pulled out another to get the grease off. He used a third napkin. He could still feel the grease on his hands when he opened the folder, but he didn't see any grease spots.

The paper on top was a list of names. Fox recognized most of the names as the people who'd witnessed the accident.

"That's all the people we talked to," Xander said. "And if you flip that page over, what you have next are all the reports on what we said to each. If we sent them an offer from Celia, it says so at the bottom of the page. If they accepted, that is marked down there too."

"How many accepted the offer," Fox asked. "How much money did you spend on that?"

"No much," Xander said. "The figures are in there. I think it was something like $1,000 or maybe $1,500. It was all in cash, of course."

Fox flipped through the pages. Each had a report on a different person.

"Just so we're clear here," Fox said, "how do you see me using this information? Do I wait until Celia tries something?" He hoped that wasn't the case. What he really wanted was for Celia to say nothing at all.

"I wouldn't," Xander said. "If you want, you can show it to her anytime. If I were her, I would back off."

"Let's hope she's like you," Fox said.

"Now there's the matter of my money," Xander said. "I'd like to get paid before I head home and I'm planning on leaving right after this."

"Is the bill in here?" Fox flipped through the last few pages of the folder, but there was no bill.

"Here it is." Xander passed Fox another sheet of paper.

This sheet had a list of dollar figures next to expense items. Most of it was typed, but Xander had used an ink pen to change the figures at the bottom. He had added the cost of the burgers.

"Can I write you a check?"

"If you must," Xander said, "But I prefer cash."

The way he said it made Fox think he would avoid taxes, if he could. "That's the best I can do. I don't carry that much cash with me."

"Then a check will have to do," Xander said.

Fox pulled out his checkbook. As he made out the check, he felt liberated. That feeling was well worth every penny that he had spent to get this done. The check would make Xander a very happy man, but what was in the folder was even better.

Fox could hardly wait for his opportunity to show Celia that he'd won this fight.

But Xander seemed as eager to get moving as Fox. As soon as Xander had the check in hand, he explained that he needed to get on the road soon. He stood up and left Fox sitting there with his food and his folder full of stuff. Xander was finished and as Fox later discovered, if Fox had tried to call him, Xander wasn't answering his calls. But that was okay because Fox had everything he needed to see an end to the problems Celia and Jack Abrams had caused.

Chapter Thirty-Eight

She could've done it right after she'd met Xander, but she had so much work that had to be done before Sunday and she was ready to have Saturday off. So, after Amber finished her work, she went into the office and dialed Grayson's number. A woman—not Celia—picked up the phone.

"Grayson went home," the woman told her.

She had to switch buses, but she made her way downtown and found herself standing at the door of Grayson's condo. She knocked on the door, hoping that Lizi would be the one to let her in. But no one answered. She knocked again. It was too early for them to be in bed.

After coming so far, she wasn't about to just leave. She sat down on the floor and leaned against the door. The work she had done that week must have taken its toll because the next thing she knew, Grayson was crouched beside her and was shaking her shoulder.

"Are you alright?" he asked.

It took a few seconds for the fog of her mind to clear.

"I'm alright," she said. "You weren't here, so I waited."

"How long have you been out here?"

"I don't know," she said. "I fell asleep."

"Yeah, we noticed," Grayson said. "Do you think you can stand up so I can open the door? Then, if you want to sleep, I'll offer you a couch to crash on."

"No, that's alright." Amber pushed herself up from the floor. Once she was standing up, she was rewarded with a hug from Lizi.

"We went to see you," Lizi said.

"You mean just now?"

"Funny, isn't it?" Grayson said as he pushed the door open. "I still say you need a cellphone."

"What did you need?" Amber asked. "Was it important?"

"Important enough," Grayson said, "but it'll wait until you're awake. Why did you come over here?"

"I had a strange visitor at church today," Amber said. "He's a private investigator your father hired."

"That doesn't surprise me," Grayson said. "Dad doesn't like having you around. You've got him scared."

"He shouldn't be," Amber said. "I don't want to hurt him." Just because she didn't like him didn't mean she would do anything against him.

"I know that," Grayson said, "but that's the way he is. Are you worried about what you told the guy you saw today?"

"No," Amber said, "that's not it. This guy isn't investigating me right now. The odd thing is that he wanted my advice. He's been working for your dad, but he's also done some work for Celia. He wanted to know how he could help your dad without getting Celia too upset."

"That seems like a funny thing to ask about," Grayson said.

"That's why I thought you should know. I'm not sure what's going on between your dad and Celia, but when it has a private investigator concerned, it might be something to worry about."

"Thanks for telling me," Grayson said.

Amber wondered if he was about to finish the thought by telling her to mind her own business.

"Something's been going on for a while now," Grayson said. "This merger with Jack Abrams has turned into something really scary. I'm ready to back out, but Dad won't even let me talk about that. Right now, Jack Abrams is so worthless that they should be paying us to take it. I'd be willing to bet anything that this private investigator has something to do with that. It wouldn't surprise me at all if Celia and Jack Abrams are doing something to force us into the merger. That would make some sense."

"But Celia's still your girlfriend," Amber said.

"In a manner of speaking," Grayson said. "That all started because it seemed like a good thing at the time, but I don't know her all that well."

"But you're still seeing her."

"What would you have me do?" Grayson asked. "Dump her when I'm not sure what's going on between her and Dad? If she's trying to pull something, I don't want to upset her any more than I just have to."

"You don't trust her, but you don't have a problem with her being around Lizi."

"I never said that," Grayson said. "I never leave Lizi alone with Celia. I've just been hoping that I'd figure things out before I set Celia off. If Dad would tell me something, I might have figured it out ages ago."

"I should've pushed Xander harder for information," Amber said. "Then I could've told you what was going on."

"No, what you did is fine. What I'd really like to see happen is for Dad to tell me what's going on."

Amber could agree with that.

"Well, since we talked about all that, let's talk about why Lizi and I went to see you."

"Okay."

"I've been doing some thinking. Lizi really needs a mother."

Celia's face flashed before Amber's mind, even though she just heard that she was out. She pushed that thought aside. "Who did you have in mind?"

"Let me rephrase that," Grayson said. "Lizi needs her mother. Don't get me wrong, I love that she's my daughter and she's a great kid, but this parenthood thing is—let's just say I wasn't ready for it."

"Her mother is dead," Amber said.

"Her mother is sitting right here in front of me," Grayson said. "You don't have to give me an answer right now, but I'd like you to consider it."

"Just what am I considering?"

"Marriage," Grayson said. "We can do the whole dating thing, if you like, but I'm too busy right now to play games. I think I could love you and Lizi thinks you should be interested in me, whether you are or not."

"You really know how to sweep a girl off her feet."

"Yeah, I was afraid of that," Grayson said. "It's just a little too weird, isn't it? Well, anyway, you know where I stand. If you're not interested, I guess that's understandable."

"Hold on," Amber said. "I haven't shot you down yet. You're springing a life changing event on me all the sudden and I'm not sure I'm thinking straight. I need time to think. Can you ask me again when I've had some time?"

"Sure," Grayson said. "I'll do that."

"You realize that you're doing what Fox was afraid you would do."

"Yeah, I know," Grayson said, "but I can't worry about that right now. I have to do what's best for my daughter and if I get a good Christian wife in the process, that is just that much better."

"I'm afraid you may be asking for more trouble with me," Amber said. "If you knew half the things I've done…"

"Well, I figure God knows all of what you've done and you're okay with him, and it's not like Lizi has more than one mother for me to choose from."

"I'm not really her mother," Amber said.

"You're the closest thing to one that she remembers," Grayson said. "You've done an excellent job of raising her so far. I'd like to see you finish the job."

"I'll have to have time to think about it," Amber said. "Like I said, you're springing this on me all the sudden. So ask me again in a few days."

"All I can ask is that you think about it."

She would think about it. It would be hard to get out of her mind, but she already knew how she would answer.

Chapter Thirty-Nine

Fox rolled out of bed even earlier than usual on Saturday morning. Fiona was still nestled beneath the sheets. If he didn't disturb her, she would stay there for some time. It was dark outside and everything was quiet. He shaved and dressed in the bathroom before going downstairs.

He willed the sun to rise. The sooner the sun came up, the closer he was to meeting with Celia. Ten o'clock was when she'd agreed to meet him at her office. He preferred to meet her there than at home or in his office at work. There wouldn't be many people working over the weekend, but the less chance of his family overhearing something the better.

Fox turned off the alarm and opened the front door. He crossed the drive and picked up the paper from the lawn, still wet from the sprinkler being on the night before. He pulled the paper out of the plastic sleeve and unfolded it. The headlines were nothing to take notice of. He carried it inside and dropped it on one of the small tables in the great room. He might read it later, when he didn't have so much on his mind.

He was never one for fidgeting, but on this morning he opened the folder, leafed through the pages, closed it and opened it again more times than he could count. It was after nine when he went back upstairs to tell Fiona he was heading out. She was still in bed, but her eyes were open and she was staring at the ceiling.

"You shouldn't be working so much," Fiona said. "It's time for you to retire."

"I'm trying to cut back," Fox said, not wanting to tell her that this wasn't work. That pleased her and he left her staring at the ceiling.

As far as he could tell, Celia was the only person in the office when he got there. She poured coffee into a white cup. "Would you like some?"

"No, I've had plenty," Fox said, ready to get this business over.

Carrying her coffee with her, she led him back to her office. She sat in the big chair and put the cup in front of her.

"We won't be going through with the merger," Fox said. "I wanted you to be the first to know."

With a plastic spoon, she stirred her coffee. She scooped it up and sipped from the spoon. "That's up to you, of course, but I've warned you what would happen if it doesn't go through."

"I didn't make this decision lightly," Fox said, "but under the circumstances, it's the only choice I have. Y'all owe too much for us to take on."

"You'll be talking to Dad too," Celia said.

"I have to," Fox said.

"And I'll be talking to your family," Celia said. "Are you sure you want to go through with this?"

"I'm looking forward to it," Fox said. "The sooner you tell them, the sooner I can get this behind me."

"You're awfully sure of yourself," Celia said. "I'm not sure you fully appreciate the information I've found. Do you need me to remind you?" She opened a drawer and pulled out a large envelope.

"I don't need to see it," Fox said. He'd already spent too much time looking at the copy Celia had given him. Thankfully, it had little meaning to anyone without Celia's explanation. "What I've got trumps what you've got." He patted the folder he held.

"Just what have you got?" Celia asked. "Are you going to show it to me?"

"Let's just say that if you talk to my family, I have a way to make sure that they don't believe you."

"If that's what you've got, then I can understand why you would want me to talk to your family."

"You're not the only one who can play this game."

Celia put the envelope away. "I guess that's that. What can I say? You got me. You understand that I had to try."

It couldn't be this easy. Nothing was this easy.

"I understand," Fox said.

"No hard feelings?" Celia asked.

He felt compelled to tell her that all was forgiven, when it wasn't. He'd never forgiven anyone who'd tried to rip him off and he wasn't about to start now.

"Can you give me a few days, so I can break it to Dad easily?" Celia asked.

A voice in Fox's head screamed at him to say no. Whatever she planned to do with that time, it was not to tell Jack that the deal was off. She was too unperturbed. Something was going on. She was planning something and it wasn't good.

"Sure," Fox said, "I'll give you a few days. How long do you need?"

Celia leaned back in her chair. "A week—no more than that. I need some time to think about how to break it to him. But a week should be plenty."

"Then I'll plan on announcing it to everyone a week from Monday," Fox said. "That should give you all the time you need."

He feared the truth of his words. It was more than enough time for her to tell her father, but what else could she accomplish during that time?

"Dad is going to be disappointed."

"I'm sure he'll get over it," Fox said.

"Sure he will," Celia said. "I just shouldn't have tried pulling something over on you. I knew you were smarter than me."

If her flattery was supposed to make him like her better, it wasn't working. He had the feeling that he was missing something important—something that he shouldn't have missed.

"I wouldn't say that," Fox said. "I was just lucky."

"You're much too modest. Who else would've thought to use the same private investigator that I used? Most people would've been afraid that he would tell me what he was doing for you. Especially with the scruples that Xander has, but not you. No, you went right ahead with it because you knew he was the right man for the job. And look what it got you. I've got to applaud you for that." Celia clapped her hands, the sound echoing off the walls of the room.

"I only did what I was forced to do," Fox said, Celia's mock praise made him all the more nervous.

"Of course you did," she said, "but a lesser man wouldn't have known what he needed to do. You knew exactly what needed to be done and you did it. Congratulations"

"I'm not looking for congratulations from you," Fox said.

"No, of course not," Celia said, "but who else is there to congratulate you? It was a well-played match, it's only fitting that I offer you my congratulations. Your friends and family can't do it because that would require you to tell them what happened the day of the accident."

"This isn't a sport," Fox said. "We're talking about my life here."

"Yeah, I know," Celia said. "And the lives of your grandchildren and your son-in-law and the guy in the cement mixer. Now people will never know who really killed them."

The familiar sickness in the pit of Fox's stomach returned. He faced their killer every day when he looked in the mirror.

He had to live with that, but it wasn't right for his family to live with it too.

"We should celebrate your victory," Celia said. "What do you want to do to celebrate?"

"No, we don't need to celebrate," Fox said.

"Spoilsport!" Celia said. She pulled the envelope from her desk again. "I know what we should do. You should shred the envelope as a way to celebrate. It'll be like a note burning. Don't some people do that when thy pay off a loan?"

"No, I'm not going to do it," Fox said. The longer he sat there, the angrier he became. Celia seemed to feed on his anger.

"Oh, come on," Celia said. "It'll be fun. I've got a shredder over here."

"No," Fox said. "I've told you what I came to tell you. Now, I'm leaving."

"If you must, you must," Celia said. "But I just can't get over how well you handled this situation. You really taught me a lesson."

As Fox left, he could only wonder what lesson she was about to teach him.

Chapter Forty

The bus lumbered toward her, the driver in no hurry get anywhere, as Amber waited at the bus stop on Sunday morning. A small sign on a metal post marked the bus stop. There was no covering or even a bench. Amber would've leaned against the post, but she was afraid she would get her dress dirty. It was early in the day, but the Texas sun beat down on her, making the bus a welcome sight.

A gray sedan swerved into the lane beside the bus. The driver accelerated to get past the bus and then swerved back to the right before hitting the brakes and coming to a stop right next to Amber.

She heard the whine of the motor as the passenger side glass descended into the door. She looked through the window to see who was inside.

"Need a ride?" Grayson leaned across the seat so that he could see her. Lizi was in the back seat.

Amber looked at the bus, still making its way to the bus stop. She put her hand on the handle and opened the door. She sunk into the plush seat and closed the door. "I'm not sure I want one. I saw the way you came around that bus."

"I didn't want him grabbing my passenger," Grayson said. "I thought we had plenty of time, but I got through the light and saw you already at the bus stop."

"It takes longer on the bus," Amber said, fastening her seat-belt.

"Yeah, I know." Grayson pushed on the accelerator. "That's why we came to pick you up, but I didn't know you left this early."

He said nothing of his previous proposal, though Amber wished he would. They could get it out of the way. She worried he'd thought about it and changed his mind. It was under-standable if he did.

"I talked to Dad yesterday," Grayson said. "It looks like the merger with Jack Abrams is on hold."

Fox and the merger were the last things that Amber wanted to talk about. Anything to do with Fox just made her mad, but she could understand that Grayson was more concerned about his father and the company than he was with the possible fu-ture with her. It served her right for thinking otherwise. Why hadn't she just told him she would marry him when he'd asked? Then he would have to tell her that he'd changed his mind instead of just avoiding the subject.

"You must be happy about that," Amber said. "I know you were nervous about it."

"To say the least," Grayson said. "But I'm still nervous about it. For some reason, he doesn't want to come right out and say that it's off, but he doesn't want anyone working on it either. I'm afraid he's going to decide later that he really does want the merger."

"Have you talked to him about it?"

"I've tried to," Grayson said. "But he won't talk about it."

"Do you think it has anything to do with what was going on with Celia?"

"I'm sure it might," Grayson said, "But he wouldn't tell me anything. I asked him why the sudden change of heart and he just said to make sure no one was working on the merger."

"Did that surprise everyone when you told them?"

"I didn't have to tell anyone," Grayson said. "There was already an understanding that they weren't supposed to be working on it. I should probably tell them that it's okay to tell Dad that they aren't working on the merger now."

"What happens if your dad finds out you were going behind his back on that?"

"It won't be pretty," Grayson said. "But at least the end result was something that Dad wants now. It wouldn't be the first time I did something behind his back. Here lately, he's been so out of everything that I do what I have to do."

"Why has he been out of it?" Amber asked. "Is he just getting too old to run the business?"

"Dad, too old?" Grayson laughed. "No, he's not too old. He's still as sharp as a tack and there's a lot I could learn from him. No, he's not too old."

Grayson flipped the signal light on and pulled over into the left turn lane behind two other cars at the light. For the longest time, the only sound was the click of the signal light. The light turned green and he followed the cars onto the intersecting street.

He passed them both in the far left lane before signaling and bringing the car back to the center. They'd gone several blocks and reached the next light before Grayson spoke again.

"He's just never been himself since the accident," Grayson said. "I think he blames himself, but I can't get him to talk about it. After it happened, he just stopped going in to work. He said it was because he was worried about Mom. I'm sure she needed someone to look after her, but I think there was more to it than that."

"What happened," Amber asked. "Or is that none of my business?"

"With what?"

"The accident," Amber said. "One of your employees told me that it happened on the traffic circle and she thought I might know more about it than she did. Is the traffic circle dangerous?"

"Not particularly," Grayson said. "At least, I don't think so. Every once in a while you'll see someone that's had a wreck there, but there's a lot of traffic that goes through there. Stuff happens. Someone will be in the wrong lane and swing out across traffic because they don't want to miss their turn. Someone will get impatient and decide to go instead of waiting for the traffic to clear. If other people don't react in time, stuff happens. I doubt it's less safe than one of these intersections with people running red lights. There one goes now!" Grayson pointed at a car that was still in the intersection as the lights turned green.

"Then what happened with Fox?"

"It was just one of those things," Grayson said. "A cement mixer flipped over and crushed the car. The way it landed, there wasn't any chance at all for the kids or Dave, but somehow, Dad walked away from it. He had some bruises and a few scratches, but considering what happened, he wasn't hurt. Even the guy in the cement mixer died, but Dad walked away. I think that must be really hard on him."

"You say he blames himself; was it really his fault?"

Grayson looked in the rearview mirror. Amber could tell he was looking for Lizi in the back seat.

"Perhaps, now isn't the best time to talk about this," Grayson said. "Sometimes, family is more important."

"I shouldn't have pushed you for an answer," Amber said. But she didn't need to push further. Grayson had answered her question by not answering it. She knew that was what he intended and she wouldn't bring it up again.

"There's no harm in asking," Grayson said, "as long as you understand that I may not always give you an answer right away."

"I get that," Amber said.

"There's something you need to understand about Dad," Grayson said, making Amber wonder if he was changing the subject or talking about the same thing. "There's nothing more important to him than his family. Not business, not church— nothing. Whatever demons he's facing right now, he'll do anything to keep them from hurting his family."

"And I came in and stepped right in the middle of that," Amber said.

"In a word, yes," Grayson said.

"What about you?" Amber asked. "What are your priorities? Do you put your family first too?"

"What is this? Ask Grayson Questions He Can't Answer Day?"

"I wasn't trying to ask a hard question."

"Yeah, I know," Grayson said, "but it's something I haven't really thought about. I guess I could give you the rote answer and say that I put God first, but it's been so long since I've had to make that choice that I'm not sure if I can back it up with action or not. I had a couple of good years with Victoria and then she left and it was just me for several years. Then last year, the accident happened and I had to take on so much of the family responsibility. It wasn't really a choice; it just had to be done. And now there's Lizi. She and I are still getting to know each other, but I want what's best for her. Wherever that puts my priorities, that's where they are."

"I'm sure they're right where they ought to be," Amber said. She looked up and realized they'd reached the church.

Chapter Forty-One

After thinking about his encounter with Celia for a few days, Fox dropped by Alex's office early Tuesday morning. The secretary at the front desk told him that Alex was with a client, but she told him he could either schedule an appointment or wait until Alex was through.

Fox chose the chair that looked the least worn and picked up a magazine. For the next half-hour, he read about the most recent rulings passed down from higher courts and the impact those rulings had on one's understanding of the law. Most of it had little meaning to Fox, but it was either that or a magazine aimed at teen girls. He'd just finished an article on the correct wording of a will when the door to Alex's office opened and a couple stepped out. Alex shook their hands, assured them that they had nothing to worry about and they were on their way out.

"Come on back," Alex said, gesturing to Fox. He extended his hand as Fox approached the door. "What can we do for you today?"

Fox waited until the door of Alex's office closed before he said, "I talked to Celia."

"Is she causing more trouble?" Alex walked over to the coffee maker in the corner of his office. "Can I get you cup?"

It reminded him of the cup he'd refused from Celia. "As a matter of fact, I would like a cup."

Alex poured two cups and placed one on the desk in front of Fox before sitting down in his own chair. "So what's going on with Celia?"

"I told her that the merger is off," Fox said.

"Wow!" Alex said. "That's really good news. I know that was a tough decision, but I'm glad to hear it."

"It wasn't as tough as you might think," Fox said. "I had a guy do some groundwork for me so that if Celia started talking about that information she has, she would have a hard time getting people to believe her."

"I'm not sure I even want to know how he accomplished that," Alex said, "But Celia must not have taken that very well."

"That's the thing," Fox said. "I showed up there ready to take her down a peg or two and it's like she was ready for me. She didn't act surprised at all and she started congratulating me on how well I played the game. She just wanted a few days to tell Jack."

"She's a real class act."

"I'm really starting to worry now," Fox said. "I told her I'd give her a week, but I'm worried about what she's planning. I'm afraid I may have walked off into one of her traps."

"Yeah, I can see where you might be worried," Alex said, "but I don't know what you can do about it. At this point, I think the ball's in her court. I guess you can try to anticipate her next move and counter it before she makes it."

"That's what worries me," Fox said. "I have no idea what her next move will be. She backed down way too easily. I'm sure she's going to make another move, but what? I'm sure she needs this merger to happen, so I'm sure that whatever she does will be aimed at making sure that happens, but I can't think of what she could possibly do that would force me to agree to the merger."

"Maybe that's your answer," Alex said. "Maybe there is nothing she can do. If you can't think of anything, then maybe she can't either."

"No," Fox said, "you weren't there. You didn't hear her talking. I've never heard someone more condescending. It was like she knew she had me beat, but she wanted me to think that I'd won."

"Let's assume that's true," Alex said. "She has something up her sleeve that will cause you to change your mind and do what she wants. Don't you think we ought to be able to figure out what that is? There can't be too many things that would cause you to make such a poor financial decision."

"Just because we can't think of something doesn't mean she isn't planning something."

"What about kidnapping?" Alex asked. "If she kidnapped a member of your family—like Fiona or Lizi—don't you think that would make you change your mind?"

"I'm sure it might," Fox said, "But it's too risky. There's no exit strategy. Once we agreed to the terms and signed the papers, we could say that we were forced to sign them under duress and the contract wouldn't be valid, right?"

"Yeah, that's right," Alex said. "I was just throwing something out there to help get the creative juices flowing. What else might she do?"

"I don't know," Fox said. "I told you that I don't know."

"Calm down," Alex said. "Let's think this through. You can't expect me to come up with an answer right off. I don't deal with kind of law. I'm not an expert on scams and I don't know anyone who is."

It only took a moment for the statement to register in Fox's mind.

"Wait! I do," Fox said, standing up. He took another sip of his coffee and left the cup on the desk. "You've helped me more than you know. Send me the bill."

Before Alex could respond, Fox was out the door.

When Fox reached the church parking lot, he parked his car beside some of the cars parked closest to the building and followed the sign that said "office." He pushed the button for the buzzer and waited. A woman with a bright smile on her face opened the door.

"I need to see Amber," Fox said.

The woman looked puzzled for a moment. "I saw her earlier, so I know she's here, but I'm not sure where she is now."

"What do you usually do when you need her and you don't know where she is?"

"I go looking for her," the woman said. "If you like, you can wait here and I'll go find her."

"Well, if all you're going to do is walk around the building until you find her, I can do that."

"You might check the classrooms first," the woman said. "I think I heard her saying something about having trouble cleaning the whiteboards."

"Where are the classrooms?"

"Just follow that hall and you'll see the signs," the woman said, pointing. "If she isn't on the first floor, you can take the elevator up to the second."

The hallway the woman had directed Fox to follow was dark and when he reached the end of it he could barely make out the signs pointing to classrooms in both directions. A little light filtered into the hall from the windows in the doors, and that was limited by the amount of light coming through the blinds in the classrooms. He turned to the right, looking in each classroom as he went. At the end of the hall, he found the elevator and a sign pointing to the sanctuary, but based on what the woman had told him, he went back down the hall and checked the other classrooms. At the end of the hall, Fox found an exit to the outside, but no sign of Amber. He walked all the way back to the elevator and pushed the button.

The elevator was slow. He waited impatiently for the door to open on the second floor. When it did, he stepped out and saw another sign pointing toward the sanctuary that pointed toward the right. He could see the wide staircase going down and the windows of the foyer. He went the other way, once more checking each classroom. When he got back to the elevator, he decided to take the stairs instead of waiting for the elevator.

When he reached the top step, he looked down and saw Amber sitting on the landing, scraping the carpet with a knife. She was dressed in worn jeans and her hair was tied behind her head. She didn't notice him, but kept scraping.

"Amber, I need to talk to you," he said, coming down the stairs.

She put down the knife and stood up.

"I can explain," she said. "He asked me; I didn't say anything about it. I haven't given him an answer yet."

Fox looked at her, wondering what she was talking about. "Who asked you what?"

"You mean you didn't know?" She stared at him. "Grayson asked me to marry him, but I haven't given him an answer yet. He may have changed his mind."

"No, I doubt that," Fox said. "If Grayson asked, he isn't going to take it back."

Amber looked relieved.

"Of course your answer will be yes, whenever you get around to giving him your answer."

"Well, yeah," Amber said, "But you aren't too happy about it."

"I don't have time to worry about that right now," Fox said. "I need your help, and then I'll worry about it."

"You need my help," Amber echoed.

"That's what I said."

"And after I help you, you're going to find a way to get me out of the way."

"Look, I need your help and because you're the only person I know who might be able to help me, I don't have time to worry about what I'm going to do about you and Grayson right now. But I'm not going to promise to bless your marriage, just so you'll help me."

"What is it you need help with?" Amber sounded like she sighed as she spoke. "I don't know what you think I could possibly help you with."

"You're a con artist, right?"

"Is that a trick question?" Amber asked. "Should I be worried you've got a voice recorder going?"

"No," Fox said. "I meant it more as a statement. I know you're a con artist and I think you can help me figure out what another con artist is doing. I don't think like a con artist, but you do."

"Okay, fine," Amber said. "I was a con artist. I'm going to be talking to some of the ladies next week on things they can do to keep from getting swindled. You can come sit in, if you would like."

"That's not the kind of help I'm looking for," Fox said. "I need help figuring out what Celia is up to."

"That's easy," Amber said. "She wants money."

"Yeah, I know," Fox said. "And she intends to get it by forcing me to merge my company with her dad's company. My problem is that I don't know how she's going to do that."

"I'm not a mind reader," Amber said. "I can't tell you what Celia is planning. Even if I were, I'm not sure I want to help you. If I do, how do I know you aren't going to use it against me."

"You've got my word," Fox said. "I promise I won't use anything you do to help me against you. I can't promise I won't use something else to keep you and Grayson apart, but as far as what you do to help…"

"What makes you think I trust your promises? You lied before when you were afraid of me. I've got to hand it to you, the guy who my handwriting knew what he was doing, but you couldn't have used that to prove anything."

"Your word against mine," Fox said. "What makes you think I couldn't have used it? And if that's true, why did you leave?"

"It got Lizi out of your house, didn't it?" Amber said, instead of telling him it was because he told her to. It made Fox fear she'd known more of what she was doing than being fearful like he'd originally thought. "But the real problem is the postmark on the envelope. I couldn't have mailed it because I was boarding at the county jail. I remember because I was in there on Lizi's birthday. They had to drop the charges, but there's still a public record of my stay."

"You could've dropped it in the mail and it didn't get postmarked until later."

"Reasonable doubt," Amber said.

"Maybe."

"It doesn't matter," Amber said. "Either way, we both know you fabricated that note and that is all the proof I need to tell me that you can't be trusted. If you're looking for a con artist, maybe you should look in the mirror."

"I know what I see in the mirror," Fox said, "and it's far worse than you can imagine."

"I've seen enough to imagine quite a bit," Amber said. "That's why I'm not sure I want to help you."

"What if I tell you the rest?" Fox asked. "What if I tell you what really happened the day of the accident? You'll know something that even my family doesn't know. It would give you something you could hold over my head."

"I don't want something I can hold over your head," Amber said. "I just want to know I can trust you. Why would you want to give me that kind of power?"

"Because I know you won't use it," Fox said. It wasn't until his words left his mouth and entered his ears that he realized the truth of that statement. "I know that what you want is for Lizi to have what's best for her. You've sacrificed a lot for her and once you hear what happened, you'll know that the best thing for her is that no one else finds out about it."

"Okay, maybe," Amber said. "But Grayson already told me what happened."

"Yeah, but Grayson doesn't know it was my fault. All he knows is that the cement mixer flipped over and there may have been another car that forced it over."

"Grayson didn't say anything about another car," Amber said.

"It wasn't involved anyway. It was just there and it didn't stop. The driver may not have realized how close he came to being in a wreck."

"Just because that driver didn't cause it doesn't mean that you were at fault."

"I was there," Fox said. "I know I was at fault. Dave and I decided we'd take the kids out and get some ice cream. After that, we were just driving around because we wanted to take a little extra time getting back to the house. We weren't in a hurry or anything, but I got to that yield sign and I saw that traffic coming. Instead of stopping to wait, like I should've, I gunned it. I don't really remember the accident, but I remember the sitting there with glass all over me and the top of the car pushing down against me. There was just enough room for me to lean forward to the left and have a little space, but I couldn't turn around. All I could see of Dave was his hand sticking out. I had to sit there like that until they came and cut me out. If I'd stopped instead of deciding I could make it..."

"That's your big secret?" Amber asked. "All you did was accelerating when you should've been braking. It would be so easy to get out of that in court, just say your foot slipped."

"I'm not worried about court," Fox said. "That's already been taken care of, but Celia found some witnesses who saw what happened. She threatened to show that information to my family if I didn't go through with the merger."

"So, what if she does? I still don't think it's anything to worry about."

"You don't know my family," Fox said. "Fiona and Abby would be devastated if they found out it was my fault. Steve and Donna might handle it a little better, but it would make it difficult. And I know that Grayson would be disappointed with me. But that's really not the issue. I fixed it so I knew Celia couldn't use that information and I told her about it. It didn't bother her at all. All she did was ask for some time. I don't know what she's planning, but I know she's planning something. That's why I need your help. I need you to help me figure out what she's up to."

Amber sat back down on the landing and started scraping again. "I can't help you with that. I've got to get this gum out of the carpet."

"Look, if this is about you and Grayson…"

"It isn't," Amber said.

"Then what is it?"

"There's no way anyone can guess what Celia is planning," Amber said. "I know what I would do if I wanted to do what she's trying to do, but I wouldn't have tried the approach she already tried, so I doubt she'll try what I would."

"So, you think you're better than she is?"

"I didn't say that," Amber said. "One of the biggest mistakes you can make with a con artist is to think that they can't trick you."

"But you see a problem with the approach she used."

"Well, yeah," Amber said. "I wouldn't open myself up to that much risk. It's all built on the assumption that you would be so afraid that she would reveal your secret that you would do what she wanted. I suppose she wasn't completely wrong, not that I understand why you think it's such big secret. The problem is that as soon as you call her bluff, she gains nothing by revealing the secret. We might call it revenge, but once she takes her revenge, she has no power over you. Even if you're right and the consequences would be bad, she has no power to reverse what she did."

"Can you, at least, give me some idea of what you would try? Maybe I can protect against that and protect against Celia at the same time."

"That won't do you any good," Amber said. "If it were me, you would be begging Jack Abrams to go through with that merger. You wouldn't realize I'd conned you until it was too late."

"You talk big," Fox said.

"It's easy to talk big when you aren't going to do something," Amber said. "But what you really need is a way to persuade Jack and Celia that they want to withdraw from the discussion of the merger."

"We've looked for something Celia is afraid of. I thought we could give her some of her own medicine, but we didn't find anything."

"That's the wrong approach," Amber said. "You've got to convince Celia and Jack that it was their idea to call off the merger. Give me a few days and I think I can pull that off."

"What do you need from me?" Fox asked.

Amber put down the knife and stood up. "First, I need you to call Jack Abrams and ask him to confirm that he still wants the merger."

"Are you out of your mind?"

"Do you trust me?" Amber asked

"Not really, but if it's absolutely necessary…"

"It is."

"What else do you need?"

"I'll need a round trip ticket from St. Louis and money for a hotel room."

"Why?"

"It's for a friend," Amber said. "You'll understand later."

"Okay, what else?"

"I need a list of Jack Abrams divisions ranked in order of the most valuable to an investor to the least valuable. And I need to know about what you think they're worth."

"That shouldn't be too hard," Fox said. He knew he had a document like that at his desk; all he had to do was find it. "What else?"

"Five thousand dollars cash," Amber said. "I won't use all of it and I'll return what I don't spend, but I need some spending money."

Fox wondered if he should make a point to ask for a receipt for all her expenses, but if he could get rid of Celia for so little, it didn't matter whether Amber kept the leftover cash or not. "Okay, what else do you need?"

"That'll do for now," Amber said.

Chapter Forty-Two

The police car made its way down the street. The last thing Amber needed was for the police to spot her suspicious looking Japanese man. John Matthews was as American as he could be, but his mother was Japanese, and that was close enough. As much as she hated calling in favors, Amber was glad he owed her one. The police car continued along the road. John pulled out his camera and started taking pictures. There wasn't much he could take pictures of. It was just a big brown rectangular building with a glass entryway, a truck dock on the side and "Jack Abrams Inc. Computer Vision" written in big letters across the front.

Amber could feel the sun warming up the interior of the rental car. She turned the key and rolled down all the windows. There was no reason to cook herself just to keep from being discovered. She crouched down in the passenger's seat. Having the windows down would make it easier to see that someone was in the car.

John took pictures for several minutes and was beginning to look toward the car, as if he wanted some sign from her that he'd done enough and could quit. She was about to motion him back to the car when the front door opened and two men wearing the uniforms of security guards came out. One was tall with silver hair. The other, a younger guy, was short and skinny, but John, a short guy who spent too much time playing video games, would be no match for either of them.

Amber strained to understand what the guards said to John as they approached, but she could only make out three words out of ten and even fewer when they were face to face with him. She couldn't understand John at all, but she could see him pointing at the camera and then the building. He pulled out his billfold and handed them something he carried inside— probably a business card. The tall guard looked at it and shoved it in his pocket. The three of them walked to the entrance and disappeared inside.

Amber settled down in the car. She picked of the novel she'd checked out of the church library. There was nothing she could do now but wait.

Chapter Forty-Three

Fox sat at his desk looking at the report on the screen. That's what he was trying to do anyway. His heart wasn't in it. The year away had proven one thing: Grayson didn't need his help running the company. Maybe it really was time to retire. He'd gotten a taste of retired life and it would be hard to give it up completely. Merger or no merger, it was time to officially hand Grayson the reins. Fox stood up and idly wondered out of his office into Grayson's. Just being in Grayson's office gave one a sense that work was being done. Grayson was on the phone and typing something on the computer. But Fox could tell that Grayson was reaching the end of a conference call.

"Alright guys," Grayson said, "if no one else has anything to add, we'll meet again next week."

Fox sat down across from Grayson as Grayson removed his headset.

"I hoped you would be part of that meeting," Grayson said, "I'm sure I sent you an invite."

"You probably did," Fox said. He hadn't seen the need to attend. He had little to add to most of the meetings and they had nothing to do with his primary concern.

"You're welcome to dial in anytime, or you and I can sit in the same room together and get on the speaker phone."

"Maybe next week," Fox said, more to quiet Grayson than to make any form of commitment.

"Well, just so you know you can attend." Grayson continued what he was typing on the computer.

"I spoke to you fiancée," Fox said.

Grayson looked up. "You spoke to who?"

"Who do you think?" Fox asked. "Just how many fiancées do you have?"

"None," Grayson said.

"I spoke to Amber," Fox said. "She said you asked her to marry you."

"I did," Grayson said, "but she hasn't told me one way or the other yet. She told me to ask again in a few days. Now I'm afraid she'll say no."

"She won't," Fox said. "She's afraid that you changed your mind. I told her you wouldn't do that."

"I know you think this is the wrong thing to do," Grayson said. "But I've got to think about what's best for Lizi. Amber is the only mother she's ever known."

"Are you sure you want a marriage based on that alone? In a few years, Lizi will be out on her own and Amber will still be around."

"I know that," Grayson said. "That's not an unappealing thought."

"Well, if you're sure you'll be happy," Fox said, "just be sure to invite me to the wedding."

"Of course," Grayson said, "but why the change of heart?"

"Let's just say I owe your fiancée," Fox said. "She's helping me out with something."

"Does this have something to do with this?" Grayson pulled a large envelope from his desk. Fox didn't have to open it to know what was inside.

"That was locked in my desk."

"You gave me a key," Grayson said. "I was looking for something and I found this. I don't care what Celia thinks she found, the accident wasn't your fault."

"Yes, it was," Fox said. It was time for his family to know the truth, whatever trouble that truth would cause. "I knew I didn't have time and I didn't stop."

"I know," Grayson said.

"You know?"

"Yeah, I couldn't leave it alone. After it happened, I had to make some kind of sense out of it, so I talked to everyone who might have seen anything. I talked to all the people in the cars that I could find. I talked to the people who own the businesses along the traffic circle. I even found the guy who was driving the car on the other side of the cement mixer."

"So you've known it was my fault all this time and didn't say anything."

"No," Grayson said. "I know you didn't stop when you should have, but that's not what caused the cement mixer to tip over and even if you had stopped, the accident might have happened the same way. Your car wasn't in the other traffic's lane when the accident happened. If you'd stopped, you would've stopped right where you were anyway."

"So, if you're right, what caused the accident?"

"He was drunk and he was driving too fast. I think he must have gotten up close to the circle and realized he needed to turn the wheel. He turned it too quickly and with him carrying so much weight up top, it tipped over."

"You're saying it was because he was drunk."

"It's in the accident report. They tested his blood and it was enough to have impaired his driving ability. He shouldn't have been driving that truck."

Fox wouldn't be so quick to turn loose of his guilt, but hearing Grayson adamantly say that he wasn't at fault made him feel a little better, if only a little. If Grayson had looked at everything there was to see and was sure that Fox wasn't at fault, the rest of the family might agree.

"I'm kind of relieved you found that," Fox said, "but that's not what Amber is helping me with. After I called off the merger, Celia said some things that made me think she has something else up her sleeve. I figured Amber would be the perfect person to help me figure out what that was."

"And did she?"

"No, not really, but she seemed to think she could make the problem go away. That's what I came to tell you. Amber said that if Celia or Jack asks about some Japanese investors that we're supposed to tell them that we don't know what they're talking about."

"That should be easy enough," Grayson said. "I don't know anything about any Japanese investors."

"She said not to let them think that we're trying to cover anything up, just tell them that we don't know anything."

"Well, I'm sure going to be looking forward to her explaining herself," Grayson said, "because I don't have a clue what this is about."

They didn't have long to wait. Before Fox left Grayson's office, Sandra came to the door. "Jack and Celia are here."

"Send them in," Grayson said, standing up. "Let's see what they have to say."

"I don't know how you thought you could get away with this," Jack said, coming into the office. Celia was right behind him. "All this talk about how little my company is worth and then you try pulling something like this!"

"Jack, I can assure you that I have no idea what you're talking about," Grayson said. "You know even better than we do that you're so deep in debt right now that we couldn't sell every asset you have and make enough to pay it all off."

"Yeah, you'd like us to think you believe that. All this time, I thought you needed us for the software side of the business and all the while it's been about Computer Vision," Jack said.

"It's no wonder you were so quick to say you wanted to continue with the merger. You want that division in your control so you can sell it off."

"Look, I'm not sure why we decided we changed our mind again," Grayson said, looking at Fox.

Fox wondered if he should've tried to give Grayson an explanation. Telling him that Amber had told him to didn't seem like the right answer.

"But we were open with you from the beginning," Grayson said. "We told you that we intended to sell off that division because the technology we have is further along in its development than yours."

"Yeah, but you didn't tell us how much you were getting from it. Does the number 427 million sound familiar?"

"427 million?" Grayson suppressed a laugh. "In what currency?"

"What? You think it might be in Japanese yen?"

"Japanese?" Grayson asked. "I don't know anything about that."

"Sure you don't," Jack said. "Well I do and I'm not giving my company away so that you can make a killing by selling it off to the Japanese. We're pulling out of the merger and don't even pretend that you don't know why."

"Honestly, we don't," Grayson said.

Jack and Celia walked out.

"That was unexpected," Grayson said.

"Yeah, I don't know what Amber did, but it must have worked."

"We could still use Jack Abrams' software guys," Grayson said. "It's a shame it couldn't work out better."

"All may not be lost," Fox said. "Maybe we can buy that division from the Japanese investors."

"I wouldn't hold my breath," Grayson said.

Chapter Forty-Four

Amber sat on the couch in Fox's house. Grayson was on one side of her and had his arm draped around her. Lizi was on the other and was tugging at the diamond ring on Amber's finger. Amber wasn't sure how much it was worth, but she was sure it was worth more than everything she owned when they bought their tickets in St. Louis and boarded a southbound train.

The whole family was there. Fox had sat himself down in his favorite chair. Fiona was in another chair near his. Abby was in the chair to Grayson's left and Donna was sitting on the arm of Steve's chair to Lizi's right.

"Alright young lady," Fox said—it was about as close to a term endearment Amber had heard Fox use in reference to her, "You've kept us waiting long enough. You owe us an explanation of what you did to convince Jack to back out of the merger."

"It really wasn't that hard," Amber said. "It's easy to get someone to believe almost anything if you know what they want to believe. I just convinced them that they had an opportunity for a better deal somewhere else."

"You mean the Japanese investors," Grayson said.

"Yeah," Amber said. "It had to be someone believable and I figured the Japanese were the most likely to want a company like that."

"But how did you do that?" Fox asked. "I'm sure you didn't just call Jack and tell him he should ask the Japanese if they wanted his company. And it doesn't explain why they stormed in saying that we were trying to cheat them."

"I'm sorry about that," Amber said. "It couldn't be helped. There's this guy I know in St. Louis who owed me a favor. Put him in a suit and tie and he really looks the part of a Japanese business man. I had him come down and take some pictures of that division."

"Why that division?" Fox asked.

"A couple of reasons," Amber said. "It was here in town, so I knew Jack and Celia might actually drive out to see what was going on. I knew it was a division that you didn't have much use for, so it would seem believable that you would want to sell it off."

"That was our plan from the beginning," Grayson said.

"I figured it was," Amber said. "And another reason I picked that one was because they have security guards."

"Why would that be important?" Fox asked. "I would think you wouldn't want to mess with security guards."

"Well, but if there aren't security guards then they're more likely to call the cops. I was counting on the security guards going out to talk to my friend. Once they did, he told them that his employer had sent him to take pictures of the facility because they're looking into buying it. He gave them a business card with a Japanese company on it and told them that the owners of the building had cleared it. They couldn't call the police or send him on his way until they checked it out, so they took him inside and someone called Jack. Jack didn't know anything about it. After they ask my friend a few more questions, they find out he thinks it's you who owns the division instead of Jack Abrams. All he had to do then was to let it slip that his employers were going to offer 426 million dollars for the division."

"You should've talked to me first," Grayson said. "There's no way that division is worth that much."

"I know what it's worth," Amber said. "Fox gave me a listing with all of their divisions on it. I had to make sure the Japanese were offering a lot more than what you guys were saying it was worth."

"So, what happens when they find that there isn't a Japanese investor who wants to buy that division?"

"It'll take them a while to figure that out," Amber said. "If we're lucky, they won't look too hard for that one investor, they'll try finding some other investors who might be interested too. If one investor will give you 426 million, another might give you 500 million, right?"

"Yeah, could be," Grayson said. "But they're eventually going to figure out they've been had."

"They might," Amber said. It was always a good idea to plan for that possibility.

"No, I don't think they will," Fox said. "Amber knows what she's doing. Besides, they've burned their bridges already. And even if they do, we'll have a member of this family that knows how to handle them."

And with that, Amber began to believe that she was wanted.

Final Thoughts

One of the questions that reader frequently ask authors is *where do you get your ideas?* While most people who ask intend it as a compliment of the author's ability to spin a yarn, many authors have trouble answering the question. Who is to say where ideas come from? They just come and with work we form them into stories. That answer is unsatisfactory, so let's take a look at how the tale you just read came into being.

Back in the spring of 2008, I entered a first page contest on literary agent Rachelle Gardner's blog. We were given a first line and a limit of 300 words, which is about the number of words on one page of a novel. Other than that, we allowed to write what we wanted with the goal being that a reader would want to continue reading after reaching the end of that page. I took what I knew of the contest judge into account and I wrote a page that I thought would appeal to her.

I had recently watched an episode of *Murder She Wrote* in which one of the suspects was taking care of a boy that wasn't her own, but had somehow been left in her care. I explored that idea a little and two characters, Hannah and Ashley were born. For the first page contest, I wrote a scene in which Hannah had dressed Ashley up in some foul smelling clothes and they visited a church to ask for clothes, but it ends with Hannah thinking about how she would get money from a wealthy man who was talking to the pastor.

While I didn't win first prize in that contest, I was a runner up, so when I later carried through with that idea. Hannah became Amber and Ashley became Lizi. But the idea began to morph. I started with that same first page I had written, but I discovered that it didn't fit with the rest of their story. Had I left that page in, the beginning of the story would have spent a great deal of time with Amber debating with herself about what she should do with Lizi. I decided to skip that part and jump immediately to when she is taking Lizi to her family.

I completed that story, but after that it sat in my closet for a couple of years. In the story I had written, Fox didn't want either Amber or Lizi because he saw himself as above them. Also, the business was not going through a merger, but Grayson wanted them to purchase another company, but Fox wanted nothing to do with it because it too was beneath him. While I liked the story, I began to wonder if readers would have trouble connecting with it. So I pulled it back out and I changed some things. I put less significance on Victoria's death and more on the accident. In the original, Fox was at home when the accident happened rather than being in the car. Celia's role changed also. The last 100 pages of the story are completely new.

So, as you can see, while an idea might start with some curious thought like, *what would it be like if a woman was raising a child that wasn't her own?*, it is a long arduous process to take that idea an turn it into a story.

Other Books By Timothy Fish

- Searching For Mom
  (ISBN 978-1-4196-7039-8)
- How to Become a Bible Character
  (ISBN 978-1-4196-8331-2)
- For the Love of a Devil
  (ISBN 978-1-4392-1425-1)
- And Thy House
  (ISBN 978-1-4392-6871-1)
- Church Website Design: A Step By Step Approach
  (ISBN 1-4196-5971-5)

Did you enjoy the book?

If you enjoyed reading this book, please tell others about it. Many of the online stores encourage you to write reviews of the books you have read. Help other readers by taking the time to review this book.

Also, feel free to e-mail the author at:

bookcomments@timothyfish.net

Timothy Fish is the author of five novels and a book on website design. He is actively involved in his church and association work. He has the proud distinction of being able to carry a tune in a bucket, but he makes no claims that his musical ability is much better than that.

He encourages you to visit his website at:
http://www.timothyfish.com

And his blog at:
http://timothyfish.blogspot.com